DISCARD

Death
and
Sensibility

Also available by Elizabeth Blake

JANE AUSTEN SOCIETY MYSTERIES

Pride, Prejudice, and Poison

Death
and
Sensibility

A Jane Austen Society Mystery

~

ELIZABETH BLAKE

CROOKED
LANE

NEW YORK
David M. Hunt
Library
63 Main Street, PO Box 217
Falls Village, CT 06031-0217
860-824-7424 / huntlibrary.org

Copyright © 2021 by Carole Bugge

Published in the United States by Crooked Lane Books, an imprint of The Quick Brown Fox & Company LLC.

Crooked Lane Books and its logo are trademarks of The Quick Brown Fox & Company LLC.

Library of Congress Catalog-in-Publication data available upon request.

ISBN (hardcover): 978-1-64385-730-5
ISBN (ebook): 978-1-64385-731-2

Cover design by Ben Perini

Printed in the United States.

www.crookedlanebooks.com

Crooked Lane Books
34 West 27th St., 10th Floor
New York, NY 10001

First Edition: August 2021

10 9 8 7 6 5 4 3 2 1

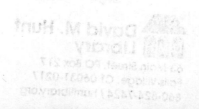

For my niece, Ariana "Bones" Farren,
a young woman of great talent and
accomplishments

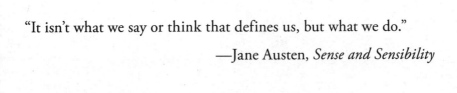

"It isn't what we say or think that defines us, but what we do."

—Jane Austen, *Sense and Sensibility*

Chapter One

The December wind whipped at the trees outside her cottage as Erin Coleridge lugged her battered gray suitcase from the bedroom closet. She hated packing. No matter the occasion, it was always exhausting to choose what to bring and what to leave behind. How could you know what you will need until the need arises? Consequently, she invariably overpacked.

Determined not to fall into that trap this time, Erin pulled a couple of shirts from their hangers and tossed them into the suitcase. She would be away from her Kirkbymoorside book store and cottage for a week, but she could buy anything she needed in the much larger city of York.

Tossed by the wind, the branches of the yew tree outside her window tapped at the panes, and she shivered at the sound. Weather on the North Yorkshire moors was unpredictable—sometimes mild weather lingered lazily well into November, but you could just as easily find yourself in an early snowstorm or torrential rains. Today, wind advisories had been all over the news. They'd been predicting over fifty-mile-an-hour gusts with heavy rain and Erin didn't fancy driving down to York in a rainstorm. Worse, she knew her best friend, Farnsworth Appleby, would absolutely freak out about the weather. She hated storms. Many years ago, a tree fell on her car, and she had been spooked ever since.

As if on cue, Erin's landline rang. She reached for the receiver on the bedside table and cradled it to her ear while she continued packing.

"Hello, Farnsworth."

"I just heard the weather report. Hurricane force winds, Erin. *Hurricane force.*"

"They're only predicting gusts of fifty miles per hour. Hurricane force would be seventy or more."

"Still," Farnsworth said. "Maybe we should wait it out a day."

"Our reservation at the Grand York starts tomorrow, and at those prices, I'm not wasting a single minute. I'm packing now."

"You're upstairs?"

"Yes. In the bedroom."

"How did you know it was me, by the way?" asked Farnsworth. She sounded like she was chewing something. "You don't have caller ID on that phone."

"I'm psychic."

"And I'm Maggie Smith."

"More like Dame Edna, I should think."

"This is nothing to joke about."

"I expected you'd be in a massive panic over the weather just about now."

Farnsworth sighed. "If there's one thing I hate, it's being predictable. It's so dreary. Stop it, Willoughby! Leave Marianne alone!" Farnsworth had a large assortment of cats, all named after Jane Austen characters.

"Willoughby?" said Erin. "Is he new?"

"I got him from the shelter last week. Very handsome, but quite the cad. Always going after the females."

"Isn't he neutered?"

"He still fancies himself a ladies' man. *Stop* it, Willoughby, or I'll have to separate you! There," she said. "That seemed to put the fear of God into him."

"You don't really believe he understands English?"

"Of course not. Elinor might, though . . . she's pretty sharp."

"So are you excited about the conference?"

"What if there's flooding? And the wind—that little car of yours will fly around like papier-mâché."

"We can take yours if you like."

"You know I don't fancy driving in bad weather. I'm just going for the food, you know. The restaurant is meant to be fabulous."

"I can't imagine a little rain getting between you and lobster thermidor."

"I've been looking at the menu online," Farnsworth said mistily. "Oak-smoked salmon, crab mayonnaise, fennel toast . . ."

"Think of it this way. If we arrive late, that's one day less of dining."

"The person, be it gentleman or lady, who has not pleasure in a good meal, must be intolerably stupid."

"Prudence won't like hearing you misquote Austen."

"Then we won't tell her." Prudence Pettibone was a key member of the Jane Austen Society's Northern Branch, and a good friend. However, she could be a bit fervent and was very competitive about her knowledge of Austen's work. Farnsworth sighed, "I do hope the panels aren't too boring. Which ones are you on?"

"My first one is *Feminine Identity in the Jane Austen Heroine*."

"How very trendy. I'm doing *Sense or Sensibility? Jane Austen and the Role of Reason in Contemporary Romance Fiction*."

"What time shall I pick you up?"

Farnsworth whimpered a little, "Are you sure we'll be all right?"

"It's the first Jane Austen conference of its kind in the UK, and we're the hosting society branch. What would it look like if we were late?"

"It's not just the two of us, you know. Hetty and Prudence will be there. And Jonathan. Mustn't forget him," she said slyly, referring to Erin's recent flirtation with him.

"Your first panel is tomorrow, isn't it?"

"Yes."

"I'm sure Prudence would jump at the chance to take your place."

There was a silence. Then Farnsworth said, "You can be really horrid, you know that?"

Erin laughed. "I'll pick you up at noon. We'll have lunch on the way."

"I'll be the one wearing the sou'wester and hip waders."

"Good night, Farnsworth."

After hanging up, Erin threw a few more things into the suitcase, then suddenly felt very hungry. Abandoning her task, she padded down the narrow stairs to the ground floor, where she puttered around in the little kitchen in the rear of the cottage that overlooked the stream. She could hear the brook burbling and rushing outside the window, the water level higher than usual because of the storm. In the middle of summer, the stream was often reduced to a thin trickle, but now it sounded like a waterfall.

"You're not really hungry," she muttered to herself as she grabbed a jar of Sainsbury's crunchy peanut butter. "You're just trying to avoid packing." But the thought of peanut butter and pickles on toast made her stomach grumble, and she devoured it standing at the kitchen counter, surrounded by all the good and familiar things in her small but cozy kitchen, the walls painted bumblebee yellow. It had been her mother's favorite color. Gwyneth Coleridge was the most cheerful person Erin had ever known, but that hadn't saved her from the disease that devoured her from the inside out like an evil parasite. It was almost as if the sickness had fed on her energy and light. Erin wished her mother could see her little cottage by the stream, with its footbridge leading to the wide sweep of rolling meadows bordered by hedgerows.

She also wished she believed in an afterlife. Though she sometimes fancied that she sensed her mother's presence, Erin thought it was simply a manifestation of her own consciousness.

"All right," she muttered, yawning as she headed back upstairs. "No more procrastination."

It was near midnight when she finally finished packing, and after a bath in the lion's paw tub, she fell into bed as the wind whistled and howled in the eaves outside her cottage. Snug under the blankets, she dug her feet into the down comforter and slipped into a deep, untroubled sleep.

Chapter Two

❧

"That wasn't so bad, was it?" Erin said to Farnsworth as they entered the lobby of the York Grand Hotel Friday afternoon.

"I'll let you know when the circulation returns to my extremities," she replied, lumbering behind her. Farnsworth was a rather large woman who usually carried herself gracefully, so Erin took the heavy stride as a reproach for being forced out in inclement weather. "Do you think you brought enough clothes?" Farnsworth asked, with a glance at Erin's compact suitcase.

"I always overpack, so I tried to travel light this time, she shrugged, taking in the spacious lobby with its inlaid marble floors, wrought iron railings, and elegant arches. "This place is quite something. I can see why it's a five-star hotel."

"A splendid example of Edwardian architecture," Farnsworth said. "Or so the guidebooks say." The building really was beautiful. It was all red brick with long, elegant windows, gables, and cupolas. Ornate, but not overdone.

A familiar voice floated across the marble lobby.

"If adventures will not befall a young lady in her village, she must seek them abroad."

Erin turned to see Prudence Pettibone, flanked by her best friend, Hetty Miller. A more unlikely pair was hard to imagine—Prudence, short and frumpy, with dull brown hair and clothing that seemed to have been plucked from a jumble sale remainder bin—and Hetty, tall, slim, and decked out like a store window mannequin, with rouged cheeks and mascara so thick it appeared to have been applied by a bricklayer. She spent more on a single outfit than Erin spent on clothing in a year. Hetty and Pru were inseparable, though they argued frequently and competed compulsively. As co-chairs of the Conference Planning Committee, they had been at one another's throats quite a bit over the past few weeks.

"Hello, Pru—hi, Hetty," Erin said warmly, glad to see them. For all their oddness, Pru and Hetty had been loyal friends to her since her arrival in Yorkshire less than two years ago. The four women met once a month for dinner, each taking turns hosting.

"Hello, Prudence—grand master of the Austen quote, as always," Farnsworth remarked. "Though you might find some competition within the ranks this week."

"If any one faculty of our nature may be called more wonderful than the rest, I do think it is memory," Prudence replied with a little smile, no doubt intended to be mysterious, but which came off as smug.

"You're looking gorgeous as always," Farnsworth told Hetty.

"Thank you, dearie," she replied, rewarding her with a glittering smile. "Isn't this just too exciting?" she asked, adjusting her very short black leather skirt over knee-high matching boots. Even in this weather, she wore three-inch heels; her outfits were never designed for practicality. She gave her dyed crimson curls a shake. "I can't wait to hit the spa. I'm going to get the massage *and* facial package." She turned to Farnsworth. "I expect you're going to the restaurant straightaway."

"I think we're all quite keen on the food here," said Erin.

"Not Hetty," Prudence replied. "She lives on wheat grass and kimchi."

"That's absurd," said Hetty. "I just have a fast metabolism. You're not wearing your eyeglasses," she said, peering at Erin.

"She finally took my advice and got contacts," said Farnsworth.

"Well done, you," Hetty said. "Mustn't hide those nice blue eyes."

"You've done a wonderful job spearheading the organization of this conference," said Erin. "I know how much work went into it."

"A lot of people lent a hand," said Prudence. "We couldn't have done it without your web mastery, posting it all over social media."

"Don't forget Carolyn's wonderful artwork," said Farnsworth. Carolyn Hardacre, who taught at York University, was a talented artist, and had designed the logo and conference programs. Her husband Owen was president of the North Yorkshire branch of the Jane Austen Society.

"Is she coming?" asked Pru.

"I don't think so," said Erin. "She had family obligations."

"And Owen would never show up without her," Farnsworth added.

"Are you going to see that sexy detective of yours?" Hetty asked Erin.

"If he's around."

"Why wouldn't he be around?" said Prudence.

"His mother's been ill. He's been going over to Manchester to see her."

Hetty shuddered. "The traffic around Manchester is dreadful, especially at rush hour."

"Well, *I'd* like to go see my room," said Farnsworth. "If you'll excuse me, I'm going to check in."

"Good idea," Erin agreed.

The pert young woman at the concierge counter had made a show of busying herself during their conversation, but she had obviously been listening intently as she pretended to sort papers. Now she smiled sweetly as they approached.

"Welcome to the York Grand Hotel," she said, all polished teeth and glimmering red lipstick. Her name tag identified her as Tricia.

"Why, thank you, Tricia," said Farnsworth.

She cocked her head to one side, her tight blonde curls brushing the shoulder of her starched uniform. "Is this your first time here?"

"Yes," Farnsworth replied. "Though *hopefully* not our last."

Erin glanced at her friend, hoping she wasn't about to say something naughty; she had that look in her eye. Just to be sure, Erin gave her a gentle nudge in the ribs. Farnsworth emitted a little squeak.

"Are you all right?" asked Tricia, her voice carrying just a hint of condescension.

"It's my lumbago," Farnsworth replied. "Acts up from time to time."

"What exactly is lumbago?" said Tricia.

"I have no idea, but mine is terrible in rainy weather."

Erin poked Farnsworth harder, which her friend ignored, smiling sweetly at Tricia. "You do have a lift, don't you?"

"Yes, indeed, though you can have a first floor room if you prefer."

Farnsworth shook her head. "Oh, no—I can't bear the thought of people looking in the window at me. My ex-husband was a Peeping Tom," she explained in response to Tricia's bewildered look.

Check-in concluded without incident, but as the four friends boarded the lift, Erin said, "Why were you so beastly to that poor concierge?"

"Didn't you see her eavesdropping on us?"

"We made it rather difficult for her not to overhear us," Erin replied.

"What do you mean?" asked Hetty.

"Your voice," said Prudence. "It could cut through glass."

"Rubbish," Hetty retorted. She turned to Farnsworth. "Do I have a loud voice?"

Farnsworth coughed delicately.

"Well?" Hetty demanded.

"The term 'clarion' comes to mind."

Hetty frowned. "What does that mean?"

"It means you sound like a bloody trumpet," said Pru.

"Isn't this your floor?" Farnsworth asked as the doors opened onto the third floor.

"Yes. Come along, Hetty," said Prudence.

"Coming," Hetty said, stumbling as her high-heeled boot caught in the gap between the door and the carpet.

"Mind your step," said Farnsworth, offering her hand.

"Thanks—I'm all right," Hetty replied, righting herself.

"Don't know why you insist on wearing heels at your age," Pru muttered, but Hetty pretended not to hear. No one really knew Hetty's age, and she did her best to keep it at bay, like a wary fighter facing a dangerous opponent. Rumor had it she had spent a small fortune on cosmetic surgery. Prudence gave her friend a hard time about the endless primping and posing, but Erin thought she secretly admired Hetty's energy and style. No one could accuse Prudence Pettibone of having anything that remotely resembled style.

Farnsworth had booked a suite on the fourth floor, and after helping her insert the key card correctly into the lock, Erin went up to her room one floor above. She had requested a gabled room on the top floor, and was glad the hotel had obliged. It was smaller than the ones on lower floors, but the slanted ceilings and the view more than made up for it. It reminded her of her childhood room in Oxford, where she had the entire floor to herself.

Pulling back the sheer white window curtains, Erin was delighted to see the Gothic towers of York Minster across the River

Ouse. York was a medieval fortified city and the multiple spires of the famed cathedral thrust at the sky like spears, as if the very air was a threat to the town's security.

There was a knock on the door. Erin opened it to see a slight young man in a bellman's uniform holding an enormous bouquet of flowers.

"Ms. Erin Coleridge?"

"Yes."

"Delivery for you. Shall I put them inside?"

"Uh, yes, thank you," she said, rifling through her purse in search of a tip.

"Ta, Miss," he said, tipping his hat when she handed him a couple of pounds.

She read the card on the flowers.

"Welcome to York. Hope these aren't too 'Austentacious.'—P. Hemming"

"Oh," she groaned. "How long did it take you to come up with that one?" Detective Peter Hemming had confessed early on his fondness for bad puns (though, Erin wondered if there was any other kind). Still, as her mother always said, you take the bad with the good if you want to have any people at all in your life. "These must have cost a bundle," Erin murmured, putting the flowers on the dresser. "And on a policeman's salary."

She had barely spoken to him since he concluded the Kirkby-moorside murder investigation in late October, much less seen him. Erin had been nervous at the thought of coming to York, where he lived. If he didn't have time to see her here, the only reasonable conclusion was that he wasn't interested, in spite of the obvious chemistry between them.

As she unpacked, Erin thought about the politics of sexual attraction. Her mother, for all her energy and strong personality, had been surprisingly conservative in that respect. She discouraged Erin from pursuing boys, insisting that "males enjoyed the thrill of the hunt." Thrill or not, if Erin liked someone, she had no qualms about making the first move. But with Peter Hemming, the situation was complicated. They had met while he was the lead detective overseeing a homicide investigation in which Erin was a potential suspect, so their relationship—such as it was—was a delicate dance, an avoidance of impropriety.

But now with the case solved (mostly thanks to her), things were simpler—weren't they? Did he resent her intervention, because she was ultimately responsible for solving what was, after all, his case? Or was she the one avoiding further intimacy? She contemplated all of this as she took her copy of *Sense and Sensibility* from her suitcase. Erin was rereading it, and was a bit taken aback at how well she understood Elinor, with her distrust of sentiment, her reliance on reason. Erin suspected her mother's untimely and shocking death made her shy away from emotional involvement, but was that too easy an answer? After all, even Elinor found love eventually, as all good Austen heroines do.

If only real life fell into place as smoothly as it did for characters between the covers of romance novels, she thought, putting the book on the bedside table. She puttered around her room, unpacking and examining the various amenities. The flat-screen television was ample and the room was large enough for two armchairs and a small settee at the foot of its queen-size bed. There was a well-stocked minibar, which she intended to avoid. She was unaware of how much time had passed before there was another knock on the door. Erin opened it to see Farnsworth, dressed to the nines in a deep-blue evening frock.

Farnsworth frowned. "Why aren't you dressed? It's almost time for the meet and greet."

"Really?"

"It's nearly four thirty. Cocktail hour starts at five."

"Sorry—I lost track of time."

"We agreed to be early, seeing as we're the hosting branch."

"You go ahead—I'll only be a few minutes."

Erin quickly slipped on a slinky black dress and heels, applying some mascara and a bit of rouge. The tower clock high atop York Minster was just chiming the hour as she headed downstairs.

Chapter Three

～

On the way to the party, Erin stopped by the conference bookstore to pick up her name badge and attendance packet, including the panel and event schedule. The bookstore was set up in one of the smaller meeting rooms, and had been organized by members of the Society's Southern Branch. Tables of books lined the walls, and included Jane Austen novels, works by her contemporaries, as well as historical studies, nonfiction pieces, and books by conference attendees. She was amused to see there were even a few copies of *Pride and Prejudice and Zombies*. There was also a section where people sold other wares such as period clothing, baked goods, herbs and spices which Jane Austen might have eaten, and other Regency era items, like fancy canes, gloves, hats, and ladies' fans.

A few people were gathered in the 1906 Bar when she arrived, but Erin didn't recognize anyone from the Society's North Yorkshire Branch. The décor was reminiscent of an exclusive London club, in muted grays and burgundy with inlaid parquet flooring.

"First round is on me," said Farnsworth, beckoning to her table in the middle of the room. She looked resplendent in her deep-blue, off-the-shoulder evening dress and creamy silk shawl, her dark hair in loose curls around her neck. "What would you like?"

"You go ahead," said Erin. "I'm just going to pop into the loo. I forgot to put on lipstick."

"You're pretty enough without it."

"As long as we're trading compliments, you look fabulous."

"I do, don't I?" Farnsworth said with an angelic smile, and headed off to the bar.

On her way to the toilet, Erin spied a young couple embracing in a secluded corner of the corridor leading to the cloak room. When they saw her, they quickly disengaged, and the young man, who was very blond, hurried away, nearly bumping into her as he passed. He muttered an apology and rounded the corner quickly, nearly colliding with a waiter carrying a tray of hot hors d'oeuvres. Erin did not get a good look at the girl, who retreated into the cloakroom, but thought she was wearing a hotel staff uniform.

When Erin returned, Farnsworth handed her a tall glass of tawny liquid topped with a slice of pineapple.

"It's one of their signature drinks."

"What's in it?"

"Rye whiskey, Frangelico, pineapple, lemon, toffee syrup . . . I forget what else. Here, try it."

Erin took a sip of the concoction. She expected it to be too sweet, but the lemon juice cut the sugary syrup, and the Frangelico gave it a nutty flavor. "Brilliant," she said. "Maybe I'll order one. What's it called?"

"Alice in Wonderland."

"I never really fancied that book. Too weird. Even as a kid, I didn't get the point of it all."

Farnsworth patted her arm. "I knew there was a reason I liked you."

"And then it turned out to be all a dream, which I hate. Good illustrations, though."

"I'm going to get you one of those drinks," said Farnsworth.

"You don't need to—"

"You can buy the next round," she said, and headed toward the bar.

It was just after five, and the room was already filling up. Looking around, Erin saw mostly unfamiliar faces. There hadn't been much communication between the various branches of the Society—until now, of course. More people had signed up for the conference than she expected—the Grand was completely booked, with spillover to other York hotels. Many of the attendees were members of various Jane Austen Society branches but according to Prudence, there were also a fair number of people who just liked Jane Austen or the Regency period.

Someone brushed against her, and Erin turned to see a striking young woman with ebony skin and lustrous, almond-shaped eyes.

"Sorry," the woman said. She wore a long fitted black jacket over cream-colored fitted pants and a high-necked lilac blouse. The outfit vaguely resembled a Regency gentleman's clothing.

"No worries. I'm Erin Coleridge," she said, extending her hand.

"Khari Butari," she said. Her grip was firm, her hand cool and dry. Erin was suddenly worried her own palms were sweating, as they did sometimes when she was nervous.

"Your name is familiar," she said. "Are you a filmmaker?"

"Yes, I am."

"I knew it! I saw your documentary about Senegal—*Girls of Dakar.*"

"Then you are one of a very select few," Khari said with a wry smile.

"It was wonderful. I learned so much about Senegal. What a fascinating place."

"You are very kind."

"She is not," said Farnsworth, handing Erin her drink. "But she *is* honest. Hello—I'm Farnsworth."

"Khari Butari."

"Khari is a filmmaker," said Erin.

16

"Are you making a film about Jane Austen?" asked Farnsworth.

"Actually, I got a grant to make a documentary about her life."

"That's quite a change of subject from *Girls of Dakar*," said Erin.

"I'm interested in female agency, and Jane Austen made an impact on the world at a time when most women were dependent upon male relatives for their survival."

"Speaking of agency, what are you drinking?" said Farnsworth. "I'm buying the first round."

"What are you having?" said Khari.

"A wicked concoction called Alice in Wonderland."

"*Parfait.* Sounds perfect."

"Be right back," Farnsworth said, pushing her way through the increasingly dense press of bodies.

"I'm going to grab a seat while I can," Khari said, sinking into a plush burgundy armchair.

"I'll join you," said Erin, sitting opposite her.

"Isn't that Barry Wolf, the keynote speaker?" Khari said, pointing to a short, balding, middle-aged man standing at the bar.

"And his much younger wife," Erin added, eyeing the attractive young woman on his arm.

It was hard not to stare at such a mismatched couple. She was sleek and svelte, her straight black hair shiny as sealskin. She looked like a '30s French movie star. Short and unathletic, with pasty skin and an unsuccessful comb-over, Barry didn't even look like her father. He looked like her accountant.

"Pru and Hetty said he was a pain in the—neck," Erin said, glancing at Khari, who smiled.

"Do not worry about using bad language in front of me," she said. "My mother swore like a drunken sailor."

"Pru said he complained about everything. She was regretting inviting him in the first place."

"But his biography of Jane Austen was brilliant. Did you read it?"

"Absolutely. It won the Baillie Gifford Prize."

"I like his previous book even better," Khari said.

"*Jane Austen and Her Contemporaries*?"

"Yes. It was fascinating."

"We thought we were lucky to book him for this conference, but—"

"Great writers aren't always equally wonderful human beings."

"Exactly," said Erin.

At the bar, Barry Wolf put an arm around his wife, who was chatting with a slim, black-haired man closer to her own age. The gesture was remarkably possessive.

"Who's that young man talking with Mrs. Wolf?" Erin asked Farnsworth when she arrived with Khari's drink.

"I think that's Barry's assistant, Stephen Mahoney. Barry told Hetty and Pru he was bringing his 'secretary.' He's quite the looker, isn't he? Someone to give Jonathan Alder a run for his money."

"He is attractive, in a neurasthenic kind of way."

"'Neurasthenic'? How positively nineteenth-century of you," Farnsworth said.

"I know what she means," Khari said. "He looks like something out of a Poe story. What does he use on his hair—motor oil?"

Stephen Mahoney's thick black hair was so heavily slicked down it stuck to his skull as if it had been glued there. It emitted an unnatural oily sheen, glistening beneath the room's soft track lighting. He wore a tight-fitting black suit that hugged his narrow frame, snug as a straitjacket.

"And that suit," said Erin. "It's so tight he can barely breathe."

"That's all the rage these days," Farnsworth said breezily. "The boys like to look as if they've been poured into their clothes."

"It only works if you're really, really thin," said Erin.

"Which shouldn't be a problem for you," Farnsworth remarked.

"I hope the society members aren't paying for Stephen's room," said Khari.

"No fear of that," said Farnsworth. "We could barely scrape together the funds to cover Barry's."

"What's his wife's name again?" asked Erin.

"Luca," said Farnsworth. "She's Hungarian."

"Mail order bride?" asked Khari.

"I wouldn't be surprised. Pretty odd couple."

Erin raised her glass. "Here's to a successful conference."

"Cheers," said Khari.

But Erin's attention was already taken by the subtle drama at the bar. The body language was unmistakable. Luca Wolf was leaning into Stephen Mahoney, laughing, her head thrown back in what was literally a throat-baring gesture, while he said something that they both obviously considered witty. Her forehead was shiny her lips were parted so invitingly that it was almost shockingly obvious. Stephen wore a smug little smile, his body slightly inclined toward hers with his shoulders thrown back.

Barry Wolf bore an expression of such pure malice that Erin could feel his rage all the way across the room. It was hard to believe the other two were unaware of it. He tightened his grip on his wife, pulling her to him in an almost violent gesture.

Watching them, Erin wondered what sort of man they had engaged to be their keynote speaker.

Chapter Four

∾

"I see you're looking at our guest of honor and his wife," Farnsworth remarked, leaning back in her chair. "I know women like her are supposed to be a trophy, but I always wonder what men like him think people are saying behind his back."

"Probably, 'I wonder what *she* sees in *him*'?" said Khari.

"'There goes another gold digger and her fool.'"

"Steady on," said Erin. "You *are* talking about our keynote speaker. He is a literary celebrity."

Farnsworth sighed. "I hate it when you're right. Fortunately, it doesn't happen too often."

Khari laughed, showing perfectly symmetrical, pearly teeth. "I can see you're really good friends."

"How so?" said Farnsworth.

"Only very good friends could insult one another so casually."

"Wait 'til she meets Hetty and Pru," said Erin.

"Oh yes," Farnsworth agreed. "They're *really* good friends." She stood up. "I'm going to powder my face."

As she turned, a waiter carrying a tray of appetizers brushed by, catching her shawl on the edge of the tray. Caught off balance, Farnsworth stumbled and lurched forward, twisting her ankle. Erin gasped as she fell, but her fall was intercepted by a pair of strong arms. Erin looked up to see a tall, solidly built man with a strong, square face and a sweep of steel-gray hair.

"All you all right?" he asked in a deep voice.

"I—I've just twisted my ankle a bit," Farnsworth said, gritting her teeth.

The waiter hovered over her, looking very distressed. He was slight, with a long nose, tiny mustache, and curly brown hair. "I'm *so* sorry! Are you sure you're all right?"

"Quite all right, thank you. Please don't worry."

"Let's get you sorted," the tall man said, gently helping her up. Farnsworth was not a small woman, but he lifted her back into her chair as if she were a sylph. He was about the same age as Barry Wolf, but unlike the other man, his stature and presence commanded respect. "Could you fetch a bag of ice?" he asked the waiter, who scurried off quickly. "You mind if I take a look at that?" he asked Farnsworth.

"I don't think it's broken," she replied.

"Still, best to have a look just to be sure."

"All right."

Was she *blushing*? Erin wondered.

He knelt and examined her foot and lower leg. Erin had to admit; Farnsworth did have nice ankles, shapely and delicately tapered. Her own mother dismissed women with thick ankles as having "peasant legs."

"It doesn't appear to be broken," he said, straightening up. "Still, best to keep it elevated," he added, pulling over a footstool and placing her leg gently on it. "Does it hurt?"

"Not much. I'm just embarrassed."

"It could happen to anyone," Khari said, just as the waiter returned with a bag of ice.

"The bartender saw the whole thing and had this ready," he said, giving it to the tall man, who placed it carefully on Farnsworth's ankle. "Again, I'm *so* sorry."

"Not your fault, Sam," she replied, glancing at his name tag. "I'll be fine, and you have things to do."

He nodded and gave a little bow before darting off into the crowd.

The tall man remained standing where he was. "Is this seat taken?"

"It is now," Farnsworth replied with a sweep of her arm. "I'm Farnsworth Applebee."

"Grant Apthorp," he said, taking her hand and kissing it lightly.

"Thank you so much for—for—"

"Coming to her rescue," Erin finished for her.

He smiled majestically. "It's not often one has the chance to save a beautiful woman."

Farnsworth made a gurgling noise that Erin had never heard before. It appeared to be some version of a giggle. "How very genteel," she said.

"I'm Erin Coleridge, and this is Khari Butari," said Erin.

"Pleased to meet you. Isn't Khari usually a male name?"

Khari gave him a wry smile. "My parents wanted a boy."

"How fortunate their wish was not granted."

"How did you know it was a boy's name?"

"I've spent some time in Senegal. Not as much as I'd like, alas."

"Are you the same Grant Apthorp I heard quoted on a BBC documentary about Jane Austen?" said Erin. "From Cardiff University?"

"Guilty as charged."

"I saw that!" said Farnsworth. "Have you really translated Austen's books into Welsh?"

"Some of them, yes."

"I liked what you said about Austen inventing the trope of the virtuous man who initially appears cold and remote—"

"Like Darcy?" said Khari.

"Or reserved and taciturn, like Colonel Brandon," he said.

"Yes," Farnsworth agreed. "But don't forget the flip side—"

"The cad who first appears as a romantic hero," said Erin.

"Like Willoughby," said Khari.

"I'm not the first to point that out, of course," he said, smiling. He had very thick, dark eyebrows, and when he smiled, they rose in unison, like obedient caterpillars.

"But the way you framed it in the social mores of her time period was incredibly compelling," said Farnsworth.

"Actually, what I like most about Austen's works is that women are always the central characters. For all their political and social power, men exist as satellites in their world."

"Surely as a woman, it was natural for Austen to put females in the center of her stories," said Khari.

"Indeed," he said, raising his glass. His hands were broad and muscular, with thick, strong fingers. He was, Erin thought, a man you would want on your side. "Let's drink to the centrality of women in culture."

He winked at Farnsworth and Erin saw her friend blush. She wondered if Apthorp was laying it on a bit thick, playing the enlightened male, or if he was indeed what he appeared to be. Whatever his intentions were, she thought, he had better be more Colonel Brandon than Willoughby, or he would have Erin to reckon with.

By the time they finished their first round, Farnsworth was flushed and boisterous, her silk shawl fallen around her elbows, displaying plump white shoulders. Her rosy cheeks shone, and her eyes—her best feature—sparkled. Erin thought she looked fetching, and suspected Grant Apthorp did too. The cues were all there—he was smiling at her and touching her hand or arm from time to time. He was definitely paying her attention and Erin was glad to see her friend so animated.

"My turn to buy," Grant said, rising from his chair. "Same again?"

"It's too late to desert Alice now," said Farnsworth.

The others agreed, and he maneuvered his way through the crowd toward the bar. The room was packed now, the din of voices having long reached what Erin's mother would call "the danger decibel." She was afraid of damaging her hearing, a fear she communicated to Erin, who also disliked loud noises of any kind. The volume of conversation was so loud now it was impossible to communicate in a normal voice.

* * *

"What do you think?" Farnsworth shouted.

"About what?" said Erin.

"Grant Apthorp, of course!"

"He seems to be a nice gentleman," Erin replied. "Wouldn't you agree?" she asked Khari.

"Yes, and very articulate."

"Speaking of which," said Farnsworth, "you have a beautiful accent. Is English your first language? You seem so at home in it."

"Along with Wolof and French, yes."

"Wow," said Erin. "That's so amazing, to be fluent in three languages."

Khari shrugged. "My parents were teachers, and insisted we keep up our studies. But Senegal is multilingual, like a lot of other African countries."

Apthorp returned carrying four drinks, which wasn't much of a challenge; his massive hands were as capacious as the rest of him. Unusually tall and broad shouldered, he carried a fair amount of weight on his generous frame. Erin's mother would have referred to him as "heavyset." Erin thought it suited him, though. It only added to his already impressive presence.

As he set the drinks down, Erin's eyes were drawn back to the bar. "Barry Wolf and an elegant middle-aged woman in a striking green cocktail dress were having an intense conversation, and he looked angry." His face was red, and he jabbed his index finger at her repeatedly. Wolf never quite touched her, but the gesture struck Erin as violent and threatening.

"Who's that?" she asked Grant. "Do you know that woman?"

"That's Barry's ex-wife, Judith Eton. She's quite the scholar herself—a historian and author of a number of important academic publications."

"You know them well?" asked Farnsworth.

"Barry and I worked at the same university years ago, and it was during that time he and Judith met. She was my research assistant at the time, but I didn't introduce them. He's always had an eye for beautiful women."

"She /is/ very attractive," agreed Farnsworth.

"They have a son, too—Jeremy. He's at uni here in York. I saw him in the lobby earlier today."

"Oh yes, please," Farnsworth said to a waiter hoovering nearby, carrying a tray of hors d'oeuvres, as she plucking a salmon croquette from the plate. Erin chose a piece of sushi, while Grant and Khari went for the puffed cheese balls.

"You should have seen Judith when they met," Apthorp said. "What a stunner. Mr. Wolf always had an eye for the ladies. Lived up to his name in that regard."

"The mystery is why the ladies had an eye for him," Farnsworth mused.

"Maybe he has money," Khari suggested.

"Or maybe he's a really nice guy," said Erin.

"He's not," said Grant. "He's a tosser. I suppose some women go for that."

"Rubbish," said Farnsworth. Yikes. Harsh.

"I am glad to hear it," Grant replied, smiling.

The argument between Barry Wolf and his ex-wife seemed to be nearing its climax. Wolf's face was so red that Erin feared he might have a stroke. Judith Eton listened to him, stony-faced, arms crossed, her weight settled onto one spiky-heeled sandal. She really was a handsome woman, with high cheekbones and full lips. Her dark hair as fastened in a smooth chignon at the nape of her neck.

While Wolf was still talking, she turned abruptly and stalked away as rapidly as her high heels would allow. He watched after her for a moment, then turned back toward his current wife and attempted to put an arm around her, but she shrank from him. Erin's mind whirled, trying to come up with scenarios explaining this curious behavior, until Farnsworth tapped her on the arm.

"Earth to Erin," she whispered.

"What?"

"You're staring."

"Who's for another round?" Erin said, a little too heartily. "My turn to buy."

The cocktail party went on until nearly the end of the dinner hour. Fortunately, Farnsworth summoned everyone to the dining room just in time. The the hotel's renowned cuisine lived up to its reputation, with locally sourced ingredients and an imaginative menu. Erin had the seared hake with orange braised chicory. Farnsworth and Grant went for the duck, while Khari ordered the vegetable filo tart, explaining she was mostly vegetarian.

"At least you're not a vegan," Farnsworth said as the waiter filled up their wine glasses. Erin could only imagine what kind of hangover they would all have tomorrow.

"I do eat fish sometimes," Khari admitted. "But I never found meat very appealing."

"More for us," Grant said with a wink at Farnsworth.

It was nearly midnight by the time they left the restaurant, full of good food and bonhomie. Grant and Khari had rooms on the ground floor, so Erin and Farnsworth bade them goodnight and headed for the lift.

"What time is your panel?" Farnsworth, stifling a yawn as she pressed the button.

"Two o'clock," Erin said, yawning in response.

"Lucky you. Mine's at ten. Did you bring your hangover remedy?

"Of course. Thought we might need it."

"Will you marry me?"

"What about Grant Apthorp?"

"He *is* lush, isn't he?" Farnsworth said as they got off the lift.

"And he clearly thinks a lot of you."

"Rubbish. I'm too old for romance."

"Stop fishing for compliments. You're gorgeous and you know it," Erin said, fiddling with her key card. It took three tries before she got it—she was more affected by the alcohol than she realized. "Here you are," she said, retrieving a packet of crystallized ginger from the dresser drawer. "Cup of tea to go with that?"

"I won't say no," Farnsworth said, sinking into the settee. She looked around the room. "Your place is smaller than mine. But then, I got a suite."

"All right for some," Erin said, turning on the kettle.

"You could have had one too."

"I wanted a top-floor room."

"Why?"

"I like slanted ceilings."

Farnsworth shivered. "It's too *La Bohème* for me. Mimi coughing herself to death in her garret room."

"Where's your sense of romance?"

"Sitting in front of a roaring fire with a snifter of brandy."

There was the sound of giggling and low voices in the hall.

"You hear that?" Farnsworth whispered.

"Yeah. I wonder who it is?"

"Let's find out," Farnsworth said. Getting off the couch, she tiptoed to the door and peered through the peephole.

"Who is it?"

"A young couple. I can't see their faces. Wait—they're leaving."

"Can I look?" said Erin, but she got to the door just in time to see them retreating down the hall toward the lift. She thought the young man had blond hair, just like the one she had seen earlier near the cloakroom. The girl appeared to have dark hair, but it was hard to be sure.

"Wonder why they'd come up here to canoodle?" Farnsworth said.

"My guess is that they can't meet in their rooms—"

"Because they're here with someone else!"

"Tea's ready," Erin said, pouring them each a mug.

"Nice flowers," said Farnsworth. "Let me guess who sent them. Now you'll *have* to call him."

"Why?"

"To thank him for the flowers, of course."

When they had finished their tea, Erin offered to walk Farnsworth to her room.

"Very kind of you, but—"

"I want to pop down to the front desk anyway and get an eye mask. I forgot to bring mine," Erin said. She was a light sleeper, and preferred total darkness at night.

"You could have one sent up."

"I don't want to be that much trouble."

"I'll come with you."

"But—"

"Then you can walk me to my room."

She agreed, and the two women rode the lift to the nearly deserted lobby.

"Good lord, is it that late?" Farnsworth said, looking at the wall clock over the desk. It was a few minutes before twelve.

The hotel clerk, a very bright-eyed, cheery young man, seemed only too glad to fetch Erin an eye mask.

"I'll just nip down to housekeeping," he said, coming around from behind the desk. "Won't be a minute."

Before she could protest, he darted down the hall and around the corner.

Glancing down the hall in the other direction, toward the restaurant, Erin saw Barry Wolf talking to a tall, wiry man of about fifty. He wore his thick gray hair slicked back from his angular face, which reminded her of a crow, with its beakish nose and sharp, dark eyes. In fact, he was a dead ringer for the Irish writer, Samuel Beckett. The two men seemed to be engaged in deep discussion— the wiry man's arms were crossed; he was nodding and biting his lip.

"Who's that talking to Barry Wolf?" she asked Farnsworth.

Her friend peered down the hall. "Oh, that's Terrence Rogers. He's a leading literary scholar specializing in eighteenth- and nineteenth-century women writers. We nearly asked him to deliver the keynote speech, but decided on Wolf in the end."

It was clear that Rogers did not like what Wolf was saying; his face darkened and he turned away. Wolf followed up the remark with something else, and for a moment, Erin thought Rogers was going to turn and slug him, but he just shook his head and walked away. Wolf waited a moment before heading in the other direction, toward the cloakroom.

"Could you hear what they were saying?" Farnsworth whispered.

"No," Erin replied, as Terrence Rogers entered the lobby. He gave the women a brief, preoccupied smile before ringing for the lift.

"You can't lie to me, remember? I always see through you."

"I really didn't hear them," Erin said as the hotel clerk returned.

"Here you are," he said. "I brought two in case your friend wants one."

"How very thoughtful," said Farnsworth. "Cheers."

"My pleasure, madam. Anything else I can do to be of service?"

"No, thank you," said Erin. "Much appreciated, thanks."

By the time Erin got back to her room, she was so tired that she flung herself into bed without flossing her teeth. The last thing she saw before she drifted off was the red lights of the alarm clock flashing 12:30 AM.

Chapter Five

∼

"Erin! Erin, wake up!"

Erin was dreaming about having tea with her mother at Vaults & Garden Café, located in the back of the Church of St. Mary the Virgin, where her father was vicar. As the sun filtered in through the tall fourteenth-century windows, she was just about to take a bite of raisin scone with clotted cream and jam when she heard the sound of loud knocking.

"Erin! Open the door!"

She inhaled the aroma of fresh scone, opening her mouth for a bite . . .

"If you don't open this door, I'll break it down!"

The café slowly dissolved, giving way to her room in the Grand Hotel, the scone becoming a knob of bedsheet clutched between her fingers. Her disappointment was replaced by concern, as she realized the voice belonged to Farnsworth, who continued knocking insistently.

"Be right there," Erin called, still half asleep. Throwing her legs over the side of the bed, she stumbled to the door, images from the dream trailing after her. But when she opened it, her mother's smiling face was replaced by Farnsworth's alarmed one. "What is it?" Erin said. "What's happened?"

"Barry Wolf—he's dead!" Farnsworth exclaimed, unable to hide a certain glee in her voice. She appeared to have dressed hastily, in tan slacks and long wool cardigan over an untucked white shirt, her dark hair pulled into an untidy bun.

"What—how?"

"He was found in the cloakroom this morning."

"Who found him?"

"One of the hotel staff."

"How did he die?"

"I don't know."

"Give me a minute to get dressed," Erin said, opening the door to let Farnsworth in. "What time is it?"

"It's after nine."

"What about your panel?"

"We canceled all the morning events."

"Tell me what you know so far," Erin called from the bathroom.

"Not much—I went down for breakfast and saw all these EMT workers. Sam filled me in on the details."

"Sam?" Erin said, shoving a toothbrush into her mouth.

"Our waiter from last night."

Erin poked her head out of the bathroom. "So you're on a first-name basis now?"

"He's quite nice, you know—insisted on buying me breakfast to make up for last night."

"You're making friends everywhere, aren't you?"

"I refused, of course, but it was a nice gesture."

"Did you have breakfast?"

"There was too much going on—I didn't want to miss anything."

"Why didn't you come get me?" Erin said, pulling on a black jumper over jeans.

"Don't be cross with me because you slept in."

"I fell asleep before I could set the alarm."

"I'm a natural early riser. I never sleep past eight."

"How's your ankle?"

"Still a bit swollen, but much better."

"I'm ready," Erin said, slipping on some sandals and grabbing a cardigan from the closet. "Let's go see the scene of the crime."

"No one said anything about a crime," Farnsworth replied as they left the room, the door closing behind them with a fatalistic clunk. "Do you think we might have a bit of breakfast? I'm starving."

"Crime solving should never be done on an empty stomach," Erin said as they strode down the carpeted hallway toward the lift.

Downstairs, the atmosphere in the hotel was completely transformed. The air was charged with a strangely exhilarating excitement, a contagious electricity that made Erin's skin tingle. The hotel desk staff looked a bit stunned, as if they were extras who had ended up on the wrong movie set. Tricia, the perky young eavesdropper from the day before, had been replaced by a soft, middle-aged woman with a sweet, heavily powdered face. Several younger staff members scurried about, answering phones and peering at computer screens intensely as if they held the key to explain what had just happened.

The kindly concierge, whose name was Harriet, informed them the body had already been removed, but Erin spied an emergency vehicle outside the front entrance, lights flashing. A couple of medics perched on its bumper, drinking from paper coffee cups.

"Come along," Erin told Farnsworth, striding across the lobby's inlaid marble floor. "Let's have a chat." Pushing open the heavy front door, Erin was surprised at how biting the air was. The temperature had dropped overnight, the rain giving way to a bone-chilling cold. She immediately regretted neglecting to throw on a coat.

"Ugh," Farnsworth said as a gust of wind swooped across the broad street. "Must we talk with them *now?*"

"You can go back inside. I won't think less of you."

"Bollocks," Farnsworth said, pulling her cardigan tight around her generous frame. "Just make it quick."

"Can I help?" said the older of the two medics, a tall woman with tightly braided hair over high cheekbones. She had a Jamaican accent and a regal bearing, and Erin tried not to be intimidated. According to her name tag, her name was Shanise.

"We were just wondering if you could tell us anything," Erin said.

"You see, we know the vic—the, uh, man who died," Farnsworth added.

"Our mates jes' took 'im away," said the other medic, a pale young man with thinning sandy hair and pale eyes. He was sucking on an unfiltered cigarette; his accent was pure East End. The name "Henry" was stitched on his green jumpsuit. "They arrived jes' before we did, but it was too late t'save the poor fella. 'Fraid he's brown bread."

Farnsworth stared at him. "That's Cockney rhyming slang for dead," Erin whispered to her. "Can you tell us anything about what happened?" she asked them, stifling a cough as a gust of wind blew tobacco smoke in her face.

"We are not allowed to comment to the public," Shanise said sternly.

"Unless a'course you're family," Henry added.

"Indeed we are," Farnsworth replied. "Barry's my . . . cousin."

"Sorry," said Henry. "Tough, that, losin' yer baker's dozen."

"Rhyming slang for 'cousin,'" Erin told Farnsworth in response to her bewildered look.

"Yes, he was a good—uh, baker's dozen," Farnsworth replied. Henry nodded, but Shanise eyed them dubiously. "You see, we came here with him," Farnsworth continued. "He adored travel, poor Cousin Barry."

"What about you?" Shanise, peering at Erin.

"I'm his niece," Erin said, meeting her gaze.

"Did you happen to see the body?" Farnsworth asked eagerly. "I mean, he was such a lively man. It's hard to think of him—you know, as brown bread," she added, dabbing at an imaginary tear.

"Yeah, sad, innit?" said Henry, taking a thoughtful drag on his cigarette. The smoke curled upward before dissipating in the cold air.

"So did you get a look at him?" asked Erin, moving upwind of him.

"We did, yeah. Our mates were already here when we arrived, an'—"

"Did you happen to notice anything unusual? Any signs of trauma on the body?"

"It's all in the report," Shanise interrupted. "It will be made available to *family* members."

"Poor Cousin Barry," Farnsworth said mournfully.

"Come t'think of it," Henry said, "there was somethin' a bit odd."

"What was it?" said Erin.

"See here—" Shanise began, but Henry ignored her.

"Looked like he'd vomited quite a bit," he said.

"That's not unknown in sudden cardiac arrest," Shanise snapped.

"So that was the cause of death? Cardiac arrest?" said Erin.

"That's what it looked like," said Henry, flicking a piece of tobacco clinging to his lips. "'Course that could change on the coroner's final report."

"What about the time of death?" said Farnsworth.

"Dunno, but looked like he'd been dead fer a while."

"That's enough," Shanise said, stepping forward. "If you really *are* family members, you'd best contact the coroner's office for further details."

"Oh, we will," Farnsworth said. "Dear Cousin Barry."

"Thank you for your time," Erin said. "We appreciate it."

Henry nodded and tossed his cigarette into the gutter. "It's hard losin' a family member."

"Uncle Barry was more than family," said Farnsworth. "He was—"

"I thought you said he was your cousin," Shanise said, her eyes narrowing suspiciously.

"He wore many hats," Farnsworth replied.

"Thanks again," Erin said quickly, pulling her away. "We'll just go slip on a pair of daisy roots."

"What on earth are daisy roots?" said Farnsworth as they entered the lobby.

"Boots," said Erin, wishing she was wearing hers.

"Where did you pick up so much Cockney rhyming slang?"

"From one of the books in my shop. Excuse me—uh, Harriet," she said to the middle-aged woman with the kind eyes behind the desk. "I wonder if I could ask you something."

"Yes, dear?"

"Would you happen to know which staff member discovered the . . . body?"

Harriet shook her head sorrowfully. "That would be Christine," she said in a soft Scottish borders accent. "Poor girl, had to go home straightaway. Very upsetting, it was."

"Christine—?"

"Christine Brooks. She came in early to set up the dining room for breakfast, and, well, poor thing was nearly hysterical."

"And were the police here?"

"Aye, but not for long. They stayed less than an hour. Didn't even mark it off as a crime scene." She sighed. "Nice looking they were, too—handsome blond fella and his tall, dark sergeant. Very polite, he was—quite the cheerful lad."

"Thank you," said Erin. "I appreciate it."

"Did you know the poor fella, then?"

"Yes," said Farnsworth. "We did. He was our—"

"Well, I'm very sorry for your loss," said Harriet as the front desk phone rang. "Excuse me," she said, picking it up. "I've got to take this."

"Thanks again," said Erin, turning to leave. "Weren't you laying it on a bit thick with the medics?" Erin said to Farnsworth as they walked through the lobby.

"Do you think they bought it?"

"Definitely not. You couldn't even decide if he was your cousin or uncle."

Farnsworth sighed. "Poor Barry."

"You can knock it off now," Erin said they approached the restaurant.

"I mean it. No one should die alone in a cloakroom."

"We don't know yet that he was alone—or that he died in the cloakroom."

Farnsworth's eyes widened. "You think—?"

"I don't know, but I mean to find out," Erin said with more conviction than she actually felt.

Chapter Six

It was too late for breakfast at the restaurant, so they agreed to return to their rooms and meet for an early lunch. Erin arrived at her room to find the maid had come and gone; the bed was neatly made, and fresh towels hung from the bathroom rack.

Tossing her key card on the bureau, Erin sat heavily on the edge of the bed, feeling unexpectedly melancholic. Her opulent surroundings, with a glorious view of York Minster, suddenly felt unimportant in the face of something as solemn as the passing of another human being. Her initial reaction to the news had been rather shallow but now that reality was sinking in, she felt ashamed. This wasn't one of the mystery novels lining the shelves of her beloved bookstore—this was *real*. A man had been breathing and talking and going about his life, with perhaps no more thought than what to have for breakfast, and now he was no more. All that remained of what was once Barry Wolf was a cold and lonely lump of flesh on a bare metal slab somewhere in the bowels of the hospital morgue, awaiting the medical examiner's knife.

Farnsworth was right, of course—Barry Wolf might have been an unpleasant person, vain and ignoble, but no one deserved to die alone in a cloakroom. That was the question, of course—*did* he die alone, or did he have help? A voice deep inside her insisted that his death was not a tragic medical occurrence, but something far more sinister. Yet what did she have in the way of proof? Merely an observation that Barry Wolf had a knack for making enemies, and a stray comment from a young EMT worker with a Cockney accent and an addiction to unfiltered cigarettes.

It would never hold up in a court of law. Her father's voice flitted through her head; it was one of his favorite sayings, even though he was an Anglican minister, not a lawyer. But he also believed in trusting your instinct, and hers told her that something was not right. Erin gazed at the landline on the bedside table. If she picked it up and called Peter Hemming to tell him her suspicions, would he think her a fool? She could thank him for the flowers, and slip in a mention of Barry's death—or would that be hopelessly maladroit?

Her mobile phone lay on the small desk along the opposite wall, still attached to its charger. Her father's number was at the top of the Favorites list, and all she had to do was press one button to speak with him. But what sort of advice did she long for, really?

"Get it together," she muttered to herself, and reached for her mobile. But as if reading her mind, the phone chimed the first few notes of the Bach Fugue in B Minor, the ring tone reserved for her father.

"Hiya," she said, flopping onto the bed after disengaging the phone from its charger.

"Morning, Pumpkin. Sleep well?"

"Very well," she said, gazing up at a faint yellow water stain on the ceiling. It was probably her morbid imagination, but the stain reminded her of a forensic body outline.

"Is the place as nice as it looked online?" her father said.

"Even nicer."

Now that he was on the phone, she was reluctant to mention Barry's death, or her suspicions. Her father would only worry, tell her not to get involved, and no doubt remind her of what happened the last time she stuck her nose where it didn't belong.

But he had the instinct of a bloodhound. "Something wrong?" he said.

She sighed. Try as she might, she couldn't seem to keep secrets from him.

"What is it?" he said. "What's happened?"

She told him everything, starting with being awakened by Farnsworth, up to the conversation with the paramedics.

There was a pause, and then he said, "You read too many murder mysteries."

"Perhaps from now on I should restrict my reading to the Old Testament. No violence there, surely."

"Mind you don't get involved in all this. Remember what happened last time."

"I knew you'd say that."

"Sorry to be so predictable."

"It is disappointing. One does hope one's father will set an example."

"That's what I'm trying to do."

"By being stodgy and predictable?"

"Now see here—" he began, but heard the call waiting beep on her phone.

"Sorry," she said. "I've got another call."

"You sure you're all right?"

"I'm fine. I'll call you later."

"Erin—" he said, but she rang off and pressed "Answer".

"Hello," said a smooth, cultivated baritone with a tired, somber edge. It was the voice of Peter Hemming.

The sound him made her stomach tingle.

"Hello," she replied, trying to sound casual. In truth, she felt unprepared, a bit giddy and nervous. They had not met since their farewell in front of her bookshop on that crisp fall day several weeks ago, and since then had spoken only a few times on the phone.

"Are you in York?" he asked.

"Yes—we arrived yesterday. How's your mother?"

"Not so good."

"I'm sorry to hear that. Thank you for the flowers."

"They arrived intact?"

"Yes—they're beautiful. And not too Austentacious."

"Sorry. I did warn you about my bad puns."

She groaned. "That was definitely one of the worst."

"Look," he said. "About that poor fellow who died in your hotel. I just wanted to caution you—"

Not necessary here, I don't think.

"To keep my nose out of it."

"Or words to that effect."

"The ME's report should clear up—"

There was a knock at the door.

"Sorry," she said, relieved. "I have to go—I'm meeting Farnsworth for lunch."

"For God's sake, stay out of trouble. Please."

"I'll call you later," she said, ringing off before he could reply. Lurching for the door, she yanked it open to find Farnsworth, looking much more put together than earlier. Her dark hair was combed and curled, a brown wool cardigan neatly buttoned at her throat. Her linen cream pants looked freshly ironed.

"Come along," said Farnsworth. "I'm starving. We're meeting Hetty and Pru to decide what to do about the keynote address."

"Don't you look smart."

"How kind of you to say so, Miss Coleridge. One never knows who one may encounter in a public restaurant, after all."

"Nonetheless, you set a most admirable standard for sartorial splendor."

"I endeavor to display appropriate dress at all times, but I fear you flatter me."

"Your humility does you credit, Miss Appleby. Shall we make our way to the dining room?"

"By all means," Farnsworth said. "After you."

As they walked down the hall, Erin heard a door opening behind them, then closing quickly. It sounded like it came from the room across from hers, but by the time she turned around, it was too late to tell.

Chapter Seven

◞

The dining room was nearly full, the servers scurrying around like squirrels gathering nuts for the winter. Apparently, the keynote speaker's untimely death had not diminished the appetites of conference attendees. The air buzzed with the same heightened sense of anticipation she had noticed earlier. It was similar to the energy after a concert or play, the feeling that Something Important had occurred.

Hetty and Prudence had garnered a table near the window, and Hetty waved Erin and Farnsworth over as they entered.

"Have a croissant," she said, holding up a basket of freshly baked pastries. The buttery aroma made Erin's stomach contract with hunger.

"Is there room for us?" asked Farnsworth.

"Of course," said Pru. "We just need to grab a couple of chairs."

"I'll do it," said Erin.

"I'll help," said Farnsworth.

"You need to rest your ankle," Erin said, pulling up the only chair she could find. Farnsworth lowered herself onto it gingerly.

"How is it feeling, dearie?" Hetty said, patting Farnsworth's knee. She was clad in a bright pink dress, so tight Erin could see the outline of her bra strap.

"I'll live," Farnsworth replied.

"Oh, there's that dishy waiter from last night," Hetty said, peering across the room. She was nearsighted, but refused to wear glasses.

"You mean Sam?" said Farnsworth. "You think he's dishy?"

Prudence speared a pat of butter and smeared it over her croissant. "If he has two legs and two arms, he's a catch as far as Hetty's concerned."

"Have you forgotten that nice one-armed man I dated a few years back?" said Hetty.

"He was lovely," said Farnsworth. "What was his profession again?"

"He was a tennis pro."

"Overachiever," Pru muttered. "Why are you still standing?" she asked Erin.

"I don't see any other free chairs."

"May I be of assistance, ladies?" Sam asked, approaching with a chair.

"The cavalry arrives," said Farnsworth. "Well done!"

"It's the least I could do after my clumsiness last night," he replied, placing the chair with a flourish. "How's your ankle?"

"Better, thank you."

"Let me know if there's anything else you need," he said with a little bow.

Hetty sighed as she watched Sam's slim hips swaying as he walked away.

"I thought you were seeing Reverend Motley," Erin said.

Hetty wiped a bit of lipstick from the corner of her mouth with her forefinger. "We never said we were exclusive. And when the cat's away . . ." she added with a wink.

"So does that make you the cat or the mouse?" said Farnsworth, studying the menu.

"You've got the wrong end of the stick, dearie," Pru told Hetty.

"What do you mean?"

"He's gay."

Hetty snorted. "Ridiculous. I have the best gaydar in North Yorkshire."

"You'd best get it checked, then," Prudence remarked. "Because that lad is definitely playing for the other team."

"How do you know? Did you chat him up?"

Prudence smiled. "Maybe."

"Excuse me for a moment," Erin said to the others. Rising from her chair, she followed Sam to the servers' station.

"Hello again," he said, turning to see her. "What can I get you?"

"I was just wondering if you saw anything unusual yesterday."

"How do you mean?"

"Anything out of the ordinary—suspicious."

He frowned. "Do the police think that gentleman's death was foul play?"

"They haven't decided yet," she said, which was technically true. "He might have been poisoned."

"Now you mention it," he said, "there was one thing. I didn't think much of it at the time, but—"

"What was it?"

"When I went into the kitchen to serve the salads, someone bumped into me going out the swinging door as I was coming in."

"Did you get a look at them?"

"No—they were in a big hurry. Nearly knocked me down. By the time I regained my balance, they were gone. And I didn't linger—I had plates to serve."

"Can you tell me anything about them?"

"Couldn't even say if it was a man or woman. Sorry."

"Do you think anyone in the kitchen saw this person?"

"Not likely. The salads are served from a little antechamber with its own refrigerator. It's not really in view of the whole kitchen."

"Did Barry Wolf have salad that night?"

"He would've done, yeah—it came with the entrée. Unless he had the soup instead."

"Do you remember which it was?"

Sam thought for a moment. "His wife ordered the soup—I remember, because of her sexy accent. I liked the way she said 'butternut squash.'"

"And Barry?"

"He had the salad."

"Are you sure?"

"Yeah."

"Was there anything unusual about it?"

"Actually, I thought the rocket was a funny shape. I even said something about it at the time."

Another young man poked his head into the servers' station. "Oiy, Sam—you've got tables waitin'!"

"Sorry," Sam told Erin. "Gotta go."

When Erin returned to the table, Prudence gazed at her with one raised eyebrow. "So, did you get a date with him?"

"Hardly," Erin replied, sitting down. "Shouldn't we discuss how to proceed with the conference?" she asked, to forestall any more questions. "We did just lose the keynote speaker."

"Tragic death," said Hetty. "Even if he was a total wanker."

"He was definitely the sort of person who makes enemies everywhere he goes," Pru added. "Wait a minute," she said, looking at Erin with wide eyes. "You don't think—"

"Oh, yes," Farnsworth replied. "She very much does."

"*Seriously?*" Hetty said. "You think someone did him in?"

"I think it's within the realm of possibility," said Erin.

"Is that why you were talking to Sam?" asked Prudence.

"He served Barry Wolf's dinner last night."

At that moment, every female head in the room turned toward the entrance. Temperatures rose, hearts fluttered and beat faster, and bosoms shuddered with sighs as the object of all the attention sauntered gracefully across the room.

"Jonathan Alder has arrived," Farnsworth murmured. "Let the games begin."

"It's each woman for herself," Hetty said, licking her lips. Jonathan Alder had set hearts aflutter when he moved to Kirkbymoorside two years ago to teach at the middle school. He lost little time in joining the Jane Austen Society, where he was responsible for a sudden influx in female membership.

"He fancies you," Prudence told Erin.

"I don't know about that," she replied as he approached their table.

"But then there's your sexy detective," Farnsworth murmured. "What's a girl to do?"

"Hello, ladies," Jonathan said, swiping a hand across his forehead to brush away a lock of dark wavy hair. Erin's own heart beat a little faster as his blue eyes locked with hers. He was absurdly good looking, with soft pale skin and cheeks rosy as a milkmaid's. He was only average height, but so well-proportioned he looked taller.

"When did you arrive?" Prudence asked him.

"Just a few minutes ago. What's this about the keynote speaker suddenly dropping dead?"

"Terrible, isn't it?" said Hetty, batting her false eyelashes. One had come loose at one end, flapping precariously like a small black wing.

After they filled him in on the details of Barry Wolf's unexpected demise, Jonathan shook his head. "Rotten luck. What are you going to do?"

"Carry on as best we can," Hetty said. "Stiff upper lip and all that."

"Do we have a backup speaker?"

"There are several people here who would do in a pinch," said Prudence. "What about your new boyfriend?" she asked Farnsworth. "He's an experienced lecturer."

"New boyfriend?" said Jonathan. "It appears I've missed quite a lot."

Farnsworth flapped her napkin dismissively. "Prudence is being whimsical."

Prudence sat up straighter and gave a little sniff. "Whimsicality is foreign to my nature."

"I only met the gentleman last night," Farnsworth explained.

"It is not time or opportunity that is to determine intimacy—it is disposition alone," Prudence declared.

"Well done," said Jonathan. "What's it from?"

"*Sense and Sensibility*," Prudence said, dabbing smugly at the corner of her mouth with her napkin. She could turn the simplest gesture into a victory lap.

"Really, *must* you always show off?" Hetty muttered.

"Well, my 'disposition' is to have some food before I pass out from hunger," Farnsworth said, rising from her chair. "Anyone else care to join me at the buffet?"

"I will," said Erin.

"Why not?" said Jonathan.

"Might as well," Prudence said, hanging her ratty wool jacket on the back of her chair. It was scuffed and frayed, as if it had been chewed on by goats. Though she lived in a tidy little cottage not far from the center of Kirkbymoorside, Pru always looked as though she had come straight from working on a farm. "Are you coming, Hetty?"

"Very well," her friend replied with a sigh, as though she was doing everyone a great favor. Erin didn't think Hetty had the naturally high metabolism as she liked to claim that she did. On the contrary, she rather thought that Hetty worked very hard to maintain her slim figure, and admired her for it. Erin was naturally thin, though she had noticed in the last few years she couldn't eat the way she used to. An extra scone for tea meant an added mile of jogging the next day. She had come to the reluctant conclusion it was easier simply to avoid the scone.

The buffet was a potential diet breaker, Erin thought with dismay as she surveyed the lavish arrangement of hot and cold dishes. Eventually, she settled on filet of Dover sole with rosemary roasted potatoes and fried baby artichokes, avoiding the béchamel sauce and opting for a slice of lemon instead. She did indulge in a spoonful of hollandaise, which looked too delicious to pass up. Her mother used to make it at home, and taught her how to slowly pour the egg yolks into the hot butter, so that they cooked without curdling.

Erin felt a nudge at her elbow and turned to see Farnsworth, a plate in her hand, staring at the far end of the buffet.

"Who is *that*?" she whispered.

Erin followed her gaze to see an extremely short woman of early middle age. Other than her lack of height, there was nothing unusual about her. She had rather thick, light-brown hair, flecked with gray, which she wore in a kind of pageboy, tapered around her neck, with thick bangs in front. It befitted her pixie-like face, with its sharp little nose and pouty lips, marred by a rather recessive chin. Her protruding lower lip was the most prominent point in the architecture of her face, giving her a perpetually dissatisfied expression. Her outfit was unremarkable; she wore a light-blue dress sprinkled with tiny daisies and bumblebees. It was exactly the kind of thing you might see on any respectable British matron weekday shopping at Sainsbury's or M&S.

"Never saw her before," Erin whispered.

"Just watch," said Farnsworth.

The woman's arm snaked toward the platter of stuffed mushrooms, but instead of putting the food on her plate, she tucked it quickly into the folds of her voluminous handbag.

"Did you see that?" said Farnsworth.

"Yes. What on earth—?"

"Keep watching—she's not done yet."

While they watched, the woman managed to steal a roast chicken breast, sautéed beets, and half a loaf of French bread, all secreted away in the enormous satchel on her arm.

"You're not suggesting we rat her out?" said Erin.

"Good heavens, no! It would embarrass her terribly. And you never know about people—in spite of her respectable appearance, she may be truly destitute. Besides, think of all the entertainment we'd deprive ourselves of."

"But is it fair to the restaurant?"

"She's only here for a few days. I'm sure they can spare it."

"Are you watching the buffet thief?" said Jonathan, coming up beside them.

"Yes," said Erin. "Do you know her?"

"I'm beginning to wish I did."

Hetty sauntered by holding a salad plate, a few string beans and cucumbers scattered across it like an abstract painting. "That's Winnifred Hogsworthy."

"Hogsworthy by name, Hogsworthy by nature," Farnsworth murmured. "Oh, no—she did *not* just put a custard in her bag."

"At least it wasn't chocolate," said Jonathan, pouring a generous serving of hollandaise onto his eggs Benedict. "How do you know her?" he asked Hetty.

"I met her this morning at the gym."

"Looks like she worked up quite an appetite," Farnsworth remarked. "Where are you sitting?" she asked Jonathan.

"Nowhere at the moment."

"Come join us."

"That's the best invitation I've had all day."

"I doubt that," Hetty muttered under her breath.

"You'll need to steal a chair," said Erin.

"I think I'm up to that," he replied, with a lopsided grin that caused a lock of hair to fall over one eye. Erin's legs went a little hollow. She wondered if he practiced in front of a mirror. She could practically feel the jealous stares boring into her back as he followed her back to their table.

"What else do you know about her?" Erin asked Hetty as they took their seats.

"She lives in Sussex. Took a train up because she doesn't drive," Hetty said, picking at her meager serving of vegetables.

"That's a long trip," said Jonathan.

"She said she finished the sweater she was knitting and started a new one."

"What else?" asked Erin.

Hetty poked at a piece of lettuce, pushing it around the plate with her fork. "Apparently she was Barry Wolf's grad student years ago."

Erin did a quick calculation. Winnifred Hogsworthy had to be at least forty, so that meant Barry Wolf might be even older than he looked.

"He gets around," Farnsworth remarked. "Or at least he did."

"Erin thinks he was murdered," Prudence told Jonathan.

"Really? Why?"

Erin put down her fork, feeling the heat of his gaze. "It just feels fishy. What was he doing in the cloakroom in the middle of the night? Why does he seem to have so many enemies? Why is his ex-wife here with their son? What's he doing married to a woman less than half his age?"

"Sadly, that's not so uncommon," Farnsworth remarked.

"And what is the story with that young assistant, Stephen?" said Hetty. "He's the same age as Wolf's wife. Is something going on between them?"

"Exactly!" said Erin. "There's a lot that doesn't add up."

"What are you going to do?" asked Jonathan.

"I'm not sure yet."

"In the meantime, don't let your food get cold," said Farnsworth, digging into a creamy pile of fettucine Alfredo. "If you're going to solve a murder, you'll need your strength."

Erin gazed out the long, elegant French window onto the broad avenue in front of the hotel. On the other side of the street, the famous medieval wall snaked its way around York, enclosing the city in its cold embrace. Beyond its ancient bricks, the River Ouse flowed sluggishly, in no hurry on its journey to the sea. A few snowflakes cascaded lazily from the sky as a crow darted past the window, its black wings casting a brief shadow on the glass.

Erin took a bite of sole, the flaky white flesh dissolving in her mouth. Suddenly ravenous, she speared a baby artichoke, then gulped down a large piece of roasted potato. Farnsworth was right—she would need her strength. Watching the dancing snowflakes, Erin wondered what else she might need to solve a murder.

Chapter Eight

❧

In the end, they all agreed Judith Eton would be the best choice for keynote speaker if she was willing, and Prudence agreed to ask her. Farnsworth expressed satisfaction at the fact that Judith was Barry's ex-wife, calling the choice "poetic justice."

That afternoon, the weather intensified. Scattered flakes of snow gathered into flurries, then showers, finally becoming a wall of white obscuring the view of the city. Soon the hotel was enveloped in a cocoon of snow, a soft, wet blanket of fat flakes that stuck to everything. Workers were sent out to shovel walks and driveways, but as soon as they returned, the pavement was already covered with a thin layer of falling snow.

"Beautiful, isn't it?" Erin said to Farnsworth as they stood in the hall outside the meeting rooms, waiting for Erin's two o'clock panel, *Jane Austen and Her Literary Influences*. They had an excellent view of the storm through the tall windows lining the corridor.

"As long as you don't have to go out in it," Farnsworth said with a shudder.

"Where's your spirit of adventure?"

"In my hotel room, warming my slippers and preparing a cup of hot chocolate."

"You have hot chocolate in your room?"

"Have you forgotten who you're talking to?"

Erin smiled. "Of course—you brought your own. And tiny marshmallows?"

"Without them, hot chocolate is a sad and desolate beverage." Farnsworth glanced at her watch and at the closed door of Jorvik. All the meeting rooms had names relating to the city in some way—Jorvik, for instance, was the original Viking name for York. "This panel is running late."

"You don't have to attend this one just because I'm on it. You must have better things to do."

"Tragically, I do not. Please don't rub it in."

"I have a feeling your schedule is about to fill up quickly," Erin said as Grant Apthorp emerged from a meeting room at the end of the hall.

"He *is* attractive, isn't he?" Farnsworth whispered as he approached them.

When he saw them, Apthorp broke into a grin. His broad, even teeth were a few shades whiter than normal. Erin wondered if it was the result of cosmetic dentistry, though he didn't look like a man given to such vanities.

"What a pleasant surprise," he said, standing next to them. His physical presence was undeniable—solid as a boulder, with his massive shoulders and large, thick-jawed head. He reminded Erin of a Saint Bernard—friendly, attentive, exuding good will. "It's much nicer out here," he added, wiping his brow. "That little room was rather stuffy."

"What was your panel on?" asked Farnsworth.

"*Jane Austen and Female Agency in the Nineteenth Century.*"

"How very politically correct."

"Oh, dear," he said with a wry smile. "Trying too hard, am I?"

Farnsworth shrugged. "Was it interesting?"

"It was, actually."

"I'd like to remind you that title was my idea," Erin said.

"And a jolly good one it was," Grant replied. "I learned quite a lot."

"Looks like you're up," Farnsworth said to Erin, as the door to Jorvik opened. Audience members trickled out as the staff set up the front table for the next panel. "Good luck moderating."

"Oh, you're the moderator, are you?" said Grant.

"No one else wanted to do it, so I volunteered."

"Are you on this one as well?" he asked Farnsworth.

"No. I just came along to lend moral support."

"I don't suppose you could be persuaded to join me for a cocktail instead?"

Farnsworth frowned. "Bit early, isn't it?"

"Tea, then?"

"Go on," said Erin. "I'll be fine."

"But—"

"You can watch the snowstorm from the comfort of the restaurant."

"They do a lovely tea here," Farnsworth said wistfully. "Looks like you have good attendance," she added, watching the crowd of people file into the room.

"You see? We don't need you," said Erin.

"Need her for what?" said Jonathan Alder, popping out of Bootham, the conference room next door.

"Moral support," Erin replied.

Farnsworth's face fell when she saw Jonathan. "You're on this one as well?"

"Someone dropped out, so I stepped in."

"This is Grant Apthorp," Erin told Jonathan. "He's—"

"A leading nineteenth-century literary scholar and historian. I'm an admirer of your work," he told Apthorp, extending his hand. "Jonathan Alder. It's a pleasure to meet you."

"The pleasure is mine," Apthorp said, wrapping his meaty hand around Jonathan's.

"I read *Art and Commerce: Literature and the Ascension of the Middle Class* twice."

Apthorp laughed. "Well done. My publisher could barely get through it once."

"Maybe I should stay," said Farnsworth, looking at Jonathan.

"Oh, go have tea," said Erin.

"Very well, but you must tell me all about the panel later."

"Don't be silly," Erin called over her shoulder as she and Jonathan followed the press of people into the conference room.

The panel went smoothly until the time came for remarks from the audience. Jonathan was witty and charming, gaining more than a few devotees among the females in the room. A fat man in the back row advanced the notion that Jane Austen was actually a man, which set several people's teeth on edge.

A thin woman with yellow teeth and long gray hair snorted loudly. "And I suppose Christopher Marlowe wrote all of Shakespeare's plays."

"As a matter of fact," he replied, "I've written a scholarly article on the subject." Clad in a brown leather vest and matching Indiana Jones–style hat, he appeared to be dressed for an African safari. The only thing missing was a leather whip hanging from his belt.

"That's ridiculous," muttered an older man in the front row. He looked like an Oxford don, with his old-fashioned, slightly ratty jacket, complete with leather patches on the elbows. Erin imagined him at his desk in a cluttered office overlooking a college quad, a mahogany pipe tucked between his lips, and realized she missed her father.

"What do you say we stick with the subject of the panel?" she said. "Anyone have a comment or question about Jane Austen's literary influences?"

A hand went up in the back and she recognized Winnifred Hogsworthy. Erin hadn't noticed her earlier and wondered if she had come in after the panel had started. It wasn't unusual for people to slip in and out halfway through, to catch as many panels as they could, and Winnifred was so short she was easy to miss.

"You have a comment?" Erin asked.

"A question, actually. I was wondering what the panel members thought of the theory that Jane Austen was poisoned by a literary rival."

"That's a new one on me. Where did you hear that?"

"I read it somewhere—can't remember where," Winnifred replied.

"Did they specify which rival allegedly poisoned her?" asked Jonathan.

"Not that I recall. Now that I say it out loud, it does sound a bit dotty, doesn't it?"

"You shouldn't be so quick to dismiss these things," said the man in the Indiana Jones outfit. "There's more mischief afoot than anyone realizes."

"I'm afraid our time is up," Erin said, looking at the wall clock. "I'd like to thank you all for coming, and thanks to all of our panel members."

"Saved by the bell," Jonathan remarked as he and Erin left the room. "That was pretty daft."

"I've seen worse."

"Really? Where?"

"At bookseller conventions, believe it or not."

"Booksellers have quite a reputation, actually."

"They do?"

"Their drunken orgies are legendary."

"We're a wild lot, all right."

"Uncontrollable."

"Unfettered."

"Unchained."

"Massively free-spirited."

They stood in the hall for a moment as people swarmed past. Erin felt comfortable around Jonathan, unlike Detective Hemming, around whom she often felt flustered.

Jonathan gave her one of his signature grins. "This calls for a drink. You game?"

"All right," she said, wondering if they would run into Farnsworth and Grant at the bar.

"This panel was actually my idea," he said as they crossed the carpeted corridor toward the lobby.

"I remember—I'm pretty sure I voted for it in committee," she replied as they passed the waiter Sam, walking rapidly, head down. Erin smiled at him, but he didn't seem to notice them—he was obviously in a great hurry.

"That's right—you were on the panel committee, weren't you?"

"I remember thinking yours was one of the better ideas."

"Being on panels is a bit of a busman's holiday for me," Jonathan remarked. "As a teacher, I spend all day chattering away."

"At least at a conference, you have other people to do some of the talking."

"Even if they're as bonkers as that lot was," Jonathan said, brushing a loose curl from his face. Erin's breath caught at the sight. "What was with Indiana Jones? What's his story?"

"Classic eccentric," Erin said as they entered the 1906 Bar. The room was nearly empty. The afternoon panels went until five, and it was just past four. "I see his type in bookstores all the time. People like him keep me in business.'"

"He seemed to be dressed for a safari," Jonathan said as they took seats by the window. "The only thing he was missing was a necklace of lion's teeth."

"He's harmless enough."

"Until he isn't."

Erin looked at Jonathan, surprised. "I'm a bad influence on you. Not everyone is a potential killer."

"You're the expert. Given the right circumstances, isn't anyone capable of murder?"

Gazing out at the rapidly gathering storm, Erin had to admit Jonathan was probably right. If so, her list of suspects in Barry Wolf's death had just multiplied geometrically.

Chapter Nine

～

Maybe it was the storm raging outside, or the relaxed atmosphere of the quiet bar, but Erin had a little more to drink than was good for her. Or maybe it was very good for her, she thought as she stared out the window at the swirling snowflakes. Outlined by the glare of the lights on the outside of the hotel, they leapt and danced like drunken ghosts, caught in the gusts and updrafts of the fickle wind.

Inside, LED Christmas lights strung over the mahogany bar lent a soft glow to the room, with its tasteful wall sconces and oriental carpets. Erin sank deeper into the red leather armchair with a sigh of contentment as she watched Jonathan fetch their second round. She had chosen the drink called Cthulhu, after the H. P. Lovecraft character. She liked the literary references sprinkled throughout the drink menu. Though not a Lovecraft fan, she liked the rum-based drink, even if it was a little fussy in that trendy mixology way.

Jonathan really was too gorgeous to ignore, she thought as he made his way back to her, his black curls bouncing. Erin noted that his corduroy jacket was just the right shade of mustard, a little worn at the cuffs and elbows, befitting someone who enjoyed reading. That kind of unstudied, rumpled charm was impossible to fake, unlike Barry Wolf's self-conscious slickness. Jonathan seemed unaware of his charisma, whereas Barry Wolf was obviously desperate to make a good impression. She didn't mind people dressing smartly and wanting to look their best, but Wolf had tried too hard—and unsuccessfully—to hide his age. The strain gave off an unpleasant aroma, like flop sweat.

Hetty was also devoted to hiding her age, of course, but somehow managed to pull it off. She could be ridiculous but unlike Wolf who just seemed sad and overeager, Hetty's attempt was oddly admirable.

"Desperation is rarely attractive," she murmured as Jonathan approached. "But it is not usually a cause of murder."

"What's that about murder?" he asked, handing her the drink.

"Nothing."

"You really think Barry Wolf was murdered?"

"I think it's possible."

"Why?"

"The timing just seems suspicious. He has so many acquaintances here—and from what I observed, a lot of them couldn't stand him."

"So you'll ferret out the truth."

"Meanwhile, each sip of this cocktail is bringing me closer to some sort of cosmic truth."

"How do you pronounce that again?" he asked.

"H. P. Lovecraft originally said it was pronounced *Khlûl-hloo*. But he kept changing his mind, so who knows?"

"It was a monster, right?"

"Yes, a malevolent alien creature imprisoned underground, worshipped by some, but feared by most."

"Here's Lovecraft's description of it on Wikipedia," Jonathan said, studying his phone. "'A monster of vaguely anthropoid outline, but with an octopus-like head whose face was a mass of feelers, a scaly, rubbery-looking body, prodigious claws on hind and fore feet, and long, narrow wings behind.'"

"Here's to creatures from our nightmares," said Erin, raising her glass.

"Cheers," said Jonathan.

"Supposedly, the creature would return to engineer the fall of civilization."

"Speaking of the fall of civilization, here comes our buffet thief."

Erin looked up to see Winnifred Hogsworthy amble into the bar, her enormous bag tucked under her arm. She scanned the room, as if looking for someone. Apparently, unable to locate the object of her search, she turned and wandered out.

"Bit of a lost soul, isn't she?" said Jonathan.

"I wonder who she was looking for."

"Perhaps searching for another buffet to plunder."

"What did you think of her comment about Jane Austen being poisoned by a rival?"

Jonathan smiled, deepening the dimple on his chin. "Mustn't believe everything you hear."

"It would make a good story, though, wouldn't it?"

"A sort of Regency murder mystery, you mean?"

"Something like that."

"But you'd have to have someone actually die to have a proper mystery."

"And a sleuth to solve it."

"Like you?"

"I'm not a proper sleuth."

"You solved Sylvia's murder."

"I got lucky."

"You nearly got killed."

"So did you."

Jonathan shivered. "Let's change the subject."

"But it was just getting interesting," said a voice behind them.

Erin turned to see Hetty and Prudence, inseparable as always. Pru wore a forest-green sweater that would probably look good on anyone else, while Hetty was decked out like a Christmas tree, with more beads and baubles than Erin had ever seen her—or anyone—wear.

"Don't you look festive," said Jonathan.

"Well, it's nearly Christmas season," Hetty replied.

"More like Halloween, if you ask me," Pru muttered, loud enough for everyone to hear.

"Please, join us," said Erin.

"Very kind of you," Hetty replied. Casting a baleful glance at Prudence, she moved toward one of the empty chairs, staggering a bit beneath the weight of her excessive couture. Her necklace alone appeared to weigh half a stone.

"Would you ladies like something to drink?" asked Jonathan.

"Oh, don't call us ladies," said Hetty. "It makes us seem so dreadfully *old*."

Pru pursed her thin lips. "If the shoe fits . . ."

"What shall I call you, then?" asked Jonathan.

Hetty twisted her gold necklace between her fingers. "Oh, *I* don't know."

"Dames? Women? Females?"

"How about damsels?" suggested Erin.

"How medieval," said Pru.

"Like this city," said Jonathan.

"I rather like that," Hetty said. "Damsels. It's quaint."

"Well, then," said Jonathan. "What have you damsels been up to?"

Hetty batted her false eyelashes. "Searching for our knights in shining armor."

"Do they really exist?" asked Erin.

"Only in Hetty's imagination," said Pru. "Real knights are hard to come by, and armor soon loses its sheen."

"Have you ever tried on a suit of armor?" Hetty asked Jonathan.

"I have. It weighs a ton and it's extremely uncomfortable. Can't imagine trying to ride a horse wearing it."

"I imagine it rusts when it gets wet," said Erin.

Jonathan raised his glass. "Here's to rusty armor and errant knights."

Pru gave a wan smile. "As Jane Austen wrote to her niece Fanny Knight, 'Pictures of perfection, as you know, make me sick and wicked.'"

"Where's Farnsworth?" Hetty asked, looking around.

Erin exchanged a glance with Jonathan. "She went to tea with—"

She was cut off by a loud commotion at the bar.

"No, I will *not* calm down, mate! I want another drink!"

Stephen Mahoney was leaning forward on the bar, elbows resting on the edge, his long-jawed face red, eyes blurry. The bartender was leaning back, arms crossed, his face stony.

"I said I *want* a drink!"

The barkeep lifted one eyebrow. In a barely perceptible gesture, he twisted his head slightly to the left. A burly security guard appeared, all bulging muscles and shoulders in his tight blue uniform, his goatee so neatly groomed it appeared to have been done with a laser.

"Come with me, sir," he said, taking Stephen's arm. "Let's not have any trouble now."

Mahoney pulled away, but the guard tightened his grip. "Now then, sir. I'm sure you don't want to cause a fuss."

"Unhand me!" Stephen sputtered, but the guard drew his face closer, so the two men were nearly touching noses.

"Let's not escalate this to a matter for the police, sir. You don't look like a man who would care to have a criminal record."

Mahoney shuddered, as if a bucket of cold water had just been poured over him. He straightened up, opened his mouth as if to say something, then slumped into a submissive posture. "I'll leave," he said. "You can let go of me."

"Sorry, sir, but protocol demands I escort you out."

For a moment Mahoney looked as if he might protest, but then sighed deeply, his shoulders sagged, and he submitted meekly as the guard led him from the room.

"Well," said Hetty after they had gone. "*That* was interesting."

Pru rolled her eyes, but Erin noted she had watched the display with the same wide-eyed curiosity as the rest of them.

Jonathan leaned in toward Erin. She could smell his aftershave—a bit floral, but mixed with the scent of fresh lime. "You can add a personal assistant with anger issues to your suspect list."

"Ooh, are you keeping a list of suspects?" asked Hetty.

"Not as such," Erin replied, but the truth was she was already compiling a mental list.

"What about motives?" asked Pru.

"I *do* hope he wasn't killed over money," said Hetty. "That would be unbearably tedious."

"What would be a good motive?" Jonathan asked.

"Why, love, of course! Something romantically tragic—a jilted lover, a jealous husband, a heartbroken suitor."

"It doesn't have to be either-or, you know," Erin pointed out. "Sometimes the motive is love *and* money."

She wondered if this was the case with Barry Wolf. Gazing out at the swirling snow, she didn't know whether it would make finding his killer easier—or more difficult.

Chapter Ten

"This has been lovely," Hetty said, finishing her drink. "But it's time to dress for dinner."

Erin wondered how much more dressing Hetty intended to do—she already looked as though she had raided a costume jewelry store.

"And I've got papers to grade," said Jonathan.

"Isn't school term over?" asked Prudence.

"There are some final exams awaiting my attention. A teacher's lot is not a happy one."

"Lucky students," Hetty murmured, licking her lips. Her bright red lipstick had faded to a somewhat more natural color, softening her face. The bright hues she was attracted to tended to sharpen the lines on her face, making her look older. But she seemed to get so much pleasure from her outlandish sartorial style that Erin was loath to give unsolicited comments. And who was she to advise another woman on fashion? Blessed with naturally clear skin, Erin wore little makeup. Her blue eyes were rather pale, and looked better with a touch of eyeliner and mascara, though she didn't always bother with it.

"Shall we reconvene later?" said Prudence.

"I'm going to the spa first," said Hetty. "So maybe eight o'clock?"

"I'm on an eight o'clock panel," said Pru.

"Just as well if I skip dinner," Hetty said. "I ate a big lunch."

"If you consider a salad and a few green beans a big lunch," Pru remarked, wrinkling her nose, making her appear rather mole-like.

As the little group wandered out of the restaurant, Erin wondered where Farnsworth was. The last she saw her, Farnsworth was headed off to tea with Grant Apthorp. The next thing Erin knew, Jonathan Alder was walking alongside her as she headed for the lift.

"What floor are you on?" she asked as they passed the second floor.

"Top floor. I like attic rooms."

"So do I."

"Kindred spirits," he mused, giving her one of his trademark smiles, all dimples and sparkling teeth.

"Here we are," she said as the lift bell dinged. "Fifth floor. Lingerie, women's wear, dry goods."

"Dry goods?" he said, laughing. "On the same floor with lingerie?"

"It's a small store."

She stepped off the lift, and he followed.

"Well," he said after they had gone a few steps, "this is my room."

They stood for a moment in the hallway. Then, before she could stop herself, her lips connected with his. He tasted spicy, with an edge of sweetness, like mulled plum wine. She felt she should pull away, but did not. She liked the feeling of his tongue against hers. She knew she was under the influence of alcohol, but only a little tipsy. Hungrily, she leaned in for more. Time slowed, then hung still, like tea time with Lewis Carroll's Mad Hatter, where it was always six o'clock.

"Well," she said finally, pulling away to catch her breath.

"Well," he echoed. "That was unexpected."

Was it really? Hadn't they been working toward this, in a way, for a long time?

"Nothing like a hotel for bringing out naughty impulses," he said.

Erin's heart fell. He made it sound like a school prank, and nothing more. This is a little wordy and awkward. How many times had he done this and at how many hotels? She turned and started down the hall toward her room. To her relief, he did not follow. She needed to be alone, to process what had just happened.

"See you at dinner?" he called after her. It sounded like more of a question than a statement.

"Yes," she said. "See you then." She continued toward her room at the end of the hall, and did not turn around when she heard the door to his room click open before quietly shutting again.

Chapter Eleven

Erin lay on her bed, watching the snowflakes gather in volume, until she succumbed to the welcome embrace of Morpheus. She slept lightly at first, aware of nearby sounds and smells—soft footfalls on the carpeted hallway outside her room, the soft murmur of voices as people came and went, the low hum of machinery within the walls of the hotel, the occasional banging from the radiator, the pipes swelling to accommodate the flow of hot air from the boiler. The sound brought her back to her childhood home in Oxford, lying on her stomach on the living room rug on a wintery evening, puzzled by the same loud clanking emanating from deep within the ancient plumbing.

Her mother's explanation never quite satisfied her. How could pipes make such a noise unless someone was whacking at them with a hammer? Years of hearing the same sound in so many different buildings had finally convinced her that what seemed like a violent assault on the plumbing system was in fact simply the result of contraction and expansion. She found the sound oddly comforting, resonating with childhood memories of the flat at Cowley Place, just a short walk from the Botanic Garden.

She awoke from her nap with the delicious sensation that her body, so in need of rest, was completely still and comfortable. But as consciousness crept nearer, she experienced the disappointment of realizing this fleeting moment would probably be the most pleasurable of the entire day.

Dragging herself from her comfortable slumber, she flicked the switch on the electric kettle and perched in front of her laptop on the desk by the window. By the time Farnsworth knocked on her door, she was deeply engrossed in an internet search.

"Time for dinner," Farnsworth announced when Erin opened the door. She looked elegant, hair upswept in a tidy chignon, another colorful shawl thrown over her shiny, electric blue dress. Diamond earrings sparkled on her small, delicate earlobes.

"Don't you look smashing," Erin remarked.

"What are you doing?" Farnsworth asked, peering over her shoulder as Erin bent down to save links to the web pages she been browsing.

"Doing a background check," Erin said, closing her laptop.

"On whom, pray tell?"

"Grant Apthorp, if you must know."

Farnsworth glowered at her. "Why on earth—"

"Because he knows Barry Wolf, and might have a motive to kill him."

"Nonsense."

"And because he's taken an interest in you."

"So what?"

"So I've taken an interest in him."

"You've got the wrong end of the stick."

"I sincerely hope you're right."

"You're not even dressed for dinner," Farnsworth said, looking at her disapprovingly.

"I—" she started, but was interrupted by the ringing of her room phone.

"Wonder who could that be?" said Farnsworth as Erin picked up the receiver next to the bed.

"Hello?"

"Miss Coleridge? It's Peter Hemming."

"Oh, hello," she said, wondering why he was calling her by her last name.

"I wonder if it would be convenient if I dropped by?"

"When?"

"Now, if possible."

"All right," she said. It wasn't convenient at all, and she thought longingly of the trout almondine she had planned on ordering.

"It's your sexy detective, isn't it?" Farnsworth whispered, but Erin waved her off.

"How long will it take you to get here?" she asked him.

"Twenty minutes, if that's all right."

"Fine," she said, her stomach rumbling as she thought about courgettes in truffle cream sauce.

"See you then."

"My room number is—" she began, but he had already rung off.

"He's coming over?" Farnsworth said as Erin replaced the receiver.

"Apparently."

Her friend's face fell. "So you can't come to dinner."

"You go on ahead—I'll catch up with you later."

"Maybe he wants to eat."

"That would be weird."

"I don't see why."

"This isn't a social call. He's coming to talk about the case."

"How do you know?"

"He called on the hotel phone. And his tone was formal, all business."

"But when he sees you, he'll probably melt."

"Doubtful."

"He *did* send you flowers."

"He's still not the melting type."

Farnsworth sighed. "Men. Can't live with them, can't live without—"

"Goodbye, Farnsworth," Erin said, holding the door open.

"And now my best friend is kicking me out," she said, sighing mournfully.

"Don't be pathetic," Erin said, but she couldn't help smiling. Farnsworth was having her on.

"You *are* my best friend, aren't you?"

"Of course I am. Now go."

"I'll tell them to save some trout for you."

"*Go*," Erin said, laughing, and Farnsworth obeyed.

Once she was gone, Erin scurried about the room, tidying up, stopping in front of the mirror to smooth her hair, which was quite scruffy. She dug a pair of clean socks from the drawer and pulled a pair of knee-length leather boots on over her wool slacks. Spotting a couple of stains on her shirt, she yanked a rust-colored silk blouse from its hanger in the closet and pulled it over her head, topping it off with a fitted wool jacket and tiger's-eye brooch in the shape of a seahorse on the lapel. Satisfied, she studied her reflection in the mirror. She looked put together, but not fussy—business casual, they called it these days.

She glanced at the bedside clock—he would be here in less than five minutes. What if he was early? She'd best meet him in the lobby, to avoid the discomfort of seeing him in her room, which felt too intimate under the circumstances. Slipping her key in her jacket pocket, she stood in front of the bathroom mirror and swiped lipstick over her lips. The label said Passion Fruit Posh. It was a little too pink for her taste, but Farnsworth had given it to her and Erin wore it from time to time.

"There," she muttered, wiping off the excess with her index finger. "That will have to do."

She picked up the laminated sheet of hotel amenities on the desk and studied it. If she missed dinner because of Detective Hemming, she would have to rely on room service. She was already hungry, and didn't fancy a trip out in the storm to forage for food. As she perused the brochure, she heard two people talking out in the hall. It sounded like a man and a woman. Though they were speaking in low tones, their voices carried an intensity of emotion. Dropping the menu on the table, Erin crept toward the hall to listen. The glossy brochure missed its target, fluttering to the floor, but Erin ignored it, pressing her ear to the door.

"It was foolish of you," hissed the woman.

"What was I supposed to do?" said the man in a sulky voice. "Just sit and wait for the old coot to—?"

"He may be old, but he's still your father!"

"Is he, though?"

"What do you mean?"

"I've heard otherwise."

Erin put her eye to the peephole. The woman was Judith Eton, and she was talking to a lanky youth with spiky, dyed yellow hair.

"What have you heard?" asked Judith.

The boy looked down at his shoes. "Rumors."

"What rumors?"

"About my real father."

"Who have you been talking to?"

Erin felt a sneeze coming on. Pinching her nose tightly with her thumb and forefinger, she tiptoed away as quickly as possible. But her left foot landed on the discarded brochure, and shot forward too quickly for her to recover her balance. She didn't realize she had stepped on the slippery sheet until she was in the air. Before she knew it, Erin was flat on her back on the floor, but not before her kneecap collided painfully with the bedframe.

"Ow," she muttered, rubbing her knee.

As she lay there, contemplating what she had just heard, there was a knock on the door. "Oh, just perfect timing," she mumbled, struggling to her feet.

A second knock came quickly. "Just a minute!" she yelled, feeling completely out of sorts.

She opened the door to see a bemused-looking Detective Hemming, holding a somewhat battered fedora, fetchingly rumpled in a tan raincoat. Both his hat and coat were damp. At the sight of him, her irritation faded.

"Hello," he said, tilting his head to the side, a half smile on his handsome face. She had forgotten how good-looking he was, in that absent-minded professor way. Bits of blond stubble protruded from his chin. The detective looked leaner since she last saw him, even a bit gaunt. His deep-blue eyes were red-rimmed, perhaps from lack of sleep.

"Come in," she said, suddenly glad they weren't meeting in the lobby after all.

"Nice flowers," he said, removing his hat.

"Very tasteful, I think. Not too Austentacious at all."

"What happened to you?" he added, watching her limp over to the window.

"Rapped my knee against the bed. Did you see the couple talking outside my room?"

"There was no one there when I arrived."

"But they were just outside, in the hall—"

"Not when I got here."

Where could they have gone? They must have slipped through the door leading to the stairwell on the far end of the hall, spooked by the sound of her falling.

"Why do you ask?" he said.

"No reason," she lied, eyeing the folder in his hand. "What have you got there?"

"A copy of the medical examiner's report on Barry Wolf," he said, holding it out to her.

"For me?"

"You can keep it if you like."

"But why—"

"Look at the cause of death."

Her eyes fell on the information near the top of the page, the words printed neatly in the text box. *Cardiac Arrest.* Next to it, under manner of death: *Natural Causes.* Frowning, she read on. "But look at this—*No visible signs of previous arterial disease.*"

Hemming sighed and wiped his brow, which was damp—from the precipitation outside, she wondered, or was he sweating? The room wasn't particularly warm.

"Would you like to sit down?" she asked.

"Thank you," he said, sinking into one of the armchairs. He looked exhausted. "People die of heart attacks all the time, you know."

"But without a prior medical condition—"

"Do you know how many things can cause cardiac arrest? They vary from high blood pressure to hormone imbalance to stress, for God's sake."

"Was there any evidence—"

"Wasn't he to be the keynote speaker at your conference?"

"Yes."

"That sounds stressful to me."

"He was the kind of person who lived for attention."

Hemming raised an eyebrow. "One man's meat—"

"Speaking of poison," she murmured, leafing through the papers. "Where's the toxicology report?"

"The samples are still at the lab."

"Then we don't really know anything, do we?"

"There is no 'we.' You aren't—"

"You, then. You don't know anything."

"If we find anything suspicious, we'll open an investigation. Otherwise, there's no particular reason to suspect—"

"Murder?"

"Foul play."

"Whatever you want to call it."

"Look," he said wearily. "I came to ask you to give it a rest."

"You don't look well. Would you like a cup of tea?"

"Please promise me you'll let us handle this."

"Handle what? You just told me there was no cause for concern."

"I just don't want you—"

"Mucking about on my own?" she said, perching on the end of the bed.

"Yes."

"Why not?"

"It's not safe."

"See, that makes me think you don't believe the medical report. Otherwise, you wouldn't be worried about me."

"I'm always worried about you."

"Do you want to have dinner?"

"I'm sorry—I can't. I have to drive to my mother's first thing tomorrow."

"How is she?"

"Not great."

"If you ever want to talk about it—"

"Some other time, maybe." He struggled to his feet. "I should be going."

"Thanks for stopping by," she said tartly, irritated he had rebuffed her offer of help.

"Look," he said. "I'm sorry, but I have a lot on my mind right now."

"I can see that."

"Maybe later this week—"

"Sure," she said, holding the door open for him. "You look like you need a proper night's sleep."

He nodded, then looked at her with such intensity that she held her breath.

"Erin."

"Yes?"

"I . . ."

She took a step closer so that she could smell his aftershave, clean and sharp, like a pine woods after a rainstorm. Erin took another step, expecting him to back up, but he did not. He lifted a hand and cupped her face, his fingers warm on her cheek. Were they trembling a little? She wasn't sure. She leaned in toward him, her lips parted. Down the hall, a door opened and closed, breaking the spell.

He removed his hand and gave a little cough. "I have to go. Maybe we can get together while you're here—I mean . . ."

She surprised herself by putting a finger to his lips. "I'm counting on it."

Removing her hand, he held it in his for a moment. His hand was unexpectedly soft. "Please promise me that you won't do anything foolish," he said.

"All right," she replied.

"And please leave criminal investigations to the police," he said, putting on his rather soggy hat.

"Of course," she lied.

When he had gone, she felt bereft and out of sorts.

She looked at the bedside clock—if she hurried, she could just make it to the hotel restaurant before the kitchen closed.

Chapter Twelve

"It can't be *that* bad," said Farnsworth as Erin tucked into the trout almondine. She had made it to the restaurant just in time to order before the kitchen closed.

"It's brilliant," she said, breaking off a piece of fresh baguette and smearing it with butter. "Better than I even imagined."

"I meant your meeting with your sexy detective."

"Stop calling him 'my sexy detective.'"

"Well, isn't he?"

"He's most certainly not 'mine.'"

"But he is sexy."

"Yes, he is," Erin admitted, wolfing down a bite of courgettes in tarragon cream sauce. She was famished, her disappointment at the meeting with Detective Hemming channeled into an appetite for the hotel's outstanding cuisine. Erin realized now that she had hoped he would stay and have dinner with her.

"If you eat too fast you'll choke on your food," said Farnsworth.

"You sound like my mother."

"Here we are," said Grant Apthorp, arriving at the table with two mugs. "One Irish coffee and one with sambuca and whipped cream."

Sam the waiter had been on duty when Erin ordered, but his shift was over, so Grant had offered to fetch them a nightcap from the bar. He set the Irish coffee in front of Erin, handing the one with sambuca to Farnsworth.

"Ta very much," Farnsworth said, sipping it. "Lovely."

"Yes, thank you," Erin murmured, her mouth half full of flaky, fragrant fish.

"Nothing for you?" Farnsworth asked him.

"I have a panel first thing in the morning," he replied, sitting next to her. The chair creaked beneath his weight. Grant Apthorp made every piece of furniture he sat in look like it was from a doll's house. If she were a sculptor, Erin thought, he would make a perfect a model for a statue of Atlas. He looked like he could easily carry the burden of the world on his shoulders and still have strength to spare.

"How's the trout?" he asked.

"Gorgeous," Erin replied, sliding some basmati rice pilaf onto her fork.

"The food here is brilliant," said Farnsworth. "I wish your sexy detective had joined us."

"What exactly is the story with him?" Grant asked.

Farnsworth told him about the murder in Kirkbymoorside, perhaps slightly exaggerating her own role in the case.

"And you haven't seen him since then?"

"Not until tonight," said Erin.

"He sent her flowers," Farnsworth added.

"That sounds like a sign to me," Grant remarked.

"But his mother is sick, and he's very preoccupied with her illness."

"But he came to see you despite the fact. That must mean something."

"He just wanted to show me the medical examiner's report on Barry Wolf." Strictly speaking, that wasn't true, but she didn't feel like discussing her personal life with a man she had only just met.

"Why?"

"Because *she* thinks he was murdered," Farnsworth said.

"Does your detective agree?" asked Grant.

"No," Erin said, savoring the last bite of trout.

"Why did he bring you the report?"

"To show me I was wrong."

Grant smiled. "Is he afraid you'll go chasing after a murderer?"

"It wouldn't be the first time," Farnsworth said, sipping her coffee.

"Can we not talk about this anymore?" said Erin.

"I'm afraid I'm going to have to leave you ladies," Grant said, rising. "I'm all in, and I really do have an early morning tomorrow."

"Where's the bill?" asked Farnsworth.

"It's all taken care of," he said, giving her a kiss on the cheek.

"That's not right. You can't—"

"I just did," he replied, walking toward the exit.

"But—"

"It's a tax deduction. Good night."

"Thank you!" Erin called after him. Without turning around, he raised a hand and gave a little wave.

Farnsworth sighed. "Isn't he magnificent?"

Erin had to agree, though a small, ungenerous part of her envied her friend's happiness. Watching him walk away, his gait solid but graceful, she was suddenly reminded of the overheard conversation in the hall outside her room.

"Farnsworth?" she said.

"Yes, pet?"

"This might be crazy, but . . ." She paused, stirring the whipped cream into her Irish coffee, a little whirlpool of white swirling in the dark liquid.

Farnsworth leaned forward. "What? Out with it."

Erin told her about the conversation in the hall.

"Did you get a look at them?"

"The woman was Judith Eton, and I'm pretty sure the young man is her son."

"Good lord," said Farnsworth. "So if Barry Wolf isn't his father, then—"

"Shh!" Erin said, looking around, but the only other customers still lingering were a young couple spooning in a dark corner in the back of the room. Their foreheads were touching, and they gazed deeply into each other's eyes, oblivious to their surroundings. Erin leaned forward and lowered her voice. "Jeremy certainly seems to think his father may be someone other than Barry."

"Did he mention where he got that idea?"

"No."

"What about Judith?"

"She was dancing around the subject."

"It could just be rumors."

"Or he could be right. In which case—" Erin looked at her friend, not sure whether to mention her suspicion, but, as usual, Farnsworth read her mind.

"Grant Apthorp? No, I don't see it. They have totally different builds. Jeremy's thin as a sylph."

"Jeremy's still just a lad. He'll fill out as he gets older. He certainly doesn't look like Barry."

"But are genetics always so obvious? My sister and I are totally different."

"Maybe a fox snuck into your family henhouse."

Farnsworth snorted contemptuously. "Oh, *really*, Erin. You're not seriously suggesting—"

"I'm just making a point. DNA is not destiny."

"I still don't see it."

"Who, then? Who do you think could be Jeremy's father?"

"It's not necessarily anyone at this convention, you know."

"Good point," Erin said. "More likely than not, it isn't anyone here."

Farnsworth patted her arm. "Don't look so depressed, pet. You still have a chance to catch your murderer—that is, if there *is* one. Your sexy detective seems to think you've got the wrong end of the stick."

"The more he tries to dissuade me, the more convinced I become."

"Mind how you go, pet. If there really *is* a murderer at large, I doubt they'll stop at one victim if they feel threatened."

Perhaps it was her friend's warning, or maybe it was the storm gathering force outside, but a chill crept across Erin's skin. She shivered as a gust of wind blew a fistful of snow smack against the windowpanes, knocking a long, glistening icicle loose from the roof. As she watched, it plummeted to the ground, shattering into a thousand tiny shards of frozen crystals.

Chapter Thirteen

～

Back in her room, Erin had the melancholy feeling that sometimes settled over her when she read sad poetry, or thought too long about her mother. But tonight it was the combination of the storm outside and the strange vacuum left by Peter Hemming's departure. The room felt empty, too quiet, as if the air had collapsed in on itself. Outside, soft, fluffy flakes fluttered gracefully from the inky sky, illuminated by the lights outside her window. Her mother had so many ways of describing snow that Erin's father used to joke she was part Inuit. Gwyneth Coleridge transferred her love of weather to her daughter. They had bonded over their fascination with snow, a fairly uncommon weather event in Oxfordshire.

Erin had a sudden yearning for poetry, something to match her mood. Grabbing her laptop, she lay on the bed and googled one of her favorites by her illustrious ancestor, Samuel Taylor Coleridge, "Frost at Midnight". Settling back against the pillows, she read the first stanza.

> The Frost performs its secret ministry,
> Unhelped by any wind. The owlet's cry
> Came loud—and hark, again! loud as before.
> The inmates of my cottage, all at rest,
> Have left me to that solitude, which suits
> Abstruser musings: save that at my side
> My cradled infant slumbers peacefully.

'Tis calm indeed! so calm, that it disturbs
And vexes meditation with its strange
And extreme silentness.

Gazing out, she saw frost crystals were indeed forming on her own window panes. More than ever before, she felt a deep connection to her august ancestor. What was writing, if not ongoing conversations across the membrane separating the dead from the living, and the living from unborn generations yet to come?

In the poem, he was a father keeping watch over his infant son, staying up late to write poetry while frost gathered outside his window. And here she was, linked to him by mysterious strands of DNA, and by their shared love of poetry, as she watched the frost etch patterns on her own windowpanes. She shivered again, only this time it was a pleasant tingling, an inexplicable sensation that she was not alone. She read on.

Sea, hill, and wood,
This populous village! Sea, and hill, and wood,
With all the numberless goings-on of life,
Inaudible as dreams! the thin blue flame
Lies on my low-burnt fire, and quivers not;
Only that film, which fluttered on the grate,
Still flutters there, the sole unquiet creature.

So often late at night, Erin felt like the sole unquiet creature— a natural night owl like her mother, she struggled with bedtime, sometimes staying awake deep into the night. She could remember lying in bed in her third-floor room with the gabled ceilings, watching as car headlights crossed her walls, wondering where the cars were coming from, and where they were headed.

Sea, hill, and wood. She loved his use of repetition, thrilling to the thought of Coleridge in his cottage in Nether Stowey, Somerset, where the poem was written. And here she was in Yorkshire, no sleeping babe at her side, but a murderer lurking nearby. Yet, there was a strange calm, engendered by the surrounding snow enveloping the city in its soft, seductive embrace.

She read on, caught by the breathless beauty of his language. She especially liked the last stanza—after meditating on what his son's life will be like, he ends the poem by circling back to the beginning, with the image of frost on his windows.

> Therefore all seasons shall be sweet to thee,
> Whether the summer clothe the general earth
> With greenness, or the redbreast sit and sing
> Betwixt the tufts of snow on the bare branch
> Of mossy apple-tree, while the night-thatch
> Smokes in the sun-thaw; whether the eave-drops fall
> Heard only in the trances of the blast,
> Or if the secret ministry of frost
> Shall hang them up in silent icicles,
> Quietly shining to the quiet Moon.

Gazing out the window, she saw the outline of a misty moon, shrouded in snow, the pale-yellow disc, ghostly and dim in the thickening air. *The secret ministry of frost* . . . or murder, she thought. What could be more secretive than the taking of another life? Like the frost, this killer operated beneath the quiet moon . . .

Putting her computer aside, she contemplated the poem's circular structure. She knew from her own writing that returning to the beginning was often a good way of ending a poem or story. But what was the origin of murder? *Thought, word, deed*—the deed has its beginning in thought, she reasoned, so if she could find her way to the moment the murder was first conceived, she would be that much closer to solving the crime. In order to do that, she needed a motive.

She leafed through the conference bulletin until she found the list of panelists and participants. So many people seemed to have a plausible reason to want Barry Wolf dead. The question was, which of them wanted it badly enough to actually kill him?

She lay on the bed with the bulletin, studying the list of participants. Grabbing a piece of hotel stationery, she made a list of people on the left side of the page, and across from each name, possible motives. Some people had more than one potential motive. She made a third column for circumstances that might be potential evidence. In some cases, she didn't know enough about their relationship with Barry to make an apt deduction so she filled in a question mark under "Motive."

Name	Motive	Potential evidence
Judith Eton	Money/Revenge	Shared son/divorce/ argument in bar
Terrence Rogers	Revenge/Envy	Argument in hallway
Grant Apthorp	Past grievance?	Called Barry a "tosser"
Luca Wolf	Money	Did not seem to like Barry
Stephen Mahoney	Money, love?	Seems close to Luca

And so on. It was late when she finished, and she put the list aside, brushed her teeth, and fell into bed with the pale light of the misty moon shining through her windows.

Chapter Fourteen

Erin awoke to blinding sunlight streaming into the room, reflecting off the slanted ceiling. She had fallen asleep without drawing the curtains, and the storm had blown itself out during the night, giving way to cold, crisp air and brilliant sunshine. She rolled over and looked at the bedside clock; its glowing red numbers read 7:10 AM. Her first panel was at eleven, which gave her plenty of time. Pulling on her robe to shield her from the chill in the room, she put on the electric kettle, sat down at the desk, and opened her computer. Opening her browser, she typed in "Grant Apthorp". Farnsworth had interrupted her background check on him yesterday, and she meant to finish her investigation of his past before moving on to the next potential suspect.

The first link was to Cardiff University, where, according to their website, he had been teaching literature and languages for fifteen years. His bio included numerous publications, which wasn't surprising. Her father had told her of the publish-or-perish dictums at the more prestigious universities. Among the works listed was the one Jonathan had read, *Art and Commerce: Literature and the Ascension of the Middle Class*, as well as another entitled *Alluring Lies: The False Promise of Romanticism*. Erin wished she could get hold of student reviews of Grant as a professor, but that would involve starting an application to attend the school, and she didn't have time for that. For now at least, she would have to content herself with a web search, where the most negative thing she could find was an unflattering photograph at a college cocktail party.

At eight thirty, there was a knock on the door.

"Hello, Farnsworth," Erin called, getting up to open the door. She opened it to find Khari Butari, looking rested and bright-eyed in a linen pantsuit the color of fresh cream.

"*Bonjour.* I hope you're not disappointed," Khari said, smiling.

"Not at all. I just didn't expect you."

"I was wondering if you wanted to have brunch."

"Sure—I don't have a panel until eleven."

"*Jane Austen—Adaptations and Imitations?*"

"Yes."

"I'm the moderator."

"Wonderful," Erin said. "If you don't mind waiting, I'll be ready in a jiff."

"Tell you what—why don't we meet down there around nine?"

"Perfect. That will give me time to dress."

"*D'accord*," said Khari. "See you then."

Erin was still in her pajamas, her hair uncombed, teeth unbrushed. She hated rushing in the morning, and would need time to get properly dressed. Normally, she bathed in the evening, but as she had fallen asleep without her bath, she thought she'd dip into the shower, knowing she'd feel better for it. Just as she was about to step into the shower, there was another knock on the door.

"Yes?" she called from the bathroom.

"It's me." It was Farnsworth called "I've come to fetch you for breakfast."

Erin threw on a towel and went to the door, cracking it open. "It's Sunday, so I think it's brunch."

Farnsworth was dressed all in black with a lemon-yellow scarf wrapped around her neck. "Whatever. Are you going to let me in?"

Erin opened the door. "I'm just about to jump in the shower."

"I'll come back in a half hour."

"Uh—Farnsworth?"

"Yes?"

"I told Khari I'd eat with her."

There was an ominous silence.

"Farnsworth?"

"What?" she said without making eye contact. Her tone was chilly.

"I thought you might be eating with Grant. I'm sure it'd be fine for you to join us."

"It's all right," she said, turning to leave. "I'll make other plans."

"Farnsworth—" Erin said, but she could hear her friend's footsteps retreating down the hall. "Damn," she muttered, going back to the bathroom. Farnsworth was loyal and kind and generous, but she could be jealous and overly sensitive. This was just the kind of thing that might push her into a pout, Erin thought as she turned on the faucet, lifting her face to let the warm needles of water wash over her, cleansing and absolving her of her sins.

After her shower, Erin slipped on a forest-green dress over black tights, pulled on her favorite pair of knee-high boots, and ran a brush over her curly auburn hair.

Khari was already seated at a table near the windows when Erin appeared in the dining room.

"Hello," she said, smiling when she saw Erin. Her teeth glistened, a smooth, perfect row of ivory. She was, Erin thought, a very beautiful woman.

"I hope I didn't keep you waiting," she said, sliding into a chair facing the window.

"Not at all. I got here just before you."

Erin picked up the menu and squinted at it. The sun reflecting off the mounds of fallen snow hurt her eyes, so she moved her chair to the other side of the table.

"It's really bright, isn't it?" said Khari.

"The snow makes it worse. I'm not good with bright light."

"You wouldn't do well in Senegal," Khari said. "Those blue eyes of yours."

"I come from pale, northern people," Erin agreed and they both laughed.

She looked up from the menu to see Luca Wolf and Stephen Mahoney enter the room. Their body language didn't exactly proclaim they were a couple, but Luca seemed to derive comfort from his presence, leaning toward him ever so slightly as they waited to be seated. He bent down to say something to her, his lips close to her ear. As the hostess led them past Erin and Khari's table, Luca smiled at them briefly, and Erin pounced on the opportunity.

"I'm so sorry for your loss," she said, rising from her chair.

"Thank you," said Luca. Her Hungarian accent had the refined air of someone who came from money.

"Erin Coleridge, Northern Branch of the Society," Erin said, extending her hand. "If there's anything we can do, please let us know."

"You are very kind," she replied, shaking Erin's hand. Luca's hand was thin and papery, like a leaf, the skin cool and dry.

Stephen Mahoney stood quietly at her side, his eyes wandering over the room, as if he wished he were somewhere else.

"Would you care to join us?" said Erin.

"No, we really have to—" said Stephen, but Luca interrupted.

"That would be lovely, thank you."

"This is Khari Butari," Erin said as they sat down. "She makes fascinating documentaries."

"You should be my agent," Khari said with a wry smile. "Pleased to meet you," she added, turning to Barry's widow.

"I'm Luca—Wolf," she said, hesitating before saying the last name. "And this is my, uh, my husband's assistant, Stephen Mahoney."

"How do you do?" he said, sliding into the chair next to Khari.

The next few minutes were spent studying the menu and ordering. When the waiter had gone, Erin turned to Luca.

"Are you going to stay at the conference?"

She shrugged. "We come all the way up from Oxford. The room is paid for, so we stay."

"It's what Barry would have wanted," Stephen added hastily as the waiter brought them coffee. Sam was nowhere to be seen—he didn't seem to be working the brunch shift. There was no sign of Farnsworth either—maybe she and Grant had gone out to brunch. Erin just hoped she wasn't sitting in her room pouting.

"What about the funeral?" asked Khari.

Luca shrugged. "His family make arrangement for next week."

"But aren't you—"

"She means his brother and sister," said Stephen.

"Were they close with him?" asked Erin.

The two exchanged a glance.

"I don't really know," said Luca. "They talk on phone, but I don't see them very often."

"His sister lives in Durham, and the brother owns a restaurant in London," Stephen added.

"How long have you been working for—with him?" Erin asked, not wanting to suggest Stephen was subservient to Barry. The way he held himself suggested he was proud, and wouldn't like being reminded he was Wolf's employee.

Stephen exchanged a glance with Luca. "About two years."

"Did you enjoy it?"

An involuntary look of revulsion passed over his face before he rearranged his expression into an unconvincing smile. "It was very interesting."

"Do you have an academic background?" asked Khari.

Again the briefest of glances passed between him and Luca. "Hardly," he said. "I—"

"Stephen is gifted artist," Luca said, flicking a wisp of black hair from her forehead.

"A painter?" said Erin.

"Sculptor, mostly," he replied. "But I don't know how gifted I am—"

"Don't be modest," Luca said. "He's really very good," she told them proudly, her eyes shining. They were so dark they almost looked black, with the wintry light behind her.

"Have you had any shows?" asked Khari.

"Some, back home."

"Where is that?" asked Erin.

At that moment Luca knocked over her coffee, the black liquid soaking into the white linen tablecloth. "Oh, I'm so sorry!" she exclaimed, jumping up from her chair. "I'll fetch the waiter."

"Really, it's fine," Erin said, but she was already scampering across the room.

"She's always been clumsy," Stephen remarked, "though you wouldn't think so to look at her. Used to drive Barry crazy."

It was clear from the look in his eyes that there was more to the relationship between Luca and Stephen than they were willing to reveal—at least for now. Sitting in the cold, bright December light, Erin wondered what she could do to entice the information out of them.

Chapter Fifteen

～

Later, while they were walking to their panel together, Erin and Khari stopped in front of the water station to fill two glasses with ice water. The air in the hotel was dry, and Erin knew from experience conference rooms could get stuffy, especially if they were crowded. Judging by the people lined up outside, this one would be pretty full. Their meeting room was Aldwark. All of the panel rooms were named for references to York, and Aldwark was one of the city's main streets, as well as a picturesque village about fourteen miles away.

"I must apologize for asking Luca and Stephen to join us without consulting you," she told Khari.

"That's all right. What's going on between them, anyway?"

"You noticed it, too?"

"I don't see how you could miss it. They seemed pretty intimate."

"I wish I knew what his meltdown at the bar last night was about," Erin said, looking around to see if anyone was listening, but people appeared to be otherwise engaged.

"I know—that was weird," said Khari.

"I was trying to figure out how to ask him without being rude."

"He might just lie about it anyway."

"Yeah," Erin said as the people began to emerge from the previous panels. She spied the same nerdy man with the Indiana Jones hat and matching vest. Today he sported what looked like a bone necklace on a leather strap. His skin had the pasty hue of someone who spent a lot of time indoors. He nodded at her and pulled a ham sandwich from a pouch at his side, as if he always traveled with his own food. This was odd enough in a fancy hotel renowned for its cuisine, but was by no means the strangest thing about him.

"I like your poetry, by the way," he told Erin.

"You've read my poems?" she said, astonished.

"You aren't by any chance related to Samuel Taylor Coleridge?" he asked, chewing. A bit of lettuce dangled from the side of his mouth.

"As a matter of fact, I am."

"I knew it! Artistic inclination—it's in the genes, you know," he said with a satisfied smile. "Charles Kilroy, at your service," he added with a little bow.

"Where did you read my—" she began, but he shoved the rest of the sandwich into his mouth and headed toward the rapidly emptying room.

"Sorry, but I'd better find a seat," he called over his shoulder.

Erin followed, but by the time she pushed past the people spilling into the hallway, he was already seated along the far wall in the audience area.

"So you're a poet as well," Khari said as they took their places at the long table in front of the room.

"Sort of," Erin said, straightening the card with her name on it so it was parallel to the edge of the white linen tablecloth. She disliked asymmetry. In her dresser at home was a little box of single earrings whose mates she had lost. She kept them intending to wear unmatched pairs, but could never quite bring herself to do it.

"You're published," said Khari. "I'd say you're a proper poet."

"I don't know about that. My work has appeared in fairly obscure literary magazines and journals."

"But you have fans."

Erin laughed. "One fan. I have one fan." She glanced at her watch—it was nearly eleven, time to start, but they were still missing two panelists, Judith Eton and Terrence Rogers. As Erin was contemplating what to do, Judith hurried into the room, her face flushed, trailing an aroma of Chanel No. 5. She was elegantly dressed in an expensive-looking charcoal-gray pantsuit and crisp cream-colored blouse with silver pearl broach fastened to her lapel. But she looked harried and out of breath as she sank into her chair next to Khari.

"So sorry to keep you waiting," she panted, wiping her forehead with an embroidered handkerchief.

"We were just about to start," Erin said as the door flung open and Winnifred Hogsworthy stumbled into the room.

"Sorry," Winnifred said, ambling up to the front of the room, lugging her giant bag, which seemed unusually heavy. "Carry on," she added, plopping down in the front row, setting her bag next to her chair. Erin imagined what might be in it—an apple tart, a baguette, an entire roast turkey?

Just as she was leaning into her mike to introduce the panel, the door opened, and Terrence Rogers swept into the room. He wore a monogrammed burgundy jacket and bow tie, his gray hair neatly combed and moussed. Unlike Judith, Terrence looked utterly poised, as if he had just emerged from brunch with the president of Trinity College.

"Sorry," he said breezily. "I was detained." Not altering his regal bearing, he walked calmly to the far end of the table and took his place next to Judith Eton, who appeared to stiffen in his presence. Straightening his cuffs, he leaned forward, elbows on the table. "Right, then—carry on."

Erin took an instant dislike to him. He exuded the kind of overeducated, upper-class arrogance she had moved to Yorkshire to escape. Bending close to her mike, she introduced the panel.

"Good morning, and welcome to *Jane Austen—Adaptations and Imitations.*"

The first half hour went smoothly, with the panelists opining on the various screen versions of *Pride and Prejudice* and other novels. When they came around to *Sense and Sensibility*, it was widely agreed Ang Lee's 1995 movie was the best screen adaptation.

"I know it's sacrilege," said Khari, "but I liked it better than the book."

Erin thought she heard a few gasps in the audience.

"It's a very good movie, obviously," said Judith Eton. "But don't you find it's a completely different experience from the more personal one of reading a book?"

"Quite true," Terrence Rogers agreed. "In the end, there's nothing quite like the printed word, is there? I discuss that in the new edition of my book, *The Plot Thickens: The Evolution of the Modern Romance Novel.*"

"I don't disagree," said Khari. "But the fact remains—I thought the movie was an improvement on the book."

"What movie adaptation do you all most think captures the spirit of Austen?" asked Erin.

Khari again put her vote in for the Ang Lee film, while Judith nominated the 2005 *Pride and Prejudice* with Keira Knightly. When met with a storm of protest from the audience, who strongly favored the 1995 version, she dismissed the famous Colin Firth-in-a-wet-shirt scene as obvious and needlessly cheesy, scurrilously adding, "It's not really all that hot."

The discussion continued in a lively fashion, with the audience demonstrating as much knowledge of the Austen canon as the panelists. Erin was glad she was moderating, a job in which being meticulously well-informed wasn't as important as having a knack for asking good questions. She might be better read in general than some of the other conference attendees, but was by no means a specialist in Jane Austen. In her experience, fans tended to not respect panelists who couldn't match their own extensive knowledge.

"I'll tell you what I think," Judith Eton said. "If Jane Austen were alive today, she'd be writing screenplays and teleplays."

"Or stage plays," said Terrence.

"Or maybe both, like Tom Stoppard," Khari suggested.

"Why do you think she wouldn't be writing novels?" asked Erin.

"Because character and dialogue are her great strength," said Judith. "She's not much on description or poetic use of sensory details. I think she wrote novels because that's what was available to women at the time."

"But there were female playwrights in nineteenth-century Britain," Khari pointed out.

"Maybe it's because novels were more profitable than plays," said Terrence. "She did write a few short comedies as a teenager, but seems to have regarded novels as a surer road to financial gain. I have a chapter on that in the new edition of my book." Judith rolled her eyes at this; Erin agreed that Terrence was plugging his book pretty aggressively.

"Still, she had to publish anonymously," Khari pointed out, "because she was a woman."

"Good point," said Erin.

"For one thing, women didn't even have the right to sign contracts—they had to have a male, perhaps a family member, do it for them."

"But why publish anonymously?" Erin said.

"It wasn't considered ladylike to focus on a career," said Judith. "It was thought of as degrading their 'femininity,' the proper role of women being wives and mothers."

"So much for the good old days," said Khari.

Terrence sighed. "I for one will be very glad when I'm no longer considered part of the criminal class."

"You mean men?" said Erin.

"Yes, and white men in particular."

"You're *white*?" said Khari, and laughter rippled across the room. The tension that had been building in the room dissipated, and everyone looked relieved.

"Why haven't we talked about the zombie books?" said Erin's new fan, Charles Kilroy.

"Well, they're not really proper adaptations, are they?" said Terrence.

"Still," said Kilroy "We might have discussed them."

"I'm sorry," said Erin, "but we've run out of time."

"Thank God," Terrence muttered.

Charles Kilroy adjusted his bone necklace and clicked his tongue in a disappointed way, and Erin wondered if she had lost her first—and perhaps only—fan.

"I want to thank all our distinguished panelists for coming, but most of all I'd like to thank you," Erin told the audience. "We couldn't have this conference without you."

Her remark was met with enthusiastic applause, but as Terrence passed her on the way out, he murmured, "Bit of pandering to the hoi polloi, eh?"

She gave him a weak smile, uncertain if he was criticizing her or just making a joke, but she noticed his accent suddenly sounded much less posh. Was he putting on the lower-class accent, or was the refined persona fake?

As the panel room emptied, Winnifred Hogsworthy intercepted Judith Eton on her way out.

"You were wonderful," Winnifred said, tagging along behind Judith, who seemed to barely notice her. "I loved what you said about women having to publish anonymously in the nineteenth century."

"It's not exactly that they had to," Judith corrected her. "It's more that—"

"Yes, yes, I know—you made that quite clear," Winnifred interrupted. She followed Judith out of the room, her enormous bag banging on her knees.

"Looks like Judith Eton has an acolyte," Khari remarked as Erin tidied up. There was a break for lunch until the next panel at two, and she wanted to leave the room clean.

"Or a stalker," Erin muttered. There was something unsettling about Winnifred Hogsworthy, and Erin could imagine her as a rabid fan intent on destroying the object of her adoration.

"Speaking of stalkers," Khari murmured as Charles Gilroy lumbered toward them.

"I happen to have a copy of last month's edition of *Negative Capability*," he said to Erin. "The one with your poem in it."

"Oh yes," said Erin. The bit of lettuce from earlier had lodged itself in his front teeth, and she was reminded of a seaweed-covered barnacle clinging to an old whale.

"I wonder if you would be so kind as to sign it?"

"I would be honored."

"It's up in my room. If I could just—"

"Tell you what," she said. "I'm going to have a quick lie-down, so if you don't mind, we could meet at five in the bar and I could do it then."

His face fell, but he recovered and gave a wan smile. "That would be fine. I know you're busy. Much appreciated," he said, and waddled out of the room.

"You know," said Khari as they left the room, "a nap sounds like a good idea. Breakfast was so massive that I don't fancy lunch. I think I'll retire to my room."

"Catch you later," Erin said as Khari walked through the crowd of people in the hall. She really stood out, not because of the color of her skin, but because of her bearing—she was tall and regal, with the longest neck Erin had ever seen on a person. She had never met a princess—but Erin imagined that she might look very much like Khari Butari.

A few feet away, Terrence Rogers and Judith Eton were having an argument in front of the coffee urn. They were apparently trying to keep their voices down, but as they were quite nearby, Erin could hear them quite clearly.

"Always plugging your work, as usual," Judith was saying. "Some things never change."

"You should talk," he retorted. "No one ever accused you of being indifferent to money."

"There are ways to be discrete," she replied.

He snorted. "Since when has discretion been your strong point?"

"You'll find out soon enough," she said. And with that, she turned and walked away without looking and back.

Watching her, Erin made a note to herself to keep an eye on Judith Eton.

Chapter Sixteen

~

"Come in," said Farnsworth in response to Erin's knock on her door. On her way to a nap, Erin had decided to look in on her friend to see if she was still out of sorts.

Erin entered the room to see Farnsworth sprawled across the green armchair next to the bed, her stockinged feet resting on the matching stool, watching television. The air was thick with the aroma of fresh popcorn. Onscreen, an unreasonably cheerful young blonde woman in a red overcoat was walking down a charming, snow-covered street so heavily decorated for Christmas that it appeared to be an advertisement for a holiday boutique—except that she wasn't so much walking as waltzing. Or floating, her elegant boots barely touching the snow-covered ground. And no wonder, given the opulently festive surroundings. Smiling reindeer pranced atop lampposts wound with fresh greenery and frosted ornaments; houses were festooned with tasteful fairy lights nestled amid perfectly symmetrical holiday wreaths. Cheerful red bows on front doors fluttered in the softly falling snow. The spirit of Christmas radiated from every inch of the town, no less from the young woman's face, which expressed the kind of blissful joy and goodwill that could only be the result of an endorphin overload induced by a surfeit of hot chocolate and butter cookies in front of a roaring fire, while background choirs softly hummed "The Little Drummer Boy."

Farnsworth was watching a Hallmark Christmas movie.

"Have a seat," Farnsworth said without taking her eyes off the screen.

"What are you watching?" Erin said.

"I'm conducting a sociological investigation."

"Into what?"

"I can't imagine why these movies exist, let alone thrive. They are mindless, they are bland, and they are overwhelmingly popular. Have some popcorn," she added, pointing to a large bowl on the coffee table."

"Buttered?"

She gave Erin a withering look. "How long have you known me?"

Erin dug into the bowl and pulled out a generous fistful. "This doesn't taste microwaved."

Farnsworth shuddered. "Good lord, no. Dreadful stuff."

"How did you pull this off without a kitchen?"

"Sam, of course. He can't do enough for me. For the price of a twisted ankle, I'm being treated like a queen. If Sam had a tail, he'd be wagging it constantly."

"You're onto a good thing. You should sprain your ankle every time you travel." Farnsworth seemed to be over her pout, but Erin still felt she should tread lightly. "This is delicious."

"So?" Farnsworth said. "What do you think? Why do these movies exist?"

"Decoration porn."

"What?"

"Look at the optics," Erin said through a mouthful of popcorn. "Every inch of the frame is filled with Christmas decorations."

"You mean an entire genre of films has sprung up based on holiday wreaths and Christmas lights?"

"That and the wistfully optimistic storyline."

"Which is always the same."

"Exactly," said Farnsworth. "Part of me wonders why this absurdity exists as public entertainment, whilst the other, more wistful part asks why real life can't be like this."

"Wouldn't it be boring after a while?"

"No. No, it would not."

"Do you want to hear what I learned today at the panel?"

"Wait just a minute. I want to see the meet-cute. We don't even need the volume," Farnsworth added, muting the sound. "Watch."

Onscreen, the fetching young woman in the stylish boots was chasing down an apparently escaped dog before it ran into traffic. The dog was small and white and fluffy, and unbearably adorable. A long leash trailed from its neck.

"How do you know this is the—" Erin began, but Farnsworth silenced her.

"Shh! Just wait."

The young woman caught the dog, and was just lifting it up in her arms when a girl of about ten sprinted around the street corner with the quaint hardware store across from the old-fashioned pharmacy, both sporting an excess of perfectly tasteful Christmas décor.

"Wait for it," Farnsworth said as the girl broke into a smile when she saw the woman holding what was apparently her dog.

"But—"

"Shh! And . . . *now*," Farnsworth said as the two of them rounded the corner together, bumping into a perfectly dressed, impeccably coiffed young man. His jaw was so square it could have been sanded down to make a table top. He wore a dark-blue pea jacket with a matching cap on his thick, wavy brown hair.

"Ah, going with the nautical theme, I see," Farnsworth murmured, helping herself to more popcorn.

There was much merriment and laughter among the three attractive people onscreen as they dusted snow from their coats, their eyes sparkling with holiday cheer as the little girl explained to the man what had happened.

"You see?" said Farnsworth. "You don't even need the sound. In fact, you're better off without it, since the dialogue is utter drivel."

"How did you know they were about to meet?"

"Oh, pet, these movies are as preordained as a Greek tragedy. Fifteen minutes in, the heroine will have met the Man of Her Dreams Only She Doesn't Know It at First Because She's So Busy Sorting Out What She Thinks Is Important in Life." Farnsworth sighed. "And to think Jane Austen started this mess."

"But Jane Austen is full of wit and social satire."

"These movies exist in the Irony-Free Zone, pet. They wouldn't know social satire if it bit them in the big, cheerful ass. Children and dogs," she added as all three characters onscreen hugged the little white dog, which seemed confused by all the attention. "They make a great fulcrum in the meet-cute, you see, because anyone who loves children and animals can't be all bad."

"And in this case, rather dreamy, I'd say," Erin remarked, as the young man laughed, his teeth sparkling like freshly fallen snow. "What's she saying to him?"

"Probably something along the lines of how adorable his daughter is. He's a widower, of course. These people can be single, but they never divorced. If one of them has a child, the spouse is dead— tragically, in a car accident, or cancer, or something equally pitiable. Sometimes the woman is the one with the kid, but here it's him, so you *know* he's a perfect match for her. I'm guessing she's ambivalent about having kids, but not because she doesn't love children—she does—but because her sister died young, or something like that."

Erin laughed. "If you have these so well figured out, why don't you write them?"

"That would ruin everything. I'd have to stop making fun of them."

There was a knock on the door.

"Are you expecting someone?" asked Erin.

"Not really. Be a love and answer it, would you, pet?"

Rather than being annoyed by Farnsworth's demands, Erin was relieved that, evidently, all was forgiven. There would be no mention of her friend's snit fit—Farnsworth was usually embarrassed by her own bad behavior, and if she didn't outright apologize, would prefer to just forget about it. An apology might still be forthcoming, but Erin wasn't holding her breath.

She opened the door to find Hetty Miller, in a white terrycloth robe and Japanese-style bamboo flip-flops decorated with bright pink plastic flowers.

"Hello, ladies," she said cheerfully. "Anyone care to accompany me to the spa?"

"Is there a sauna?" said Farnsworth.

Hetty rolled her mascara-caked eyes. "It's a *spa*, darling."

"I could use a nice sauna," said Erin. "Good for the sinuses."

"And the skin," Hetty added hopefully.

Farnsworth looked stricken. "What about Suzie Perkycheeks and her budding romance with Johnny Squarejaw?"

"You can tell me what happened," said Erin.

"I already *told* you what's going to happen. That's not the point."

"I could really use a sauna."

"Fine—abandon me!" Farnsworth said, but her tone was only half-serious.

"Look," said Erin. "Why don't we watch another one tonight?"

"Promise?"

"Girl Guide's honor."

"You were a Girl Guide?" said Hetty.

"Briefly. The less said about it, the better."

"I'll bet you were brilliant at it. I mean, you're so outdoorsy and all."

"Girl Guides have to follow orders, pet," Farnsworth remarked without taking her eyes off the television screen. "She's not so good at that."

"Right—well, shall we go?" said Erin, pushing Hetty out the door.

"Remember to stay hydrated," Farnsworth called after them.

The spa was indeed luxurious, with a fourteen-meter swimming pool, state-of-the-art gym, whirlpool, and two kinds of saunas. Erin opted for the Aromatic Steam Room over the Nordic Dry Sauna, and Hetty agreed to join her. After a quick dip in the pool, they wrapped themselves in fluffy white bath towels and lounged on soft flowered cushions in the steam room. It looked just like the Nordic sauna, with classic teak paneling and benches. Steam seeped in from a pile of rocks in a large wooden box in one corner, and there was a variety of aromas to choose from. Hetty and Erin agreed on Lavender Rose, which the brochure claimed was "calming and meditative."

"This is the life, eh?" said Hetty as the steam rose in thick clouds around them.

"It's lovely," Erin agreed, taking a deep breath. She could feel her sinuses clearing.

The door opened and Judith Eton entered the steam room. She was clad in the same fluffy white towel, in full makeup, including lipstick and blush. Long gold earrings dangled from each lobe; a matching necklace sparkled on her chest. She clutched a mobile phone in her hand—strictly forbidden in the spa.

"Nice jewelry," said Hetty as Judith eased herself onto one of the cushions.

"Oh, hello," she said. "Almost didn't see you there through the steam."

"It is pretty cloudy in here," Erin agreed.

"Better than what's going on outside," Judith said with a shudder. "I think it's actually sleeting at the moment."

"Ugh," said Hetty.

Erin said nothing—she enjoyed extreme weather.

"That was a good panel this morning," Hetty said.

"You were there?" said Erin. "I didn't see you."

"I popped in about halfway through. I enjoyed your remarks," she told Judith.

"That's very kind of you," Judith replied.

"It reminded me how lucky we are to be alive now instead of two hundred years ago."

"We still have a long way to go," said Erin.

"True," said Judith. "But at least we don't have to rely on marrying well to survive."

"How do you know Winnifred Hogsworthy?" Erin asked.

"We were at school together."

"She seems to admire you quite a lot."

Judith sighed. "Poor Winnie. She always was an odd duck, even at school, and I was one of the few people who were nice to her."

"That reminds me," said Erin. "Did Prudence ask if you would be willing to fill in as keynote—"

"Yes," said Judith. "I'd be thrilled to bits."

"Oh," said Erin, a little surprised at her cheerful response. Judith obviously wasn't grief-stricken over her ex-husband's death. "That would be lovely."

Judith smiled grandly. "Say no more. I'm sure Barry will be turning in his grave, but then he never did think much of women's intellect."

Erin frowned. "Seriously?"

"Serves him right, then," said Hetty.

"I don't like to speak ill of the dead," said Judith, "but he could be a real tosser."

"Interesting," Erin said. "That's just what Grant Apthorp said."

"Figures," Judith said with a toss of her elegant head. Her gold earrings jingled faintly. "Barry's not exactly popular among his colleagues."

"Why's that?"

"He is—was—devious. Brilliant lecturer, of course, but in it for himself. Didn't care where the chips fell."

"Oh?"

"Take what happened to Terrence Rogers, for instance."

"What was that?" asked Hetty.

"You didn't know? Barry stole a department chair position Terrence should have had. Snatched right from under his nose."

"Where was this?"

"Oxford, of course. Terrence was up for the position, and Barry—well, let's just say he got what he wanted, but not in the most ethical way. And now Terry's stuck teaching at Newcastle Uni—not that there's anything wrong with it, mind you, but it's not Oxford."

"When was that?"

"Oh, it's been donkey's years. But if I were Terrence . . . well, let's just say it's not the sort of thing easily forgiven."

"What did Barry do, exactly?"

"Well—" she began, just as her mobile phone trilled Beethoven's "Für Elise." "Sorry, I have to take this," she said, and left the steam room.

"Mobile phones aren't allowed in the spa," Hetty said when she had gone.

"She managed to smuggle hers in."

Hetty wiped a damp lock of hair from her cheek. Her bright red hair was remarkably thick for someone her age—whatever that was. Erin wondered if she used extensions. "Wonder who called her."

"Hang on a minute," Erin said. She tiptoed to the door and listened, but the thick teak was an effective sound barrier, and she couldn't make out any words. Wiping the steam off the tiny window, Erin could make out enough of Judith's facial expression to tell she looked concerned. She wasn't doing a lot of talking, mostly just listening to whoever was on the other end.

"Catch anything?" Hetty asked when Erin sat down again.

"No," she answered. "But she looked worried."

"I'd give anything to hear what she's saying."

"So would I."

"I'll tell you something else," said Hetty. "I saw Winnifred Hogsworthy trail Judith all the way down the hall, and it looked to me like she might feel more than just admiration."

"You think?"

Hetty tended to sexualize everything, but she could also be very observant.

"I'm just saying . . . you never know with people," she said as Judith entered the sauna again.

"Sorry," Judith said. "Business call."

"Watch out for the spa attendant," Hetty said. "She's not above confiscating your mobile."

"They're very strict about that," Erin agreed.

"Tell you what," Judith said. "I have to go to the loo. Will you be a dear and watch my phone? I don't need some snarky little prat nicking my mobile."

"No problem," Erin said.

"Ta," Judith said, handing her the phone. "Back in a jiff."

When she had gone, Hetty stared at Erin. "Well? Are you going to look at it?"

"It would be wrong to spy on her."

"You're no fun," Hetty said, stretching out her long, remarkably toned legs.

"I'll just slip it into my pocket," Erin said. "And if I happen to see—oops, there it is."

"What?" Hetty said, leaning forward.

"The last call she received."

"What is it?"

"That would be telling," Erin said. She was too busy memorizing the number.

Chapter Seventeen

～

Back in her room, Erin opened her computer and typed the number into a reverse phone number search engine. The result showed up immediately: *William B. Holbrook, Solicitor. Wills and Probate Law.* So, she thought as she got dressed for her afternoon panel, Judith Eton was already sniffing around Barry Wolf's estate.

The panel, *Jane and Cassandra: Sisterhood in the Nineteenth Century*, was well attended, though not as full as the morning one. Predictably, women outnumbered men in the audience, though she was pleasantly surprised to see a number of males who actually seemed interested in the famously close relationship between Jane and her older sister. There was a lively discussion of the fact that neither sister married in a time when it was one of the few ways a woman of their class could manage to live in anything approaching comfort.

Much was made of the tragic death of Cassandra's fiancé, who succumbed to yellow fever while serving as an army chaplain in the West Indies.

"He only took the job to earn enough money to support poor Cassandra," said Winnifred Hogsworthy, who had planted herself in the front row, her enormous satchel taking up two chairs. "Another proof of how helpless women were financially during the Regency."

No one could reasonably object to this remark, but her tone was so whiny and irritating that Erin wondered if she had any idea of what she sounded like. She was one of those people who had neither grace nor charm of personality, doomed by Nature to repel her fellow humans. Erin felt sorry for her, but she too had an impulse to avoid Winnifred, which made her feel guilty. When the panel was over, Erin resolved to seek her out—perhaps she would be better company one on one.

But the sight of Jonathan Alder lingering in the doorway took her mind off poor Winnifred. Catching her eye, he grinned and waved, and a little piece of her heart couldn't help responding to that smile. Whatever gifts Nature had cruelly denied poor Winnifred, she had capriciously bestowed upon Jonathan Alder. When he walked down the hall, women parted for him like the Red Sea bending to Moses's will, falling under his spell like enchanted fairy tale princesses. Erin doubted Winnifred Hogsworthy had ever cast a spell on anyone. And so, waving at Jonathan, she marched over to Winnifred and extended her hand.

"I don't believe we've been properly introduced. I'm Erin Coleridge."

"Oh, I know who you are—indeed I do," Winnifred replied, blushing as she shook Erin's hand. "I have even sampled your poetry, thanks to my friend Charles—you know him, yes? Charles Kilroy. Built like a pillow, dresses as if he's on a safari."

"Oh, yes, I met him earlier," Erin said, relieved to hear Winnie had a friend.

"He and I have attended so many conferences together," she said, pulling absently on a strand of hair. "Anyway, he showed me some of your poetry in a literary magazine. Quite nice, quite nice indeed."

"Thank you so much," said Erin. "I wonder if you'd care to join me for a drink?"

"Well," Winnifred replied, her eyes wandering. "I'm not sure . . ."

"My treat, obviously."

She brightened instantly. "How could I refuse such a generous offer?" she said, picking up her satchel. "Certainly. Lead the way."

Erin had to smile as they walked toward the door. Winnifred Hogsworthy might be truly impoverished, but she was most certainly cheap. When they entered the hotel corridor, Erin saw Jonathan Alder at the water station chatting with a couple of young women. He caught her eye and nodded, and Erin pointed in the direction of the 1906 Bar. He nodded again, and she continued on with Winnifred in tow, with the hopeful thought that he might join them. A glance at the hotel clock told her that it wouldn't be long before Charles Kilroy showed up for her autograph, and she hoped even more fervently that Jonathan would come.

The bar was nearly empty when they arrived, though she expected it would fill up as people filtered in as the day's last panels ended. In the far corner of the room, a pint in front of him, was Charles Kilroy. Erin sighed. It was a full half hour before they were due to meet, and she didn't fancy being trapped between Winnifred and Charles. Seeing them, Charles waved.

"Oh look," said Winnifred. "It's Charles! Shall we join him?"

"Why not?" said Erin.

"Hello there," Charles said as they approached. "What a pleasant surprise, two lovely ladies instead of one."

Winnifred giggled. "How very *galante* of you, Mr. Kilroy," she said, affecting a posh accent. "If I did not know you to be a man of great integrity, I might suspect you are flattering me."

"My dear Miss Hogsworthy, nothing could be further from the truth," he replied in the same accent, rising from his chair. "You are the very vision of female pulchritude—as are you, Miss Coleridge."

Erin realized they were playing the same game she and Farnsworth did, imitating the elaborate elocution of characters in a Jane Austen novel. She felt a little put out that someone else had discovered what she had always considered their private joke, though she couldn't really begrudge them their fun. Besides, she thought, she and Farnsworth did a better job of it.

"Please allow me to offer you ladies some refreshment," Charles said with a little bow.

Erin looked at Winnifred. "But I was going to—"

"I insist. It is not often a man has the pleasure of entertaining such charming and beguiling members of the opposite sex."

"I'll have a cosmopolitan," Winnifred said, licking her lips.

"That sounds good," said Erin. "Make it two."

"My pleasure." Giving another little bow, he headed for the bar.

"So you know Charles from other conferences?" Erin asked.

"Yes, we're both literarily minded. We met at a *Game of Thrones* conference."

"I'm sorry," Erin said, seeing Jonathan enter the room. "Will you excuse me for a moment?"

"Go on, then," Winnifred said, rummaging around in her bag. "I have my knitting to amuse me."

"I'll only be a minute," said Erin, hurrying over to Jonathan, who stood near the entrance.

Jonathan winked at her as she approached. "I see you're in a nerd fest. Lucky you."

"It's not so bad."

Gazing at his shoes, he cleared his throat. "Look, about last night—"

"What about it?"

"Well, we'd both had a few drinks, and—"

"Are you implying you weren't responsible for your actions?"

"Well, I—"

"I most certainly was responsible for mine, and I'm not sorry."

"I didn't mean . . . I just wanted to—"

"To clear the air?" she said.

"Something like that, I suppose."

"From where I stand, the air is just fine. And the view isn't bad either."

A deep pink flush flared on his cheeks. "Why, Miss Coleridge, I hardly know what to say."

"Why don't you join us?" she said, pointing to Charles and Winnifred.

"I'd love to, but—"

"Coward."

"All right—one drink."

"Come along," she said, pulling him by the wrist. "Look who I found," she said to the others. Charles looked annoyed, but Winnifred broke into a wide smile.

"Why, hello. I'm Winnifred Hogsworthy. You can call me Winnie."

"Jonathan Alder, at your service," he said, kissing her hand, and she giggled again.

Erin was afraid for a moment he was mocking her, but believed Jonathan too kind for that.

He turned to Charles Kilroy. "Mr. Kilroy, I presume? I hear you are quite the expert on nineteenth-century literature."

Charles' face relaxed into a smile. "Yes, indeed, though you have me at a disadvantage, Mr.—?"

"Jonathan Alder, at your service."

"Delighted to meet you. What'll you have?"

"I'll have a whiskey, thanks, but allow me to get the next round."

"I'm supposed to buy—" said Erin, but Jonathan interrupted.

"Please."

"Very well," said Charles, returning to the bar.

"May I see what you're working on?" Jonathan asked Winnie, pointing to the pile of knitting in her lap.

"It's not finished yet," she said, blushing.

"The yarn is a beautiful color."

"Oh, all right," she said, lifting it up so he could see. It was a half-finished turtleneck, made of multicolored wool in warm earth tones.

"Your work is so skillful," he said, examining it.

Winnie smiled shyly. "Thank you, but—"

"My mother used to knit. I have happy memories of sitting at her feet while she made sweaters and socks and hats—she even let me pick out the wool sometimes.

"How lovely," Winnie said. "Is she still with us?"

"Sadly, no," Jonathan said. Erin noticed he neglected to add how she died—at the hands of his father.

Charles returned with Jonathan's drink. "Ta very much," Jonathan said, raising his glass. "Here's to mothers who knit."

"And to the patron saint of virgins," Charles added, with a wink at Winnie, who blushed and looked away.

"Who would that be?" said Erin.

"Saint Winifred," Charles replied. "We're in the presence of her namesake."

"Ah," Jonathan said to Winnie. "You're named after a saint?"

"She was a martyred Welsh princess in the seventh century," she explained.

"Beheaded by her suitor when he found she intended to become a nun," Charles added.

"How gruesome," said Erin.

"Legend has it she came back to life," said Charles. "And lived for some years afterward in a convent."

Erin googled "Winifred" on her phone. "It says here 'A girl's name of Welsh and Old English origin meaning holy, blessed reconciliation, or joy and peace.'"

"I can see that," said Jonathan. "I feel more peaceful already in your presence."

"Or maybe it's the whiskey," Erin suggested. "Malt does more than Milton can to justify God's ways to man."

"I take my Milton neat, with a chaser," Jonathan remarked.

"Speaking of great poets," Charles told Erin, "I brought the magazine for you to sign."

"I'll be glad to. But I'm hardly in Milton's company."

"I'll be the judge of that," Charles said, fishing it out of his knapsack, which was leather, like much of his outfit.

"Well done, you," Jonathan told Erin. "I'll have to get a copy."

"Here you are," Charles said, handing her the magazine.

"*Negative Capability*," Winnie said. "That's an unusual name for a magazine."

"It's named after an idea first proposed by John Keats," Erin said.

"According to him," said Charles, "it is 'when a man is capable of being in uncertainties, mysteries, doubts, without any irritable reaching after fact and reason.'"

"Well done," said Erin. "You've committed it to memory."

Charles shrugged. "Keats admired Shakespeare, who he claimed possessed this quality, but I'm afraid he made fun of your august ancestor, who he felt was too dedicated to making a philosophical statement in his poetry."

"Too invested in the *meaning* of a poem, then?" said Winnie.

"Something like that, yes."

"It's human nature to want to wring meaning out of existence," Erin said, signing the magazine. "And I don't think Shakespeare was shy about philosophizing." Not to be outdone, she added, "But as Rilke said, 'Try to live in the mystery.'"

Jonathan smiled. "Aren't we the heady lot?"

"Well, this *is* a literary convention," Charles remarked drily.

After signing the magazine, Erin volunteered to get the next round, but Jonathan insisted it was his turn. "So much for staying for one drink," Erin whispered in his ear as he reached for her glass.

"A man can change his mind, can't he?" he replied with his charmingly lopsided smile.

"I'll give you a hand," said Charles. "Too much for one fellow to carry."

"Cheers," said Jonathan, and the two of them wove their way through an increasing crowd toward the bar.

Erin turned to Winnie. "How do you know Judith?"

"We were at school together."

"When she was Grant Apthorp's research assistant?"

"I knew her before that. We were first-year college roommates. She didn't work for Grant until her third year at Oxford."

"Did they get along?"

Winnie shrugged. "I suppose." From the way she squirmed in her chair, Erin could tell she was hiding something.

"Sounds like there's more to the story."

Winnie gave a bitter little laugh, and Erin realized that, as far as Winnifred Hogsworthy was concerned, there was much, much more to the story.

Chapter Eighteen

~

"So what exactly did she say about their relationship?" said Farnsworth, looking around the dining room to make sure no one was listening.

"She was obviously upset about something," Erin said. The two friends were dining at The Rise. Farnsworth had tracked Erin down in the bar, and insisted on treating her to dinner to make up for her moody behavior earlier.

"Grant and Judith had an affair, you think?"

"Could be. Why aren't you having dinner with him?" said Erin as Farnsworth poured them each a glass of Malbec.

"He wanted an early night. Said he was knackered after a big day of panels."

"I hope his nose isn't out of joint because we asked Judith to step in and do the keynote address."

"Especially if there was some hanky-panky between them in the past. Men have such delicate egos," Farnsworth said, taking a sip of wine. "Hmm, not bad. Hey, what happened with Jonathan?"

"He went to bed early."

Farnsworth shook her head. "No stamina."

"Men are the real weaker sex," Erin agreed, taking a bite of frisée. "This lemon dressing is brilliant."

"So why did Winnifred think something was going on between Judith and Grant?"

"Apparently, Judith became more remote, in spite of what Winnie claimed was a very close friendship. She seems to blame Grant for getting between them. When I pressed for more, she clammed up."

"I think she's a bit stuck on Judith."

"She does follow her around like a puppy."

Farnsworth sighed as she poured another glass of wine. "It's sad, really."

"It's not necessarily sexual."

"Right. I've had that kind of crush on people, where it's just admiration, kind of like being starstruck. Haven't you?"

"Yes," Erin said as the waiter arrived with their entrées. "That looks wonderful," she said as he placed the elegant gold-rimmed dinner plate in front of her. She inhaled the buttery aroma of trout almondine, basmati rice pilaf, and sautéed broccoli rabe.

"You really love that fish dish," Farnsworth remarked as the server delivered her entrée of roast pork belly, peas, and golden mashed potatoes.

"Couldn't resist—it's *so* good. Is Sam not working today?" she asked the waiter, an amiable young fellow with a mass of freckles and closely cropped ginger hair.

"He was supposed to be on shift, but they called me to say he hadn't turned up." His dialect was pure Ulster, with the upward cadence and curled consonants typical of Northern Ireland. He exuded a sweetness that seemed wholly unstudied, rather than being calculated to please patrons or garner larger tips.

"Is Sam all right?" asked Farnsworth.

"I hope so—it's not like him at all," he said, frowning. "He's usually reliable, so he is."

"If you hear anything, would you mind letting us know?" said Erin.

"I'll see what I can find out."

"Thank you so much," said Farnsworth. When he had gone, she turned to Erin. "What do you suppose is going on?"

"I don't know, but I don't like it."

Back in her room after dinner, Erin took out her mobile phone and pressed the first number on her Favorites list. Her father picked up after two rings.

"Hello, Pumpkin. I was just about to call you. Are you staying out of trouble?"

"Listen, I want to ask you—"

"Any more news about that chap's death? Do the police think it was murder?"

"That's what I was calling about."

"And here I thought you just wanted to hear my voice."

"That too. I just—"

"That you missed me, you know."

"I *do*. Listen, I need a favor."

"Nothing illicit, I hope."

"I just want you to do a little digging into someone who attended Oxford. Actually, a couple of people, if you don't mind."

"When did they graduate?"

"It would be about twenty years ago. Maybe more."

"Before my time, Pumpkin."

"I know. But if you could just ask around." She opened the curtains wide and gazed out at the snowflakes fluttering in the pale glow of the hotel's outdoor LED lamps. "Also, I'm interested in any information you can dig up about one of their professors."

"Which college?"

"Trinity."

"I know a few people there."

"You know *everyone*." It wasn't that far from the truth. As vicar of the University Church of St. Mary the Virgin, the parish church of Oxford University, her father knew an astonishing number of people, some of them very influential and important.

"I'll see what I can do."

"You might try the porters," she said, kicking off her shoes and sprawling on the bed. "A lot of them have been there forever, and know everyone, see everything."

"I know the Trinity porter—I'll try him first. Who am I snooping about?"

"Two literature students, Judith Eton and Winnifred Hogsworthy."

"And the professor?"

"His name is Grant Apthorp. He was there around the same time."

"Apthorp, you say? Sounds Welsh."

"It is."

"That name rings a bell. Let me see what I can do."

"You're a darling," she said, turning on the cable television, muting the sound. The screen flared into life, and Martin Shaw appeared onscreen. It seemed like he was in everything these days. Erin didn't mind—she rather fancied him, with his tousled gray hair and soulful eyes.

"Just to be clear, even if I didn't help you, you'd still be snooping around, right?"

"Absolutely."

"That's what I thought."

"So you might as well help me," she said, channel surfing. Idris Elba's face appeared—it was a repeat episode of his popular crime show *Luther.* Like every other woman in the UK, she definitely fancied him.

Her father sighed. "Why are you so intent on putting yourself in danger?"

"Nothing's going to happen to me," she said, watching Idris Elba run down a dark alley, long legs flashing in the headlights of a car in pursuit.

There was a long pause, and then he said, "Is this about your mother?"

"Don't be daft," she said, but as soon as he said it, she knew he was right. Forced to watch helplessly as her mother died of cancer, solving murders gave her an illusion of control. She knew it was just an illusion, but also knew it was better than the alternative. "I've got an early morning," she said. "'Night, dad. And thanks."

"I'll call you when I have anything."

"Love you heaps," she said, and rang off.

Onscreen, Idris Elba was fighting the forces of evil in the dirty streets of London; outside, snow swirled in the night, and inside the hotel, who knew what forces were at work? She pulled the blankets up to her chin and stared out the window at the snowflakes doing their crazy, doomed dance in the gathering darkness.

Chapter Nineteen

〜

"The thing about creativity," said Barry Wolf, "is that it can't be learned. No matter how desperately it's sought, it can't be taught, and it can't be bought."

"Nice assonance," Farnsworth muttered, chewing on a handful of popcorn.

She and Erin were lounging in Farnsworth's hotel suite the next day, watching Barry Wolf's YouTube TED Talk on the hotel's enormous flat-screen television. Their morning panels completed, Farnsworth had made popcorn for the occasion, insisting they drink the fancy little bottles of sassafras soda from her mini fridge. When Erin protested the outrageous cost, Farnsworth dismissed it with a wave of her hand.

"Who knows how much longer I'll live? I say enjoy life while we can!"

Erin frowned. "Is there something you're not telling me?"

Her friend insisted there was nothing wrong with her—she was just being dramatic, as usual, so Erin agreed to drink the overpriced soda.

Now, watching Barry Wolf on the screen, Erin felt a shiver slide down her spine. It was odd watching someone deceased but so recently alive—stranger somehow than seeing an old movie with long-dead actors. She felt as if Barry's aura hadn't yet dissipated in this world—he seemed to hover over the conference, his presence still palpable, in the ghostly manner of those so recently dead. And here she was watching his digital imprint on a fifty-two-inch flat-screen television, eating popcorn and drinking expensive soda. It felt disrespectful, irreverent. It felt ghoulish.

"Only you can contact your own creative impulses," Barry said. Onscreen, he seemed more attractive—alone on the TED stage, it wasn't so obvious how short he was. Clad in gray pants and a fitted black shirt, he looked thinner, and not so desperate to hide his age. "You can't pay someone to do it for you, coax it out of you, or imbue you with imagination if you have none," he continued. "It doesn't work that way."

Farnsworth crunched on a hard kernel of popcorn. "Ow," she said. "Think I might have broken a tooth."

"Should we pause the film? I need to hear what he's saying."

Farnsworth sighed. "I'm all right. Carry on."

Turning to a group of women in the audience, Wolf smiled, and Erin saw the same condescension she had noticed when he was alive. "The problem is that the world is full of people who *think* they're creative, but they're not. And so they muck it up for the rest of us."

"That's rather harsh," said Erin.

"Now that everyone can self-publish, and post videos of themselves on YouTube, the world is becoming increasingly full of junk," Wolf said. "Because that's what a lot of it is—junk."

"That's true," Farnsworth murmured.

"In the days when Jane Austen was writing, you couldn't just throw your half-assed 'book' up on Amazon," he went on, his fingers making air quotes around the word "book." "In those days, there were *gatekeepers*, people whose job it was to ensure a bunch of half-baked manuscripts didn't pollute the shelves of bookstores. Because in those days, space was finite, books took up room in the shop, and quality *mattered*. Nowadays it's all digitalized, and it costs almost nothing to stick something you 'wrote'"—more air quotes—"online, and call it writing. But a lot of it isn't writing—it's self-indulgent spewing. And there's no one left to stop it anymore."

A hand shot up in the audience.

"Yes?" said Barry Wolf, licking his lips, perhaps hoping to chew on an unsuspecting grad student.

"How can we tell if we're creative or not?" The young man was thin, with slicked-down black hair and pale skin. Erin realized he was none other than Barry's assistant, Stephen Mahoney. Could he be a plant in the audience, she wondered, carefully instructed to pose the right question at the right time?

"For starters, don't take your word for it," said Wolf. "Seek advice, counsel—seek criticism from someone who isn't afraid to tell you the truth."

"So not your mum, then?" said Stephen, and everyone in the audience laughed.

"Certainly not."

"What if she's a famous author herself, for example?"

"Especially not then. She'll either want your success too badly or envy your talent. Either way, you won't get a straight answer."

There was a murmur among the crowd, a nodding of heads, and Erin realized that every single person in the room considered themselves "creative"—whatever that meant.

"Isn't that young Stephen?" Farnsworth said, pausing the video.

"Yep," said Erin.

"I wonder if he was already working for Barry then."

"There's one way to find out."

Farnsworth gave a naughty smile. "Can I join you?"

"I don't see why not."

Farnsworth scraped the last few kernels of popcorn from the bowl. "Look at all the old maids," she lamented. "Just like me."

"You are not a maid, and you are certainly not old."

"No one wants me. I'm like the hard, unpopped kernels rattling around the bottom of the bowl."

"Oh, put a sock in it," Erin said, and then saw Farnsworth was grinning broadly.

"It doesn't take much to get you going."

Erin tossed a napkin at her. "Come on, let's go."

Ten minutes later they were sitting in the bar, sipping tall glasses of fruit juice.

"We could just find his room number and knock on his door," Farnsworth suggested after a few minutes.

"I don't want his guard up. It's better if he thinks it's just a casual conversation."

Farnsworth took a sip of pineapple/mango juice. "What makes you think he'll turn up here?"

"Remember last night?"

"You mean when he was so sloshed?"

"That's not the behavior of someone with a casual relationship to alcohol."

"You think he's a boozer?"

Erin traced the lip of her glass with her finger. "Let's just say I expect Mr. Mahoney is no stranger to wicked hangovers."

"So you expect him to turn up—"

"Right about now," Erin said, just as Stephen Mahoney wandered into the room, looking around tentatively. "Don't stare," she cautioned Farnsworth. "Pretend we're not interested in him."

"I'm not a very good actress," Farnsworth said, picking up the cocktail menu. "I'll just keep my eyes glued to this."

Leaning against the bar waiting for the bartender, Stephen spotted the two women and waved. Erin waved back, and pointed to the empty seat beside her. Minutes later, Stephen sauntered over to them holding a glass of what appeared to be whiskey.

"Hello again," he said, settling into the comfortable leather armchair next to Erin. "Making any progress in your investigation?"

"What do you mean?" asked Erin.

He smiled. "Everyone knows you're looking into Barry's death. The police might not think it was murder, but word around says you do. I don't believe we've met," he said to Farnsworth. "I'm Stephen Mahoney."

"Farnsworth Appleby."

"Delighted. To Barry," he said, raising his glass.

"Cheers," said Erin, sipping her fruit juice.

"He may have been a bastard," Stephen said, "but no one deserves to be murdered."

"Was he?" said Erin. "A bastard?"

"Let's just say . . . never mind. May he rest in peace," he said, taking another swallow of whisky.

"Have you known him a long time?"

"A few years."

"Did you know him when you were in the audience for his TED Talk?"

He looked taken aback. "Uh—no. I just turned up to hear him, then went up to him afterward and he offered me a job."

Erin and Farnsworth exchanged a glance. "When was that?"

"Three years ago."

"You've worked for him ever since?"

"I know—sounds masochistic, doesn't it?"

"And have you had time to work on your art?"

"Actually, that was one of the best things about the job. I produced a lot of work, and was lucky enough to be in a couple of gallery shows."

"Where?"

"I was part of a group show in a Soho museum called Off the Wall, and later they offered me a solo show."

"Well done," said Farnsworth.

"What about Luca? How did she and Barry meet?" asked Erin.

"Look, I'd better be off," he said, draining his glass. "Nice talking with you."

"Good to meet you," said Farnsworth.

"See you later," said Erin. When he had gone, she turned to Farnsworth. "Did you hear how he pronounced that word?"

"What word?"

"Museum."

"Was it unusual?"

"He said *moozayum*."

"Interesting. What do you think it means?"

"I have a theory."

"Do tell," Farnsworth said as Hetty and Pru entered the room.

"There you are," said Hetty, striding over to Erin and Farnsworth, an urgent expression on her face. Pru scurried after her, her legs being much shorter; she too looked as if she had something pressing on her mind.

"Hello," said Farnsworth. "What's up?"

"We've just lost our moderator for the two o'clock panel. Either of you available?"

"What's the topic?" asked Erin.

"*Jane Austen's England—Paradise or Paradigm?*"

"I think I can handle that," said Farnsworth. "I'll do it. Unless you want it?" she asked Erin.

"You go ahead. I've done plenty already."

"And you need time for your sleuthing," Hetty said with a wink.

"What happened to your moderator?" asked Erin.

"He became suddenly ill," Pru said.

"What's wrong with him?"

"Apparently it's some sort of stomach thing. Come along, then," she said to Farnsworth. "The panel starts in ten minutes."

"I'll walk with you," Erin said as Farnsworth followed the other two out of the room.

As they passed through the lobby, Farnsworth pointed to a pair of large, terra-cotta pots on either side of the entrance. Each contained deep-blue plants with masses of bell-like blossoms on long, elegant stems. The interior of the blossoms were beautifully intricate, mottled patterns of white and lavender.

"Such healthy specimens of monkshood," Farnsworth remarked as they passed.

"Are you sure that's what they are?" said Erin.

"I don't lay claim to much expertise, pet, but I do know my flowers. Why do you ask?"

"I'll explain later," Erin said. "Have a good panel."

"But—"

"Come along," Pru said, taking Farnsworth's elbow. "No time to waste."

As her three friends turned off toward the conference rooms, Erin bent and carefully examined the plants. Straightening up, she headed toward the lifts. She had a theory, and she was very anxious to try it out.

Chapter Twenty

～

"York Constabulary, Detective Hemming speaking." His voice was tired, ragged.

"It's Erin."

There was a pause, as if she had taken him by surprise.

"Hello, Miss Coleridge. What can I do for you?"

"Miss Coleridge." Not a good sign. Erin took a deep breath. "Has the medical examiner completed the tox screen on Barry Wolf?"

"They haven't sent us any results yet."

"Tell them to test for aconite poisoning."

"What?"

"It's the main toxin in monkshood. It interferes with the heart—"

"I know what it does. Why do you think we should test for it?"

She described the plants in the lobby.

"What makes you think—"

"I could see where some stems had been cut or torn off."

"I'll be there in fifteen minutes."

"I'll meet you in the lobby."

Sixteen minutes later, he staggered into the hotel, looking bedraggled in his weather-beaten trench coat and herringbone tweed cap.

"Are you warm enough in that?" she said as he stamped his feet on the mat, moisture clinging to his boots.

"My ancestors were Vikings, remember?" he said, brushing the snow from his shoulders.

"You did tell me that." It seemed so long ago, their walk across the moors, the tea shared huddling in the ruins of a cottage while being pelted with rain. "Still, you might—"

"I'm wearing a jumper," he said, opening his coat to reveal a thick, dark-blue sweater. "You sound like my mother. Now, what did you want to show me?"

"This," she said, leading him over to the pair of potted plants, aware the overly perky desk clerk was watching her closely. She made eye contact with the woman, who looked a bit startled. "Tricia, isn't it?"

"Yes—can I help?" she answered warily.

"You don't mind if I show Detective Hemming these potted plants, do you?"

"Detective? No, not at all, but—"

"Thanks. Now, look here," she told him. "A large chunk has been cut off of this plant." She turned the pot round so he could see.

"Maybe it was being pruned."

"You don't prune a plant that way. You'd pinch it off a bit from the top, but you wouldn't remove entire stalks."

"Maybe it was an accident."

"You can see where it was cut cleanly, probably by a knife or sharp scissors—here, where some of the stem still remains."

He peered down at the plant. "What if you're right—what are you implying?"

She glanced at Tricia, who was pretending to organize papers, but was clearly listening intently.

"Not here," she told him.

"Where, then?"

"In the bar." Her room was too personal, and the bar was closer.

"All right."

The bartender smiled at Erin when she returned; both she and Hemming ordered cappuccino.

"What makes you think he was poisoned by aconite?" he said as they settled into a pair of armchairs by the window. His pale-yellow hair looked almost white in the winter light.

"He vomited profusely before his death."

"That's not unknown in sudden cardiac arrest."

"But it's not a common symptom. And he had no previous cardiac history."

"How do you know?"

"It was in the ME's report."

"Do you have any suspects in mind?"

"Can you just ask the medical examiner to test for aconite? And if I'm wrong, I'll back off."

He leaned back in his chair and regarded her with heavy-lidded eyes.

"You're so interested in crime. Why didn't you become a policewoman?"

"Maybe I will yet. Did you know that another name for monkshood is 'wolf's bane'?"

"Why do you ask?"

"The killer might have a dark sense of humor."

"Oh, I see—Barry Wolf. Wolf's bane. Bit of a stretch, don't you think?"

"Maybe. Maybe not."

"All right," he said, finishing his coffee. "I'll take a specimen of the plant with me."

"Thank you."

"I'll let you know the results on one condition."

"What's that?" she asked, knowing what was next.

"That you back off and stop poking around."

"I'll do my best to stay out of trouble."

"Look, Erin," he said. "I know I haven't been myself this week, but . . . I'm hoping we can get together and talk about something other than crime. In the meantime, if something happens to you—" He paused to wipe something from his eye. "I would never forgive myself."

"It wouldn't be your fault." He looked away, and she had a realization that, as far as he was concerned, everything was his fault. Suddenly, it was so clear—his exaggerated sense of responsibility, his gravitas.

She reached for his hand, but his mobile phone chirped, and he dug it out of his pocket.

"Hemming." He listened intently, his face serious. "What's the address?" Listening, he scribbled it onto a cocktail napkin. "On my way," he said, and stood up. "I have to leave right away," he told Erin.

"What about the specimen?"

"Sorry—it'll have to wait."

"Someone's been killed, haven't they?"

"What do I owe?" he asked. Digging in his pocket, he dropped the cocktail napkin.

She pounced on it as it fluttered to the floor. "My treat," she said. Glancing at the napkin, she quickly memorized the name and address before handing it back to him. When he took it from her, his fingers lingered on hers. Her breath quickened, and her stomach felt hollow.

"I'm sorry—I have to go. I'll talk to you when I can."

"Right," she said. "Thanks for coming."

When he was gone, she wrote the name and address on a little pad she always carried with her. Sam Buchanan, *41 Townsend Street*. He had scribbled something else underneath—"water?" No, it looked more like "waiter." She didn't recognize the address, but the name—could it be *their* Sam? If the word was indeed "waiter," it all fit. She tried to console herself with the idea that Buchanan was a common enough last name, but she had a bad feeling as she walked up to pay the bar bill.

Chapter Twenty-One

❧

"Here ye go, luv," said the Scottish bartender, handing Erin the bill for the cappuccinos. He was short and broad shouldered, built like a professional wrestler, with shaggy black eyebrows and thick, closely cropped dark hair. According to the tag on his red vest, his name was Spike.

"Thanks," she said. She signed with her room number before typing the address she had memorized into Google maps on her phone. She wanted to get it in as quickly as possible lest she forget it.

"Wha'd the copper want?" he asked. "Not that it's any a' my business, mind you." Judging from his truncated vowels and guttural consonants, she guessed he was from Glasgow.

"How did you know he's a policeman?"

He smiled. "Let's just say I've got a history, luv."

"He didn't want anything—I asked him to meet me."

"Oh, aye?" he said, leaning his meaty arms on the bar. On his left forearm, a tattoo protruded from the rolled-up shirt sleeve, a black-and-white cobweb. Erin recognized it as a prison tattoo, usually indicating someone who has spent a long stretch behind bars.

"How long were you inside, Spike?"

His eyes fell on the tattoo. "I'm on parole, actually, keepin' my nose clean."

"Sounds like a good idea," she said, trying to appear casual, but a little nervous in his presence—and, to be honest, a bit excited as well.

"Do you recognize this address?" she asked, showing him what she had written down.

"Aye. It's where our Sam lives."

"Sam who works here as a waiter? So his last name is Buchanan?"

"Aye."

"Are you sure?"

"Gospel truth. I've dropped 'im off after work often enough. He doesn't own a car, ye see."

Erin's head felt light, and her vision blurred momentarily.

"Come tae think of it, he daedna come in today."

"Did anyone speak to him?"

"I thaink they rang 'im but there was no answer. Why? Has somethin' happened?"

"I don't know, but I'm going to find out."

"Lemme know when ye do, eh?" Spike said, putting a tray of glasses on the shelf. "He's a good sort, Sam is."

"I will," she said, stumbling out of the room. She made it to the lift in a fog, hardly noticing anything around her. Within minutes, she was sitting in the living room of Farnsworth's suite, while her friend bustled about making the timeless British cure for all ailments and shocks to body and spirit: a cup of tea.

"Do you think if something's happened to Sam—God forbid—it's connected to Barry's death?" asked Farnsworth, pouring milk into a pair of white porcelain mugs.

"What are the chances the two *aren't* connected?" Erin said, pacing the room.

"So Detective Hemming looked upset when he got the phone call?"

"Very. He got up and left immediately. I've got to find out what happened!"

"Take it easy, pet," Farnsworth said, handing her a steaming mug of tea.

"Thanks," Erin said, taking a sip. The hot liquid was comforting in a way that defied rationality, as though the essence of succor and well-being had been distilled into the dried leaves from a modest little shrub hardy enough to grow in a wide variety of climates around the world.

"Biscuit?" said Farnsworth, holding out a tin of Scottish shortbreads.

"Ta," Erin said, taking a couple. Lunch hour was long over—it was nearing dinnertime—and she hadn't eaten anything except popcorn since an early breakfast.

"What are you going to do?"

"Drive over to the house and see what I can find out."

"Want company?"

"You don't have any panels this afternoon?"

"The ten o'clock was my only one today."

"Come along, then."

"Finish your tea," Farnsworth commanded. "I'll call the concierge and tell them to bring your car round."

Popping the second biscuit into her mouth, Erin gulped down the rest of her tea, the warmth spreading throughout her body. "That went down without touching the sides," she said, handing Farnsworth the mug.

"Auntie Farnsworth knows what's best, pet," her friend said, throwing on a long, forest-green wool cloak and matching beret. Hetty Miller might strive to be fashionable, but Farnsworth had her own, unstudied sense of style.

The snow had stopped falling, but a thick layer lay on the ground as they stepped outside the hotel.

"This must be about six inches," Farnsworth remarked as the valet drove up with their car.

"Five and a half, to be exact, mum," he said, climbing out of the car. The aroma of stale cigarette smoke hovered around him as he handed Erin the keys.

"Thanks," Erin said, taking out her wallet.

"Let me, pet," Farnsworth said, whipping out a five-pound note. "Thank you very much," she said, handing it to him.

"Thank *you*, mum," he said with a broad smile, tipping his hat. He was slight and lean, with a long jaw and protruding underbite, his skin dusky and uneven. His teeth, darkened from tobacco, were the color of weak coffee. According to the ID tag on his crisp black vest, his name was Clyde.

As they drove away, Farnsworth remarked, "If he were a character actor, he'd work all the time. Where are we going?" she said as Erin turned onto Station Street, aka the A1036, one of the thick modern arteries slicing through the medieval city.

"41 Townsend Street."

"Shall I put that in the satnav?"

"If you like. I sort of memorized the route."

"Well done, you. I'll do it anyway, just in case," she said, leaning forward to type the information into the car's GPS screen.

"It's a pretty straight shot," Erin said as they crossed the River Ouse. The water beneath them flowed sluggishly, moody and gray beneath the wintry sky, as the last feeble rays of the sun struggled to break through a thick cloud cover. York Minster loomed heavily in the foreground, its trembling spires reaching for the hand of God, a testimony to man's endless yearning. She continued forward, as Station Road became Museum Street, past the Theatre Royale, staying on the A1036 as it turned left at Duncombe Place, changing its name again to Gillygate.

They were in college territory now, bordering the campus of St. John's University. Chinese takeaways were followed by fish and chips joints and cozy coffee shops, making Erin nostalgic for her student days.

"Oh, there's the Coconut Lagoon," Farnsworth said wistfully as they passed an inviting-looking Indian restaurant. "It's meant to be really good."

"We're almost there," Erin said, turning onto Townsend Street as the aroma of curry spices and tandoori naan wafted into her nostrils.

"Maybe we can go there after?" said Farnsworth.

"We'll see," she replied, though she was feeling a bit light-headed from hunger.

Number 41 was the left half of an ordinary-looking gray stone building, the kind of rambling two-family home often occupied by students. Erin wondered if Sam was a student at St. John's, moonlighting as a waiter between classes.

It was obvious right away that something was amiss. An ambulance sat at the curb, its top light spinning, flanked by two police cars and a white police van with a band of blue and yellow stripes. Above the stripes were the words Crime Scene Investigation. Behind the van was Detective Hemming's battered blue Citroen. Cursing herself because her own car was equally unmistakable, Erin swung the Sunbeam Alpine onto Backhouse Street, the narrow side street just across from 41 Townsend. Pulling into the carpark behind a block of flats, she cut off the engine.

"What now?" said Farnsworth.

"Stay here. I'll be right back."

"Why do you get to have all the fun?"

"Because I have to be able to hide quickly if Detective Hemming comes out of the building. I can't let him see me."

"And you think I can't move fast enough?"

"Can you?"

Farnsworth sighed. Afraid she was in for another pout, Erin laid a hand on her arm. "It's just that two people are harder to hide than one."

"Right," Farnsworth said unconvincingly. "Go on, then."

"Look, if you really want to—"

"Get along—it's getting cold in here. Hurry up."

"Will you be all right?"

"I'll be fine—get on with you."

Erin climbed out of the little car and walked rapidly back toward Townsend Street. The wind whipped at her ankles as she stood at the intersection, watching the line of vehicles parked in front of the building. As she watched, one of the police cars pulled away slowly, lights silently flashing. After a couple of minutes, seeing no one enter or leave the building, she pulled her cap down over her eyes and started across the street. The back of the ambulance was open, and she could make out two figures standing just outside it. One of them was smoking. She recognized the two EMT workers she had met at the hotel – the tall, stern Jamaican woman and the friendly, chain-smoking Cockney. She strained to remember their names. He was Henry, but the woman had a more unusual name. Shanelle? Shanade? She couldn't quite bring it up.

"I dunno," Henry was saying. "What about the petechiae? Don' get that from hangin', do ye?"

Erin stopped where she was. It was a dark, moonless night, and they hadn't seen her yet. She took a few steps to the right, stopping next to a tree, so the ambulance was between her and their line of sight. Standing very still, she held her breath and listened.

"So?" said the woman.

"An' the chap from the medical examiner's office said 'is face was th' wrong color—sorta purplish."

"I see what you mean. In a hanging you would expect it to be pale."

"What d'ye think it means?"

The woman said something Erin couldn't quite make out. Taking a deep breath, she crossed the street and approached them, trying to look casual. "Hiya," she said. "What's going on here?" Glancing at the woman's uniform, Erin remembered now—her name was Shanise.

Henry's face brightened when he saw her, but Shanise looked less enthusiastic.

"What are you doing here?"

"I've come to meet my friend Sam. Sam Buchanan," she said, looking for their reaction. Henry glanced guiltily at Shanise, who stared at Erin impassively.

"You can't see him right now."

"Why not? What's happened?"

"He's—" Henry began, but Shanise silenced him with a look.

"You can't go in there," she said.

"Why not?"

"It's a crime scene," Henry blurted out.

"Oh my God," Erin said, doing her best to look shocked and surprised. Truthfully, she was distressed, but not exactly surprised. "What happened? Is Sam all right?"

The fact that there was an ambulance with two very unhurried paramedics standing next to it told her everything she needed to know.

Sam Buchanan was dead.

Chapter Twenty-Two

≈

The door of the house opened and a familiar figure emerged. Erin recognized the tall, athletic form of Sergeant Rashid Jarral, Detective Hemming's cheerful, easygoing partner. The building's porchlight glinted off his shiny black hair as he paused on the stoop for a moment before descending the steps and striding toward them. Erin turned to flee, but Jarral called out to her.

"Miss Coleridge!"

She froze in place. It was too late—the jig was up.

The two medics stared at Erin. "You know him?" said Henry.

"Sort of," Erin answered as Jarral approached, a friendly smile on his handsome face. The opposite of the moody, intense Hemming, Sergeant Jarral was open, good-natured, and trusting. And now that he was here, Erin hoped she could use that to her advantage.

"Fancy meeting you here," Jarral said, shaking her hand heartily and nodding at the two medics.

"Hello again, Sergeant," said Henry. Shanise gave him a curt nod. Erin wondered if she liked anybody.

"What brings you down to York?" Jarral asked Erin.

"I'm here for a conference. And Sam Buchanan is a friend of mine." Not exactly a lie, but not exactly the truth either.

"Oh," he said. "I'm so sorry." She could see the wheels turning in his head as he processed her response. "How did you—I mean, why are you here, exactly?"

"I just popped round to see him," she lied. "And then I saw all this," she added, pointing to the lineup of police vehicles.

"So you—I mean, what did they tell you?" he asked, indicating Shanise and Henry.

"Nothing, but it's pretty clear Sam is dead. Isn't he?" she added, swallowing hard, hoping she was wrong.

Jarral looked at the two medics. Shanise shrugged, and Henry looked away.

Erin shook her head sorrowfully.

"I'm sorry, but I can't really say anything at this time," Jarral said.

"How did he die?" Erin said.

"Listen, I have to go back in. I wish I could tell you more, but we haven't even notified the family."

"Of course," she said. "And do me a favor, would you? Don't tell Detective Hemming you saw me."

Jarral frowned. "He doesn't know you're here?"

"No, and it would upset him. You know how he is."

"Okay, I guess."

"Thanks."

"Right," he said, and turned to go. "Stay out of trouble!" he called over his shoulder as he loped toward the house.

Right, Erin thought. *Fat chance of that.*

"About bloody time," Farnsworth said when Erin climbed back into the driver's seat a few minutes later. "It's bloody cold out here."

"Language, Miss Appleby. What would Mr. Apthorp think?"

"Sod him," Farnsworth said, rubbing her hands together rapidly while breathing on them. Her breath hung white in the frosty air, and Erin felt a little guilty. She resolved to buy her friend a nice Indian meal. "So? What did you find out?"

"I'm afraid it's not good news."

"What? Tell me, please," Farnsworth said, an edge of panic in her voice.

"He died by hanging. At first glance it looked like suicide."

"*What?* Why would Sam kill himself?"

"A better question is who would kill Sam and make it look like a suicide?" Erin told Farnsworth about the petechial hemorrhaging and the purplish color of his face.

Farnsworth rubbed her hands and blew on them. "Petechial hemor—"

"Little broken blood vessels in the eyes."

"Which isn't common in hanging?"

"But you would expect to see in strangulation."

"Oh my God."

"So who wanted Sam dead?"

Farnsworth was silent for a moment.

"Could it be a coincidence?"

Erin nodded. "I don't believe in coincidences."

"There will be an autopsy?"

"I'm sure there will."

"When?"

"I expect when the CSI team finishes processing the scene they'll remove the body to the morgue. I don't know how long that would take—it depends on how backed up they are, how much of a rush there is on it, that kind of thing."

Farnsworth shook her head sorrowfully. "Poor Sam. He was such a good fellow."

"He definitely took a shine to you," Erin said, starting the engine. "Are you up for a meal at the Coconut Lagoon, or are you too upset?"

"Well, I'm very upset, but I'm also starving."

"That's what I thought you'd say," Erin said, driving out of the carpark and back onto the street.

"Why? Do you think I'm shallow?"

"Not at all—just practical," Erin said as they drove past the crime scene. The vehicles had not moved, and she could see Henry and Shanise lounging in the back of the ambulance. Henry was smoking, the glow from his cigarette like a single orange eye of a predator in the night. *Tiger, Tiger, burning bright, in the forests of the night.* William Blake's famous poem popped into Erin's head as she turned left on Gillygate Road, back in the direction they had come.

"After all, one does have to eat," Farnsworth said plaintively.

"Right," Erin said as they approached the Coconut Lagoon. The purple and pink neon lights beckoned, promising comfort and solace. Swinging the car round to park in front of the restaurant, Erin felt her shoulders relax. For the next hour or so, she resolved, she would take her mind off murder and enjoy a nice meal with her best friend. The problem was, she wasn't sure it was possible. Taking a deep breath, she unbuckled her safety belt—impossible or not, at least she would do her best to try.

Chapter Twenty-Three

❧

"That korma was gorgeous," Farnsworth said as they drove back to the hotel an hour later.

"The biryani was brilliant as well."

"Yes, but the korma! It was like what I imagine food in heaven would taste like. So rich and creamy, with just the right amount of cardamom." And then she burst into tears. "Poor Sam," she moaned. "He didn't deserve to die."

"No," Erin said. "But maybe we can help bring his killer to justice."

She sighed deeply as they drove past York Minster, its jagged spires jabbing at the sky, as if trying to poke through to heaven. Beams of klieg lights shot upward from the cathedral below, disappearing into the cloud cover. The night was quiet; the snow lay all around them, dampening the sounds of the ancient city.

Back at the hotel, Clyde was still on valet duty, and Farnsworth slipped him another fiver as Erin handed him the car keys.

"Ta, ladies—have a pleasant night," he said, tipping his cap.

"You too, pet," said Farnsworth, climbing the front steps a little unsteadily. Since she was driving, Erin had refrained from having anything from the wide selection of Indian beers at the Coconut Lagoon, but Farnsworth, being under no such restriction, had sampled several. "Well," she said when they reached the lobby, "I think I'll turn in. Thanks for the lovely dinner."

"I hope it made up for making you sit in the cold car."

"I'd sit in a cold car all night for a dinner like that."

"Good night. Sweet dreams."

"I plan to dream about that korma all night," Farnsworth said, giving her a peck on the cheek before heading toward the lifts. "Otherwise I'm afraid I'll dream about murder."

It wasn't very late, and Erin didn't feel like retiring just yet. She stood gazing at the elaborately tiled floor, with its circular blue and rose design, bordered on every side by elegant arches, reminiscent of Islamic palaces. Erin smiled absently at Harriet, the sweet, middle-aged desk clerk with the heavily powdered face, before wandering in the direction of the 1906 Bar. She was glad to see Khari Butari seated in the back, near the fireplace. Spotting her, Khari waved her over.

"Nice spot," Erin said, sliding into the burgundy leather armchair.

"It's only a gas fire," Khari said, "but it's good enough for me. Even after living here all these years, I'm still fascinated by fireplaces."

"Because it was too hot in Senegal to have them?"

"They weren't very common. I feel the same way about snow," she said, looking out the window. "It still seems amazing to me."

"We don't usually get this much, even in the north of England."

"Would you like a drink?"

"What are you having?"

"A Singapore sling. Spike makes it really well."

Erin looked up to see him vigorously shaking a martini in a silver flask, the edge of the cobweb tattoo peeking out from the sleeve of his shirt on his muscular arm. Wondering who would be drinking a martini, she looked around the bar and spotted Judith Eton and Terrence Rogers in a secluded corner, deep in conversation. She hadn't noticed them when she first entered.

"How long have Terrence and Judith been here?" she asked Khari.

"I'm not really sure. I didn't see them until you pointed them out just now. So what can I get you?"

"Let me get this round, and you can get the next one."

"Really, I'd be glad—"

"Please."

"All right."

"The same?"

"As Spike would say, you can't walk on one leg."

"Sounds like you've become very friendly with him."

Khari laughed. "He's a flirt."

"Or maybe he fancies you. Be right back," she said, heading toward the bar. Terrence and Judith took no notice of her, being engrossed in their own conversation.

Spike grinned when he saw her. "Hello, luv. What can I do ye for?"

"Two more Singapore slings, please."

"Right you are," Spike said. Grabbing several bottles from the colorful rack of liquors lined up behind him, he went to work pouring and mixing them into a beaker, tossing in ice cubes and bits of fruit.

Leaning on the bar, Erin tried to hear what Judith and Terrence were saying, without appearing to. She avoided looking in their direction, but strained to eavesdrop on their conversation. They were seated fairly close by, so she could make out some of what they were saying, but they were obviously trying to keep their voices low. Their tone was urgent, intimate, querulous.

"How do I know you aren't making this up?" Terrence said, leaning forward.

Judith snorted. "Oh, come on! Surely you suspected by now."

"No, I didn't!"

Then Judith said something Erin couldn't quite make out, and Spike presented her with two tall, festively decorated glasses filled with a pale pink liquid.

"That's gorgeous," she said, picking them up.

"Shall I put it on your room?"

"Uh, yes—it's room number—"

"I know the number, luv," he said, making a note on the bill.

"Add a few quid for yourself."

"Right. Coupla hundred, then?"

She laughed. "Will a fiver be enough?"

"Ta very much," he said, tapping his forehead with his forefinger in a salute.

"Mind if I ask you a question about Sam?"

"Wha's that, then?"

"I was just wondering whether he has any enemies you know of."

Spike snorted. "Sam? Not bloody likely. He's so good-natured sometimes I wonder if he's livin' in the same world as me. Doesn't see the bad side of people."

"Does he seem worried about anything?"

"Not really." He peered at Erin. "Do ye know where he's got off to?"

"No. I was just curious."

Spike cocked his massive head to one side and raised an eyebrow, as if he didn't believe her. Erin felt a pang at lying to him, but it would be a betrayal of her promise to Sergeant Jarral not to say anything.

"Thanks again," she said, taking the drinks. Walking as slowly as she could, trying to catch another snippet of conversation, Erin headed back toward her table. As she passed a few yards from Judith and Terrence, she heard her say, "Don't be so daft, for God's sake!"

She couldn't make out his reply, and had no choice but to continue on to join Khari by the fireplace.

"Ta," Khari said as Erin handed her the drink. "You seemed very interested in our neighbors over there."

"Was is that obvious?"

"Not to them—they hardly seemed aware of you at all."

"This really is good," Erin said, sipping her drink.

"So what were they talking about?"

"I'm not sure." She related what she had heard to Khari, who shook her head.

"You're right—it could be anything. But sounds like she was telling him something he didn't believe."

"Or didn't want to," Erin added.

They looked over to see Terrence rise from his chair, looking shaken. He walked toward the exit as if in a daze, while Judith watched, arms crossed. Whatever she had told him, Erin thought, it was not welcome news. Not she just had to find out what it was.

Chapter Twenty-Four

Erin slept restlessly, tossing and turning half the night. Finally she took a Benadryl and settled into a deep REM state, dreaming about chasing an ambulance down an endless series of dark alleys, first in her car, and finally on foot. Strangely, she was able to keep up with the vehicle, even on foot, but was always a few steps behind. As it swerved around a tight corner, the back doors suddenly swung open and Peter Hemming came lurching out, blood gushing from his head, and fell into her arms.

She awoke abruptly, a scream caught in her throat, to find her mobile phone ringing. She grabbed it from the bedside table and looked at the screen. It was her father.

"Bit early, isn't it?" she said, pressing the phone to her ear.

"Is it?"

"It's seven AM."

"Did I wake you?"

"No," she said, stifling a yawn. She didn't want him to think she was what he called a "layabed." A natural early riser, her father considered anyone who slept until after eight to be a "lazybones." Her mother had loved staying up late, and her father made an exception for her, but Erin received no such dispensation, being expected to adhere to her father's idea of virtue, which included early rising.

She turned over onto her back and propped her head up with the hotel's luxurious, king-sized down pillows. "So, what's up?"

"I thought you might like to hear the results of my research." He sounded a bit put out.

"Yes, please," she said, sitting up, suddenly alert. "What did you learn?"

"Well, it seems that Judith Eton was indeed Grant Apthorp's research assistant while he was a graduate student at Oxford. She was a freshman at the time."

"Any hanky-panky?"

"No, but there may have been with someone else."

"Who?"

"Terrence Rogers. He was a lecturer at the time."

"Really? Do tell."

"They were often together on campus, and my source tells me she was seen leaving his rooms at all hours."

"Who is your source?"

"A venerable old porter by the name of Harry Bellows. I knew him well back in the day. Has a memory like a steel trap, and a nose like a bloodhound. I wouldn't try to sneak anything past him. Come to think of it, I did once as an undergrad, and it didn't go well."

"You mean my dear old Da wasn't the blue-eyed boy I always thought he was?"

"That was a myth propagated by your dear late mother."

"What did you do, exactly?"

"Let's just say it involved a purloined llama and several bottles with pictures of a kilted man on them."

"Was Scotch whiskey outlawed on campus?"

"No. It was a bribe to procure the llama. Sorry to puncture your elevated view of me."

"No worries—it wasn't all that elevated."

"How sharper than a serpent's tooth it is—"

"—to have a thankless child. I'm a rotten daughter."

"No, just ungrateful."

"What else did Mr. Harry Bellows tell you?"

"Toward the end of Judith's freshman year, Terrence Rogers's office was vandalized."

"Did they catch the perpetrator?"

"There were several suspects, but no one was ever charged."

"Did Mr. Bellows remember who they were?"

"The man's a wonder, I tell you. Just a second—I wrote them down." There was the sound of rustling paper in the background. "Here we are. Judith was questioned, but she was out of town at the time, so she was eliminated. Several of his other students were also questioned."

"Anyone else?"

"Let's see . . . the cleaning lady, the building's maintenance man, and—oh, yes, a woman by the name of Winnifred Hogsworthy."

"Winnifred Hogsworthy? Are you sure about that?"

"Unlikely name, I know; that's why I wrote it down."

"What relationship did she have to Terrence?"

"Apparently she was a great friend of Judith's."

"Why was she questioned?"

"She was observed coming out of his office not long before the vandalism."

"Curioser and curioser."

"Why? Do you know her?"

"She's at this conference. Quite an odd duck. And she displays a greater than normal devotion to her friend Judith."

"That *is* interesting."

"I can imagine her being jealous of Terrence and taking it into her head to do something about it."

"Why do you think—" he began, but there was a knock on the door of Erin's room.

"Hang on a minute," she said. "Someone's at the door."

"There may be a murderer lurking about. Mind how you go."

Erin smiled at the quaint phrase, a reminder of her father's Norfolk roots. "Thanks for the information—talk to you later."

"Please be careful."

"I will, Dad," she said, and rang off as the knocking on her door grew more insistent. "Just a minute!" she said, throwing on her dressing gown, which was actually a black karate robe she had found in an Oxford charity shop.

She opened the door to find Hetty Miller, in sandals and a fluffy white bathrobe, tapping her foot impatiently.

"Did you forget?" said Hetty.

"Forget what?"

"You said you'd join me in the spa."

"I did?"

"I've been waiting for you."

"I'm sorry. It completely slipped my mind."

Hetty heaved an exasperated sigh. "Come along, then! I made a massage appointment for both of us, and they'll charge us even if we don't show up."

"Give me a couple of minutes—I'll meet you down there."

"All right," Hetty said. "Mind you don't take too long."

Hearing the smack of her rubber flip-flops as Hetty retreated down the hall, Erin changed out of her pajamas into shorts and a T-shirt. She always took a long bath right before bed, so she rarely needed a morning shower except in hot, sticky weather. At the moment, according to the weather app on her phone, it was minus four degrees Celsius. She slipped on a pair of sandals, threw on her karate robe, and grabbed her key card. Darting out of the room, she was halfway down the hall before she heard the door lock click in place.

Already feeling quite peckish, she was unable to resist the smell of buttery croissants coming from the restaurant. She made a quick detour to pick one up, and upon entering the breakfast room, saw Farnsworth and Grant Apthorp seated at a window table. When Farnsworth waved her over, Erin felt torn. She had already kept Hetty waiting, and was guilty about succumbing to her weakness for freshly baked croissants.

"Sleep well?" Farnsworth asked as Erin approached.

"I did," she lied. "What about you?"

Farnsworth sighed. "Not too bad, considering—" Erin glared at her, and she broke off with the pretense of a coughing fit.

"You all right?" said Grant.

"Yes, thanks—something went down the wrong way." Farnsworth said, glancing at Erin.

"I hear you had quite the feast last night," said Grant. Dressed in a forest-green cardigan over a crisp white shirt, his thick gray hair swept back, he looked like a movie star version of a college professor. Not for the first time, Erin wondered why a man like him wasn't married, and what his personal history was.

"It was *so* good," Farnsworth. "The korma was heavenly."

"Would you like to join us?" Grant asked Erin.

"Actually, I was just going to grab a croissant—I'm late to meet Hetty in the spa."

"Have one of these," said Grant, picking up the basket of fresh-baked breads from their table.

"Oh, I don't want to take yours—"

"It'll take you forever to get a waiter's attention," he said. "They're really busy, and rather understaffed today."

Erin looked around the crowded restaurant, the waiters scurrying about trying to keep up. "All right," she said, plucking a croissant from the basket. "Ta very much."

"Here," Grant said, handing her a tiny jar of bramble jelly. "Take this as well."

"Oh, I couldn't—"

"Go on—we've plenty of others," he said, pointing to the display of jams in a small silver canister.

"Thanks very much," said Erin. "You're very kind."

"You'd better get on with it, then," said Farnsworth. "Hetty hates to be kept waiting."

"Right. Good seeing you again," she told Grant.

"And you."

"I'll walk you out," said Farnsworth, rising from her chair.

"There's really no need—"

Farnsworth silenced her with a glare.

"All right," said Erin.

When they were halfway across the room, Farnsworth whispered, "Anything new about Sam?"

"Not really. I talked with Spike last night, but he said Sam didn't have any enemies he knew of."

Farnsworth shook her head. "Poor Sam. Such a lovely man."

"That's just what Spike said."

"Keep me posted."

"I will."

"See you at Grant's reading this afternoon?"

"Oh, is that today?"

"Yes, he's reading from *Alluring Lies: The False Promise of Romanticism.*"

"You sure you want to get involved with the man who wrote that?"

"He's talking about literature, not life, silly."

"Still," Erin said. "Makes you wonder."

Farnsworth rolled her eyes. "Go on then, or Hetty will have your head."

As she rounded the corner to the stairs leading down to the spa, Erin quite literally ran into Jonathan Alder as he came from the other direction.

"Oof!" she said, staggering backward.

He grabbed her shoulders to keep her from falling. His hands were warm, fine-boned but strong. "Are you all right?" he said, releasing her, his fingers lingering just a moment on her back.

"Fine," she said, her skin tingling where he had touched it.

"You're in a hurry."

"I'm late to meet Hetty. Apparently I promised to meet her in the spa."

"Apparently?"

"I have no memory of it."

"Uh-oh," he said. "Early onset of dementia?"

"More likely an attack of Spike's cocktails."

"He does make them strong, doesn't he? Hey," he said as she turned to leave. "You game to walk the wall today? I'm quite keen to do it while we're here."

"Uh—sure."

"Two o'clock?"

"Fine."

Walking along the Roman wall surrounding York was a popular pastime for tourists and locals alike. There was a website dedicated to the pursuit, complete with maps and historical narrative.

"I'll meet you in the lobby at a little before two, then."

"Great," she said, heading for the stairs, afraid Hetty would never forgive her.

The slim, immaculately groomed spa attendant—Marcia, according to her name tag—informed Erin that the two morning appointments were already in session. When Erin gave Marcia her name, she studied the desk register while Erin took in the cool, soothing décor. The blue and white tiles lining the floors and plaster busts of men's heads set into recessed wall niches suggested a Roman bath. Sound echoed through the cavernous chambers, bouncing off the smooth walls, becoming softer and softer, until all that remained was a faint whisper. Erin could smell the chlorine from the pool in the next room, and caught a glimpse of the gently rippling blue water.

Marcia looked up from her ledger, frowning. "Are you quite certain? It says here the appointments were booked for Hetty Miller and Prudence Pettibone."

"Really?" said Erin, trying to imagine Pru in the hands of a masseuse. She couldn't picture Prudence unclothed at all—it was if she came straight out of the womb wearing ratty, mismatched outfits.

Marcia turned the appointment book so Erin could read it. "You're welcome to look if you like."

"I believe you. I'm just surprised."

"They'll be finished in another ten minutes. There's no one booked just after them, so I can fit you right in."

"That's very kind of you, but—"

Just then Prudence and Hetty came sauntering out of the massage room, draped in the hotel's white terrycloth bathrobes. They both looked utterly relaxed and content. Pru's face was ruddy and shiny and beaming. Until now, Erin didn't think Prudence was capable of looking so happy.

When Hetty saw Erin, her face registered guilt. "Oh, I'm so sorry, Erin! It was Prudence who said she'd meet me, not you. Please forgive me for showing up so agitated."

"I was down here waiting for her," Prudence said, beaming.

"Let me treat you to a massage to make up for it," said Hetty.

"Let other pens dwell on guilt and misery," said Pru. "I have just seen a little bit of heaven."

"It's truly divine," Hetty agreed. "My treat."

"That's very generous," Erin said. "But I—"

"I insist—please."

"All right," Erin said, convinced by the beatific expression on Pru's face.

"We're off to the steam room," said Pru. "Ta-ta."

"See you later," said Hetty, following her friend across the sleek lobby.

"When would you like to book your massage?" asked Marcia.

"I'll check my schedule and call you. Thanks very much," she said, bounding up the stairs.

When she emerged into the hotel lobby, Erin realized she was still holding a now crumbling croissant, still faintly warm. Being very hungry, she settled into one of the small settees in the lobby's wall recesses to eat it. Fishing the tiny jar of bramble jam from the pocket of her robe, she shoved a corner of the croissant in, and took a generous bite. "Mmm," she murmured happily, as the tart jam and crispy, buttery croissant melded into an exquisite combination of taste and texture.

"You'll want some coffee to go with that, won't you?"

She turned to see Charles Kilroy, clad in his usual Indian Jones outfit, though she was relieved to see he had changed his shirt.

"The restaurant is really busy right now," she said, flicking a crumb from her arm.

"Don't you have a Keurig machine in your room?"

"Yes, but it's so far away. I'm on the top floor, all the way down the hall. I sound terribly lazy, don't I?"

"Come with me," he said with a mysterious smile.

"Where are we going?" she asked as he led her past the empty panel rooms—the first session didn't begin until ten o'clock.

"You'll see," he said, walking surprisingly fast for a man of his girth. Erin scurried to keep up with him. Across from the grand ballroom was a small antechamber with a couple of desks and a couple of hotel wall phones. "Ah, here we are," he said, stopping in front of a large metal coffee urn. "Fresh and hot. Allow me," he said, taking a cup and saucer from the stack next to the urn.

"How did you find this?"

"I'm an explorer," Charles said with a wink, handing her a steaming cup of coffee. "Actually, I suggested they include coffee along with the water pitchers for the panels. They had to put it in here because the hallway outlets shorted out yesterday for some reason. Cream?" he said, picking up a small ceramic pitcher.

"Thanks. You are a resourceful man, Mr. Charles Kilroy," Erin said, sipping the dark liquid. "This is brilliant."

"Quite acceptable for hotel coffee," he agreed, pouring himself a cup. "I'm going to drop by the bookstore—care to join me?"

"Just one more for the road," she said, pouring a second cup of coffee before following him down the carpeted corridor.

Chapter Twenty-Five

A few people were scattered around the bookstore, walking slowly past the tables, or standing, heads down, shoulders bent in the posture Erin knew so well, having observed it in her own customers in Kirkbymoorside. There was a particular concentrated calm displayed by people browsing in bookstores, a kind of focused, meditative state. It was soothing, like watching sheep grazing in a meadow. The room was quiet, the only sound the turning of pages or low murmurings of customers. Inhaling the familiar, musty scent of paper and ink, Erin felt a sense of peace; she was at home here, among these uniquely human objects, repositories of thoughts and feelings and imagination.

Minding the till was the thin, older gentleman she had seen earlier in her panel; he looked up from the book he was reading and nodded as she and Charles entered the room.

"Were you looking for something in particular?" he asked in his reedy voice, thin as paper.

"Just browsing," Charles answered.

"Let me know if I can help," he said before turning back to his book.

"Did you notice what he was reading?" Erin whispered as they perused the tables of titles, many related to Jane Austen and her time period.

"No, what?"

"Terrence Rogers's book."

"The one he was promoting so relentlessly?"

"Yep."

"*The Plot Thickens*, something like that?"

"*Jane Austen and Her Contemporaries.*"

"Right. I remember."

"Oh, here's Grant's book," Erin said.

"Which one?"

"*Alluring Lies: The False Promise of Romanticism.* That's interesting," she said, perusing the Acknowledgments. "He thanks Barry Wolf 'for his invaluable assistance and guidance.'"

"That is intriguing," Charles agreed as Erin replaced the book on the table. The cover illustration was a painting of a satyr presenting a blushing nymph with a sumptuous bouquet of red roses. The expression on his face was rapacious, vulgar, as he leered at her yielding, voluptuous body, clad only in a sheer, clinging white shroud. The message was clear: the roses were a front for aggressive male libido, thinly cloaked in a false presentation of love and romance.

"Nice cover," said a female voice behind Erin.

Erin turned to see Khari Butari, clad in a mustard-colored tunic over black pants.

"Hello," she said. "I didn't hear you come in."

Khari smiled. "I'm not surprised. These carpets are at least three inches thick."

"Hi, I'm Khari Butari," she said to Charles.

"*Girls of Dakar*, winner of Best Documentary, New York African Film Festival, 2018."

Khari's jaw dropped. "Wow. Who *are* you?"

"Charles Augustus Kilroy," he said, shaking her hand. "A pleasure to meet you."

She turned to Erin. "Who *is* he?"

"A fan," she said. "He's a fan."

"*Bien sur*," said Khari. "A superfan, I'd say."

"I prefer 'uberfan,' actually," he said.

They all laughed. The thin gentleman looked up from his book, clearly annoyed.

"Are you going to Grant's reading?" said Khari.

"When is it again?" asked Erin.

"In about fifteen minutes."

"We'd better get going. Are you coming?" she asked Charles.

"I think I'll stay here and browse a bit. I'll catch up with you later."

"Where is the reading?" Erin asked as the two women headed toward the panel rooms.

"Mickelgate."

"I just learned it's Norse for 'Great Street.' It's one of the city's most ancient and important thoroughfares."

"Someone's been doing their research."

"I like to know about places I visit."

"I wish I'd done more reading about York."

"There's still time," Erin said as they approached Mickelgate. "The Wi-Fi here is good. And the hotel has some interesting brochures."

"Good idea."

"Hello, ladies," said Farnsworth, coming up behind them.

"Hiya," said Erin.

Farnsworth smiled broadly. "So glad you could make it." Erin couldn't help noticing her friend's proprietary air, as if she were the event hostess.

"Now that I've seen his book cover, I'm curious to hear this reading," Khari said.

"It is rather provocative, isn't it?" Farnsworth agreed, pulling a copy of the book from her handbag.

"That's a different cover," Erin said, studying it. This version showed a grinning wolf wearing a sheep's skin as a "disguise"—it was still clearly a wolf—with a toothier version of the leering grin the satyr had worn. The object of the animal's intention was a little girl in a red cape—clearly a reference to Little Red Riding Hood. In addition to roses, the wolf was presenting the girl with a box of chocolates, with a candlelit dinner table in the background.

"The one we saw had a satyr and a nymph," Khari said. "Same idea, different characters."

"Grant did mention the bookstore has an earlier edition," Farnsworth explained. "Apparently this one just came out. It's been updated and has new material."

"I thought it was interesting that he thanked Barry in the Acknowledgments," said Erin.

Farnsworth looked puzzled. "I didn't notice that."

"May I have a look?"

Farnsworth handed her the book. "Be my guest."

Erin scanned the Acknowledgments for any mention of Barry Wolf—and sure enough, there was none. "That's odd," she said, handing it back to Farnsworth. "I'm certain I saw his name in the first edition."

"Well," Farnsworth said. "It's time to go in."

They shuffled in behind the gaggle of people already in line. Erin was impressed there were so many attending; often author readings didn't generate much interest at conferences.

Grant was seated at a long table in the front of the room, a pile of books beside him. The purpose of the reading, of course, was to attract potential fans—ideally, he would sell every book on the table. In Erin's experience, that only happened to celebrity authors, but Grant's presence was so commanding that she thought he would do well.

"Thank you all for coming," he said, pushing the microphone aside. He didn't need it—his voice had the depth and resonance of a trained actor, easily filling the small room. "Some people, in seeing my book cover, may get the wrong idea. I'm not suggesting romance has no place in modern life, only that as a literary genre it sets up false societal expectations. Feminists such as Naomi Wolf and Gloria Steinem have praised my work. I say this not to brag, just to put it in perspective in the context of this conference. And naturally, I consider Jane Austen to be a deeply subversive feminist—but more about that later. For now, I'd like to read from the new edition of my book."

Erin sneezed. And then she sneezed again. And again. After the fourth sneeze, she got up and crept out of the room. Fortunately, she was seated near the back, able to slip out without attracting much attention. She knew exactly what was happening—she was having an allergic reaction to something. It didn't happen often, but she knew that once she started sneezing, it was anyone's guess how long it might continue. There wasn't much to do except take a Benadryl—it might take a while to work, but would eventually shut down her allergic response.

Erin headed toward the lobby, and as she passed the entrance to the dining room, she saw Peter Hemming charging toward her. His face was red, and he looked angry. Startled, she stopped walking. She didn't have long to wait. He started talking while he was still several yards away—or rather, began shouting.

"What the devil were you *thinking*?"

"Excuse me?" she said, her stomach suddenly hollow.

"The details of a police investigation are *not* for the general public!"

"I don't know—"

"Don't pretend you don't know what I'm talking about! You tried to trick Sergeant Jarral into revealing things about an ongoing investigation."

She felt shame rising, hot and dry, to her forehead. She hated being yelled at, especially by authority figures. It made her dizzy and confused, probably because her parents never yelled at her. She didn't know how to handle it. "I—I certainly didn't mean to get him into trouble."

"What makes you thinks you have a right to classified police information?"

"I was afraid you would think Sam killed himself, but I know he didn't."

"You don't *know* anything!"

"I know Sam, and I'm certain his death is connected—"

"There you go again! Certainty is impossible in the early stages of something like this—that's why there's an investigation."

"Look, I just wanted—"

"I don't think you appreciate how dangerous it is to meddle in police affairs." He ran a hand through his thick blond hair, his face still beet red, but she could sense his anger was beginning to drain. "You don't think about the repercussions of your actions! You just barrel along like a bull in a china shop, without stopping to consider the consequences."

"I really am sorry," she said humbly, meaning it.

"One of these days, you're going to get yourself killed."

So that was it, she thought. He was worried about her. She knew that didn't fully explain his reaction, but it was some comfort knowing he cared about her.

"What can I do to make it up to you?" she asked.

"Back off. Let the professionals handle this. It's what we're trained to do."

"But what about Barry Wolf? Have you done the tox screen?"

"The lab hasn't gotten to it yet. But it isn't your place to—"

"To ask about something that was my idea?"

That shut him up, at least momentarily. He wiped sweat from his upper lip, and ran a hand through his hair again. He truly looked tormented, and she sensed there was much more on his mind than this case.

"Are you going to tell his colleagues at the hotel?"

"Not until we've notified next of kin. His parents are on a Caribbean cruise, and we haven't been able to reach them yet. So don't you say anything to anyone, you understand?" he said sternly. "Not a word."

"Right. I won't." Biting her lip, she tried a change of topic. "How's your mother?"

He didn't answer at once. "She's all right," he muttered finally.

"If there's anything I can do—"

"What you can do," he said evenly, "is keep from poking your nose where it doesn't belong. I don't want to have to worry about you on top of everything else."

"But—"

"You asked me what you can do."

"That's not what I meant—"

"I'm sorry my answer wasn't what you wanted to hear."

She was silent, fuming and embarrassed. Not that she had inserted herself into the situation, but that she had been caught. She wanted him to think well of her, and it was humiliating to think that he considered her merely an intrusion.

"I have to get back to the station house," he said. "Please stay out of trouble."

When he had gone, she pressed the lift button. While waiting for it to arrive, she thought about who might have given her up.

Surely not Sergeant Jarral—he had promised her not to tell. The only others who knew were Henry and Shanise, and she was pretty sure it wasn't Henry. That left Shanise—she had always felt the woman didn't like her, and here, she thought, was proof.

The lift arrived, and the doors opened as the bell dinged. Stepping inside, Erin remembered why she was headed to her room in the first place, then realized something else: her sneezing fit had entirely vanished.

Chapter Twenty-Six

❧

"I'm worried about Hetty," Farnsworth said, pouring herself a second cup of tea. She and Erin were having lunch later that day in the sunlit dining room, the storm of the past few days having blown itself out. Erin gazed at the sun-splattered table, with its starched linen cloth and pale blue and white tea service. The Grand did nothing by halves—there was an air of elegance in all the details and furnishings. Farnsworth buttered another scone and took a bite, her eyes glazed with pleasure. "Oh," she said. "I shall miss these scones."

Erin had never known anyone who enjoyed food more than Farnsworth. It was a pleasure watching her eat. "Why are you worried about Hetty?"

"She was confused about who was joining her in the spa this morning. She thought she was meeting you instead of Prudence."

"That's not so unusual, is it? I mean, there's a lot going on at the conference, and we did meet down there a couple of days ago."

Farnsworth shook her head, her dark hair bouncing around her shoulders. It looked shinier than usual, and in the afternoon sun, appeared to have blonde highlights. Erin wondered if her friend had secretly paid her own visit to the spa salon.

"I just think we should watch out for her, that's all. She eats like a bird—I shouldn't be surprised if years of malnutrition has caused short-term memory issues."

Erin had to smile. Farnsworth was perfectly content in her own body—at least officially—but Erin sometimes caught her watching the sylph-like Hetty Miller with something approaching envy.

Farnsworth took another bite of scone. "I'm just saying we should be aware, pet. In case there is something going on."

"Fair enough," said Erin, helping herself to a scone. "How did the reading go?"

"It was excellent. He's a good reader, and he has a very . . . commanding presence, wouldn't you say?"

"Yes. I'm sorry I missed it."

"What caused your sneezing fit?"

"An allergic reaction of some kind."

"Any idea what it was?"

"Not really. My allergist says I'm allergic to a lot of environmental stuff."

"There will be other readings, I expect. Maybe he could do one at your store?"

"Doesn't he live in Cardiff?"

"Yes, but . . . he might spend a little more time in Yorkshire," Farnsworth said with a secret smile.

"I see."

"Speak of the devil," Farnsworth said as Grant Apthorp approached their table.

"Hello, ladies," he said.

"Please, join us," said Erin.

"Just for a moment, thanks," he said, taking the chair next to Farnsworth.

"Erin was just saying how sorry she was to have missed your reading," she said. "She had an allergic reaction to something."

"Ah, yes, I heard some sneezing in the back row—that was you?"

Erin nodded. "I went to get a Benadryl, but it usually takes some time to work."

Grant shrugged. "Not to worry. I'm sure the reading was dreadfully dull anyway."

"It certainly was *not*," said Farnsworth. "And stop fishing for compliments. Oh," she added, turning to Erin. "I thought I saw Detective Hemming's car in front of the hotel earlier. What did he want?"

Erin looked down at her plate, not sure how much to reveal.

"Who's Detective Hemming?" Grant asked.

"Erin has a bit of romantic intrigue with a York police detective," Farnsworth explained.

"I do *not* have a—"

"He sent you flowers, pet."

Grant smiled. "That sounds pretty romantic to me."

"I have to go," Erin said, rising. "I'm walking the wall with Jonathan at two."

"Be sure to get back in time for dance class," said Farnsworth.

"Dance class?"

"Judith's conducting a demonstration of Regency dancing, remember? To prepare us all for the ball on Friday night."

"Oh, right—I forgot it was today."

Farnsworth raised an eyebrow. "Maybe Hetty's not the only one with memory issues."

"What's she on about?" Grant asked Erin.

"She's takin' the Mickey outta me, luv," she said in a Cockney accent.

Grant looked at Farnsworth, who batted her eyelashes. "Why, Miss Coleridge, I can assure you I would never endeavor to deprive you of any portion of your Irishness, should you indeed possess any," she said.

"And I can assure *you* that any such ancestral identity I might be party to would entirely resist an assault on your part," Erin replied. "Indeed, I should likely repel such an attack in kind, and dispossess you of any Hibernian roots you might have in your family tree."

Farnsworth wiped her mouth delicately. "I welcome the opportunity to put your theory to the test." "Do not desire it too dearly, or you shall find yourself wishing you had refrained from wishing quite so earnestly."

Grant laughed. "You two should give lessons on Regency era speech."

"Until this evening, then, Miss Coleridge?" said Farnsworth.

"I look forward to it," Erin said, and headed toward the exit. She could hear Grant chuckling as she walked away; Farnsworth giggled in response. It did her heart good to see her friend so happy, and she hoped it would last.

As she passed the servers' station, she noticed a couple of servers talking amongst themselves. Lunch was over, and it was some time before dinner, so the staff had some time on their hands—just enough for a few quick questions, she thought.

It was true that Detective Hemming's words had cut her, but she had promised him nothing, and had no intention of following his commands, come what may. She had reason to believe he was off his game, and feared that if she did not step in, a murder—or two—might go undetected. And she reasoned that if someone was capable of two murders, they were certainly capable of more.

She approached a young blonde woman, a pale waif of a girl who looked barely old enough to have a job. Erin had seen her around, working in the restaurant and the 1906 Bar, alongside Sam and the other servers. She seemed a quiet sort, the kind of person who, in Erin's experience, was often more observant than energetic, noisier types.

"Hello," she said approaching the girl. "I wonder if you have a moment to talk—uh, Christine?" she added, reading her name tag.

Christine shot a glance at her colleague, a robust, curly-haired young brunette with thick calves and a pert, toothy smile.

"Can I help?" said the brunette—Bridget, according to her ID badge.

"I'd appreciate anything either of you can tell me," said Erin.

"What's it about, then?" asked Christine, fidgeting nervously with the linen napkin in her hands. Her accent was North London working class. Her red-rimmed, pale-blue eyes and timid manner reminded Erin of a pet rabbit she had as a child.

"It's about Sam," Erin said.

"Haven't seen 'im in a few days," said Christine. "Is he awright, then?"

"As far as I know," Erin lied.

"You a friend of his, are you?" asked Bridget, studying her. Her accent was posher than Christine's, possibly Surrey or Kent.

Erin felt herself flush, and coughed to cover her reaction. "I've known him a while, yeah."

"What ya wanta know, then?" asked Christine.

"I was just wondering if he seemed like himself in the past few days."

"Meaning what?" said Bridget, crossing her arms.

"Did he seem worried in any way?"

"Not really," said Christine.

"He wasn't anxious or concerned or anything like that?"

Bridget stared at her. "Has something happened to him?"

"No," Erin said, feeling worse by the minute. She was about to drop the whole thing when Christine took a step forward.

"Wait," she said. "There was something." She turned to Bridget. "Remember what he said the other night?"

"Oh, yeah," said Bridget. "Saturday, wasn't it?"

"Right—the day that poor bloke had 'is heart attack."

"What did he say?" Erin asked, her heart quickening.

"It was an odd remark," said Christine. "Something 'bout the salad bein' diff'rent, innit?" she asked Bridget.

"Yes, that's it—something about the salad."

"What salad?" Erin asked, trying not to seem too eager. If Sam had mentioned it to them, she wondered who else might have overheard.

Christine bit her lip. "A salad he was serving. He thought it looked wrong."

"Wrong how?"

"The rocket looked funny. It was the wrong shape."

"He said that?"

"Yeah, after that poor bloke dropped dead."

"He kept saying it. Wouldn't shut up about it," Bridget added. "At first I thought he was jokin'—y'know, like it must have been the salad that killed him. Which is ridiculous, a course."

"Did anyone else hear him say that?" Erin asked.

"Pretty much everyone, I'd think," said Bridget.

"Yeah," Christine agreed. "He even implied he mighta known who'd done it."

"Done what?"

"Switched the rocket, like. Said he bumped into someone leavin' the salad area."

"But he didn't say who?"

"No. At the time I thought maybe he jus' wanted attention or sommit."

He certainly got someone's attention, Erin thought grimly.

"He was even talking about telling the police about it," said Bridget.

"But he never did?"

"Not that I know of," Bridget answered, looking at Christine, who shook her head.

"No," she said. "If he did, he didn't mention it to me."

Erin sighed. Clearly Sam hadn't gotten that far, though even if he had, it might not have saved him.

"You wouldn't happen to be the one who discovered the, uh, body, would you?" she asked Christine.

"In the cloakroom, y'mean? Yeah, that was me."

"Did you see anything . . . suspicious?"

"Like what?"

"Anything out of the ordinary?"

Christine bit her lip and wrapped her thin arms around her body. "Not really. I mean, it was pretty shockin', finding a dead person in the cloakroom."

"Of course. It must have been horrible for you."

She nodded, her eyes welling up. "I never seen a dead person before. At first I thought he was jus' drunk, got sick an' passed out, like. I seen that before."

Bridget put a protective arm around her. "It was very upsetting for her. She only just came back to work today."

"Of course. Thank you so much for your time," Erin said, slipping each of them a fiver for their trouble. As she left the restaurant, she passed a busboy carrying a bin of dirty dishes to the kitchen, wishing she had access to the used dishes the night Barry died. Somewhere, in the depths of the restaurant kitchen, valuable evidence of a devious crime had been washed away.

Chapter Twenty-Seven

≈

"What do you say—you up to walking the whole thing?" Jonathan Alder asked as he and Erin left the hotel a little after two o'clock.

"Sure," she said as they turned right on Station Rise, glad she had brought her winter hiking boots. Though the streets had been plowed, the snow lay thick all around them, cold and sparkling in the afternoon sun, like tiny diamonds sprinkled on cotton.

No point in downtown York was very far from the medieval wall that encircled the original city, and the nearest entrance was just other side of Station Road, where it met Station Rise, a few hundred yards from the hotel.

"You've done this before, right?" Jonathan said as they passed the York War Memorial, a tall stone monolith nestled next to the grassy mound that ran along much of the wall.

"Once, yeah."

"How long does it take?"

"We can walk it easily in two hours, and a little over one if we move fast," she said as they mounted the steps set in the stone archway. The wall was in excellent condition at this point—other sections of it were in ruins or nonexistent, and travelers had to either walk alongside the ruins or follow the path of where it used to be. Here, though, the wall could be seen in all its original glory, a sturdy stone barricade with square Normanesque towers that reminded Erin of Kirkbymoorside's historic All Souls Church. Here the wall was fully six feet wide, rising about thirteen feet from the ground.

"It's amazing to think of people building this, stone by stone," Jonathan said as they headed southwest along the stone walkway, the snow packed hard beneath their feet.

"I know—I always think of the sentinels who must have roamed it just as we are now."

"Except they were watching for invading enemies, and we're just out for a stroll."

"There's a wonderful coffee house just about halfway around, and we can stop in there. It's actually part of the wall."

"Oh, I've heard of this place—the Gateway, or something like that?"

"The Gatehouse," she said as they turned left just beyond the railway station. "I think part of it dates back to the twelfth century."

Jonathan pulled out his mobile and typed into the keyboard. "It says here it's the gatehouse of the Walmgate Bar."

"You know that a 'bar' is what they call the gates leading into the city, right?"

"And it says here the Walmgate Bar gatehouse is the only remaining barbican in England."

"What's a barbican again?"

"According to Wikipedia, it's a fortified outpost, or any tower situated over a gate or bridge which was used for defensive purposes."

"Wow. And here we are at the Mickelgate Bar," she said as they approached the imposing stone structure rising from the horizontal ridge of the wall. Its wide arch straddled the street below; the cars zipping through the winding street reminded Erin of a carnival ride.

"According to Wikipedia, it's the most important of the four main gates leading into the city," Erin said. "Monarchs visiting from the south would enter through the Mickelgate Bar."

Its twin towers loomed above them as they nodded to another pair of walkers, a fit-looking middle-aged couple in matching green down jackets, woolen yak hats, and sturdy hiking boots. They wore heavy rucksacks, as if ready for overnight camping.

"Swedish tourists," Jonathan remarked when they had passed.

"How do you know?"

"They always look overly prepared. Did you see those two?"

"Yeah. What's with the backpacks?"

"Exactly. You can always tell the Scandinavians. Too fit, always look ten years younger than their age, and dressed like they spend most of their lives outdoors in the winter."

Erin laughed.

"I would find them annoying," said Jonathan, "but they're too good-natured even for that."

"You seem to have traveled a bit."

"I'd like to do more of it."

They walked in silence for a while, then Jonathan said, "Poison's meant to be a woman's game, isn't it?"

"What makes you ask that?"

"I was thinking if Barry Wolf was poisoned, isn't it more likely to be a woman?"

"Not necessarily. Men kill people a lot more than women, but women are more likely to choose poison. They have less physical strength, and they tend to prefer less confrontational methods."

Jonathan stared at her. "Farnsworth is right—you really *are* a crime buff."

"Guilty as charged."

"So do you have any suspects?"

"Not really," she said. "It seems like everyone has a motive."

"He wasn't very well liked, was he? That's the impression I got when I first met him in London."

"You knew him before?"

"Briefly. He was headmaster of my public school for a couple of terms. Didn't last long."

"Why didn't you tell me earlier?"

"You didn't ask. And I don't see that it has any bearing on his death."

"You never know. What can you tell me about him?"

"He was remote, seemed keen on himself. Nothing you couldn't glean from seeing him at the conference. I never actually spoke with him—I was a first year and he was headmaster."

"What school was it?"

"Christ's Hospital, in Horsham. My family didn't have a lot of money, and they took charity students. Is that your coffee shop up ahead?"

"Yes. If I remember, the entrance is around this side," she said, leading him to it.

Erin pushed open the thick oak door to enter the interior of the shop. As she did, some snow slid from the roof above her and onto her head. Some of the snow slipped down her neck, and she quickly dug it out with her hands, getting her leather gloves quite wet in the process.

"You all right?" Jonathan said. "Need some help?"

"Thanks, I think I got it all," she said, continuing into the shop.

They were greeted by the warm, dark aroma of freshly brewed coffee; an espresso machine hissed gently behind the bar. A cheerful-looking young man in a white apron stood behind the long wooden bar laden with glass cabinets of muffins, scones, and cakes.

"Wow, this is something," Jonathan said as they stood at the entrance, taking in the room, with its thick walls and flagstone floors. Strings of fairy lights hung from the ceiling; heavy wooden tables and chairs were scattered around the room; a brown leather sofa took up one wall. The room was empty of customers except for a young couple huddled over a pot of tea in the far corner. Soft Gregorian chants streamed from wall speakers overhead.

"What an appropriate soundtrack," Jonathan said, smiling. "Suits this place."

"Glad you like it. Welcome to the Gatehouse," said the barista. He sported a neatly trimmed beard and sleek ponytail.

"Thanks," Erin said, walking up to the counter. On the wall was a gigantic chalkboard menu listing the various beverages available, everything from drip coffee to golden matcha latte.

"What'll you have?" said Jonathan. "My treat."

"Oh, that's not—"

"I never would have found this place without you," he told her, with a wink at the barista, who smiled broadly. There was something joyful about him, an appealing inner happiness. His dark hair was shiny as sealskin. Erin generally didn't like ponytails on men, but it suited him.

"It's true," said the young man. "A lot of folks walk the wall without knowing we're here. And the entrance is hard to find."

"Thanks," said Erin. "I'll have a macchiato, please."

The barista nodded. "And you, sir?"

"A flat white, please. And a raisin scone."

"Clotted cream and cherry jam?"

"Absolutely," Jonathan said, tucking three pounds into the tip jar.

"Ta very much," the barista said, flashing another smile.

"Let's go upstairs," Erin said when they got their drinks.

"There's another room?"

"Oh, yes," said their barista. "And you'll have it all to yourself. Not many people walking the wall in this weather."

"Slow day?" said Jonathan.

"A bit of a morning rush, but only a trickle after that."

Jonathan nodded and slipped a couple more pounds into the tip jar while the young barista's back was turned. Erin admired his generosity, and even more for doing it when no one was looking. She usually made sure baristas and store clerks saw her tip, but anonymous generosity was more virtuous.

The upstairs room was even more wonderful than the ground floor—deep, chocolatey armchairs and sofas lent the room an aura of comfort and warmth, in spite of the chilly air. Pale afternoon light filtered through narrow, cross-latticed windows set deep into the ancient walls, with huge, its rough-hewn stones, each one different a size and shape. More fairy lights dangled from the ceiling; an antique wooden chest served as a coffee table in front of the inviting leather sofa. It was like stepping back in time a thousand years, but with all the comforts of modern life.

"This may be the most awesome place I've ever had a coffee in," Jonathan said as they settled into matching armchairs facing each other in front of one of the windows.

"Definitely true for me as well," Erin said, sinking into the depths of the chair with a contented sigh. Removing her damp gloves, she laid them across a nearby radiator to dry.

Glancing out the latticed window, she could see Clifford's Tower looming in the distance, a bulky stone fortress perched on its earthen mound on the edge of the heavily fortified city.

Jonathan followed her gaze. "It's impossible to see that without thinking of the massacre."

"Yeah, I know."

"It's hard to think about it."

Erin had recently read about it, so it was fresh in her mind. In one of the nastiest and most famous incidents of anti-Semitism in the history of England, approximately 150 Jewish people lost their lives in a notorious mass suicide and massacre. Following a wave of virulent anti-Jewish sentiment, they took shelter in the tower, then part of the royal castle at the time, only to find an angry mob congregating outside. Rather than be murdered, most of them elected to take their own lives, setting fire to their possessions as they died. When the tower caught fire, the few who escaped after being promised amnesty were promptly slaughtered by the mob. The tower was rebuilt, now the only remaining part of the castle.

"I wonder . . ." Erin said, gazing out the window.

"What?"

"I wonder if Barry's death was in some way—"

"Related to anti-Semitism?"

"Yeah," she said, taking a sip of her coffee, already losing heat in the cool air.

"Do you have any reason to think so?"

"Just wondering."

They watched the evening light dim over the city. Like so many places in England, it had a complex past. Built by invading Romans, it was taken over by Angles, captured by Vikings, and later became the seat of Northumbrian and Norman royalty. And now they were sitting inside the walls of its ancient fortress, sipping fancy coffee.

"Time to go," Erin said finally, draining the last of her macchiato. "We have to get back for the dance lesson."

Saying goodbye to their friendly barista, they headed out into the December twilight. They walked along the parapet of the wall in companionable silence. Erin felt relaxed around Jonathan and enjoyed his presence. Still, as she stared at the silent stars flickering through the gathering darkness, her thoughts wandered to Peter Hemming, and she wondered what he was doing right now.

She had been walking with her hands in her pockets, but as it grew colder, she felt around for her gloves, but could not find them.

"Oh, no," she said. "I left my gloves on the radiator in the café."

"Let's go back."

"No, you stay—I'll be just a minute," she said. Turning, she jogged down the hard-packed path as quickly as was possible in heavy hiking boots.

As she approached the building, she thought she saw a dark form retreating rapidly, hugging the wall before disappearing down the steps to the café entrance. There was something furtive in the figure's movement that caught her eye—she had the distinct impression the person was trying to avoid being seen. In the dim light, it was impossible at that distance to see their face, and the thick winter clothing made it hard to even tell if it was a man or a woman. Clumsy in her heavy boots, Erin increased her gait as much as she could, clomping down the stairs and around the corner, but the figure had vanished. Disappointed, Erin caught her breath before entering the café.

Sure enough, the cheerful barista had her gloves behind the counter, and handed them to her with a friendly smile.

"Thanks," she said, taking them. "Did you have any more customers after us?"

"Uh, no—you were the last."

"No one came into the shop to look around?"

"Not that I saw. Actually, we were due to close, but I thought you might come back for your gloves."

"I really appreciate it—thanks again," she said, and left the shop.

"Thank *you*," he sang after her, his voice dissipating as she closed the heavy door behind her.

Part of her thought she was being fanciful, but she couldn't escape the nagging feeling that someone had been walking the wall with the sole purpose of following her.

Chapter Twenty-Eight

❧

When they arrived back at the Grand, it was nearly five o'clock. Erin dashed upstairs to change her shoes—hiking boots were hardly the best choice for a Regency dance lesson. The class had already started when she crept into the ballroom.

Judith Eton stood in the middle of the circle of dancers, elegant in a long Regency era gown. One or two of the other participants also wore period clothing—Winnifred Hogsworthy sported a yellow silk gown, and Terrence Rogers was resplendent in a striped frock coat, powder-blue waistcoat, and tan breeches—but most were in contemporary clothes. Many of them wore trainers, as Judith had told everyone to wear comfortable shoes. Charles Kilroy was dressed in his usual leather ensemble. At the far end of the room, Prudence and Hetty were side by side as usual, Pru looking like she had just stepped out of a gardening shed. Hetty wore a bright red cocktail dress and her signature high heels. She waved at Erin, which caused Farnsworth to turn and see Erin.

Farnsworth motioned her over. "Where have you been?" she muttered.

"Tell you later," Erin whispered back as Judith shot an impatient look in their direction.

"Now then," Judith said, "as I was saying, there isn't much athleticism involved in Regency dancing, but there is a bit of memory, so it should suit you lot perfectly."

There was some tittering and murmurs among the decidedly unathletic crowd. Not many in the room looked as if they had seen the inside of a gym.

"I see some of you are wearing trainers," Judith continued, "which is fine for now, but men wore leather shoes and women wore something akin to ballet slippers."

"Not me," Farnsworth whispered to Erin. "No arch support."

"As you can imagine," Judith said, "Regency dance is rather formal and proper. Most dances require at least four couples to be done properly. Some of the dances did have elaborate footwork, but we're not going to worry about that. We'll be concentrating instead on the movement and patterns on the dance floor. We'll start by learning one of the longer forms, the cotillion. This one is called "The Duchess of Devonshire's Reel." Dr. Terrence Rogers will help me demonstrate."

The two of them did a credible job showing the various patterns of what was a dance of rather complex parts. After twenty minutes or so the participants were gliding merrily—if not always gracefully—around the room. It looked to Erin as if maybe half of them had done this before, which made Judith's job easier. Of more interest to Erin was how physically comfortable Terrence and Judith seemed to be around each other—their body language indicated physical familiarity.

After about an hour, Judith looked at her watch. "Shall we take a little break—say ten minutes?"

Farnsworth wiped her brow and followed Erin to the beverage table. There were samovars of tea as well as ice water. Erin chose tea—walking in the cold had made her sleepy, and she could use the caffeine.

"Where's Jonathan?" asked Farnsworth, pouring herself a glass of cold water. "Did you wear him out, pet?"

"He probably just got cold feet," Erin said. "What about Grant?"

"He had a gout attack, poor thing."

"Ouch. My uncle had that—it's very painful."

"I might have to play nurse tonight."

"Aren't you going on the Ghost Walk?" said a voice behind them. Erin turned to see Khari Butari, clad in a stunning gold tunic and matching trousers.

"Well, don't you look gorgeous," Erin said.

"Nice boubou," said Hetty, sauntering up behind them.

"How do you know what it's called?" Farnsworth asked.

Hetty shrugged. "Fashion, darling. It's kind of my thing. A boubou is a traditional Senegalese garment, typically worn as a three-piece ensemble, often topped off with a hat."

"I'm not wearing the 'full and complete' version," said Khari, pouring herself a cup of tea. "That would be more proper."

"It suits you just as is, dearie," said Hetty.

"Yes," Prudence agreed. "One man's style must not be the rule of another's."

"Are you going to stay for the rest of the class?" Erin asked Khari.

"I thought I might."

"It might be hard to keep up," Farnsworth said. "You missed the whole first half."

"I've actually done this before," Khari said, spooning sugar into her tea.

Farnsworth frowned. "Really? Where?"

"Down in—" Khari began, but their attention was interrupted by the sound of raised voices near the doorway.

Jeremy Wolf and his mother were engaged in what looked like a rather intense discussion. Judith was doing her best to keep her voice down, but Jeremy's volume rose as he argued with his mother.

"Then *don't!*" he said. "I don't care anymore!"

Judith glanced at the other people in the room beginning to take notice, and grabbed her son's arm, dragging him out into the hall. To Erin's surprise, he submitted—even thin as he was, the young man could have easily overpowered his mother. He flicked his lank blond hair off his face with his free left hand. The door closed behind them, and there was a pause as everyone struggled to contain their curiosity.

"What was *that* all about?" said Prudence, coming to stand beside Hetty. Erin always had the impression she was accompanied by a trail of dust, like the *Peanuts* cartoon character Pig-Pen.

"Family stuff," said Farnsworth.

"After all, his father just died," Erin said, looking around the room. Her gaze stopped at Terrence Rogers. Frozen in place, still as a pointer on the trail of a grouse, he stared at the door. Then, snapping out of it, he turned away, absently brushing a lock of hair from his forehead with his left hand.

The gesture was unmistakable, an exact replica of Jeremy's, including the left-handedness. The truth hit Erin with the force of a thunderclap: Terrence Rogers was Jeremy Wolf's father.

Chapter Twenty-Nine

～

Judith soon returned to finish the class, which she did with remarkable sangfroid. She made no reference to Jeremy's appearance. By the end she had them frolicking about the room like eager children. Erin had to admire her poise; she seemed unfazed by her son's interruption. She now had a pretty good idea of what Judith and Terrence had argued about that night in the bar; the real question was whether Jeremy knew or not. She couldn't wait to tell Farnsworth her theory.

When the class was over, Hetty and Prudence headed for a quick visit to the spa. Erin thought it was sweet Hetty had convinced her friend to join her obsession—Prudence Pettibone was the last person she would have expected to find enjoying the luxuries of a high-end spa. Erin queued up with Farnsworth for another beverage—the room had heated up considerably during the class, and she felt quite parched.

"Are you going on the Ghost Walk?" Khari asked, joining them.

"Oh, is that tonight?" asked Farnsworth.

Erin had also forgotten—Sam's death weighed heavily on her mind, and she had neglected to check the daily conference schedule.

"Seven o'clock sharp in the Shambles," Khari said, holding up a flyer depicting a tall man in nineteenth-century dress, complete with long black cape and top hat.

"Fancy a Ghost Walk?" Erin asked Farnsworth. "It's only five pounds."

"I'm not so good walking long distances. And there's my injured ankle."

"It's only an hour long," said Khari.

"We'd be back in time for dinner," Erin said.

"You kids go ahead. I think I'll spend an evening with my feet up in front of some truly trashy television."

"Another Hallmark movie?" said Erin.

Farnsworth smiled. "Christmas comes but once a year."

"Farnsworth is a fan of Twee TV," Erin told Khari.

"I prefer to think of myself as a student of popular culture," Farnsworth remarked.

"Meet in the lobby in half an hour?" Erin asked Khari.

"Perfect."

Erin thought that would give her time to check in with her father. Leaving the ballroom, she took the back route to the stairwell, thinking she might walk instead of taking the lift. As she rounded the corner leading past the small antechamber Charles had shown her, she thought she would stop and see if there was any coffee left in the samovar. Stepping inside, she saw the urn had been taken away—not surprising, at this hour, she thought—and turned to leave.

She heard low voices speaking a foreign language coming from the other side of a door on one side of the antechamber. The door was unmarked, but she supposed it led to an office or lounge of some kind. Intrigued, she crept nearer to listen. It was a man and a woman, speaking quietly but urgently in what sounded like an Eastern European tongue. Definitely not Polish, she thought, and not Czech either. Maybe Scandinavian? She took a step closer.

Then she recognized the voices—it was Luca and Stephen, and she realized that of course they were speaking Hungarian. Although she couldn't understand a word of what they were saying, she remained where she was, mesmerized by the urgency in their tone. Suddenly, without any warning, she felt a sneeze well up in her nose. There was no stopping it—she clapped a hand over her mouth to stifle it, but it exploded in a loud "Ah-phew!"

The voices stopped, and for a dreadful moment there was silence. Then the door opened and Stephen appeared, a frown on his narrow face. Seeing Erin, his expression darkened and his muscles tensed. For a moment, she feared him, unsure what he might be capable of. But then Luca appeared at his side, and he drew a deep breath, his body relaxing.

Erin had to admit they were a handsome couple—and an idea popped into her head. "Hello," she said cheerfully. "I'm taking a few pictures of the conference. Mind if I take yours?"

Stephen glanced at Luca, who shrugged.

"You're both so photogenic," Erin continued. "Not everyone at the conference is so good looking," she added with a conspiratorial smile. She hoped they would buy it; she was appealing to their vanity, and it was a way out of an awkward situation for all of them.

"Okay," said Luca, looking at Stephen. "Why not?"

"All right," he said.

"Just look natural," said Erin. "You don't have to smile if you don't want to."

"It's okay," said Luca. "We smile if you like."

Putting her arm around Stephen, she gave a dazzling grin. Some people didn't look as good when they smiled, but Luca looked even prettier, if possible. Stephen's smile was less convincing, but he held it long enough for Erin to take several shots with her mobile phone.

"Now a shot of each of you separately," she said, and they complied. "Thank you so much," she said, pocketing the phone. "That will look fantastic in the brochure."

"Who will see this brochure?" asked Stephen.

"Only people who are at the conference—you know, other Austen Society members."

"Is okay," Luca said, squeezing his arm, and Erin decided to find out what he had to hide.

"Thanks very much—be seeing you," she said breezily, scooting away before they had a chance to protest. By the time she had been to her room to change back into her hiking boots, it was nearly six thirty. Her phone call to her father would have to wait—But when she did call, she would she would have a lot to tell him.

"Sorry," Erin said when she saw Khari standing near the elegant wrought iron staircase in the lobby. "I lost track of time."

"No worries—we can make it if we walk quickly. Or we can take a cab."

"I'm game to walk," said Erin, glad Farnsworth wasn't there after all. She would slow them down, and probably complain the whole way. She felt guilty for thinking it, even though it was true.

She and Khari bounded out the door and into the cold, crisp night. They headed toward the Mickelgate Bridge, past the Sainsbury's and the little Italian café right on the water's edge. The River Ouse flowed beneath them, dark and foreboding, illuminated only faintly by streetlamps and the lights of restaurants sprinkled along its shores. The moon had not yet risen; only a few stars were visible high in the night sky.

Erin was glad of her thick-soled boots as they crossed the bridge, her feet crunching with every step on the crust of hard-packed snow. The air was colder on the bridge, the wind whipping their ankles as they hurried across. Erin pulled up her parka hood and tightened the jacket's drawstrings, thinking how Farnsworth would have hated this. Hit by a wave of fatigue, she suddenly wished she were back in her friend's cozy hotel suite, sharing a bowl of popcorn and watching cheesy movies. Shoving her hands deeper into her pockets, she put her head down and followed Khari's long strides, noticing they were the only people foolish enough to venture out over the bridge on such a night. At least it wasn't snowing, she thought as they continued onto Low Ousegate. The street narrowed considerably as its name changed to High Ousegate, and just for a moment, Erin had the feeling they were being followed. She turned to look behind them, seeing nothing except a young couple a few yards back. They seemed engaged with one another, oblivious to Erin and Khari. Erin chided herself for being so on edge, and took deep breaths of frigid air to calm herself.

"Interesting name for a river, Ouse," said Khari as they crossed onto Pavement Street.

"I think it's a Celtic word meaning 'water' or 'slow flowing river.'"

"That's pretty descriptive of it," Khari said as they approached the winding cobblestones of the Shambles. There were more sight-seers in the streets now; half a dozen carolers huddled together singing "God Rest Ye Merry Gentlemen." "Hey, since you're good at these things, what about the Shambles? Is it called that because it's so higgelty-piggelty?"

"Actually, it's from 'shamel,' a medieval word for booth, because back then the street was full of butcher shops, and they displayed their meat in outdoor booths."

Khari shuddered. "That's an image I'll have trouble forgetting."

"That's right—you're a vegetarian, aren't you?"

"Pretty much, except I do eat fish."

Erin sighed. "I don't have the moral fiber to give up lamb chops."

"Hey, is that it up ahead? The flyer said meet at the head of the Shambles, in front of the Golden Fleece."

"There's a crowd gathering, so that's probably our tour."

About twenty people stood at the intersection of Pavement Street and the Shambles, looking around expectantly, so Erin and Khari joined them, their breath misting in the frosty air as the carolers broke into "Once in Royal David's City." Their voices were sweet but thin in the frigid air.

Erin and Khari only had a few minutes to wait beneath the streetlamps before a lanky, middle-aged man in a black cape and frock coat arrived. He sported a graying beard and a top hat, which made him look even taller. He wasted no time, addressing the crowd in a strong, theatrical voice.

"Good evening, ladies and victims—uh, gentlemen," he bellowed, and the crowd giggled nervously. "Welcome to the original York Ghost Tour, and thank you all for coming out on such a frosty night. I am your guide—you can call me Mr. Jack. I shall recount tales of murder, mayhem, and madness, so if you are faint of heart, now is the time to leave." This was greeted with another titter from the assembled company. "First things first," he said, pulling a small pouch from his frock coat pocket. "As Sherlock Holmes once said, there is the small matter of my fee." He proceeded to collect five pounds from each attendee, deftly slipping the change purse back into his pocket.

"Now then," he said, "follow me!" And he was off, charging across the street and into the Shambles at a brisk pace. The crowd followed, the soft click of leather heels on cobblestones reverberating in the still air, as they entered the heart of the medieval city, the darkness closing in behind them.

The timber-framed buildings of the Shambles teetered at such precarious angles that it looked as though they might tumble to the ground at any moment. They seemed animate, as if their overhanging second stories were leaning toward one another to share gossip, much as medieval housewives would have as they wandered among the butcher stalls lining the street. Erin shivered as they followed "Mr. Jack" through the narrow winding streets—he was lively and informative, clearly enjoying the darker aspects of his narrative as he led them through the old city, while delivering a litany of alleged hauntings.

"Some of you may recognize this," he said, stopping in front of a long, narrow alleyway between two buildings on Low Petergate. The sign over it read Lund's Court—beneath that, lettering proclaimed it to be Formerly Mad Alice's Lane.

"Was she the one hanged for killing her husband?" one of the men asked, a spindly lad in a tan anorak and black stocking hat.

"You are correct, sir!" said Mr. Jack. "Some say the story is apocryphal, but others claim her ghost haunts this very location when the moon is full—as it is tonight," he added ominously, pointing toward the sky. Sure enough, a pale round moon was poking through the cloud cover, a faint halo shimmering around its outer edge. "They say the crime took place in 1823, and the weapon of choice was poison, as is so often true when the fairer sex is involved," he added, his gaze lingering for a moment on Erin.

He continued his spiel, but Erin's attention was taken by a flickering light at the end of Mad Alice's Lane. It looked as though someone was waving a lantern or a torch—it seemed like a signal of some kind. When the guide wasn't looking, she slipped into the alley, following along the narrow passageway until it emptied out into a small flagstone courtyard bordered on all four sides by buildings. Three of them had second floor balconies with wrought iron railings. Standing in the courtyard, she looked around for the source of the flickering light, but it had vanished. She was about to leave when movement on one of the balconies caught the corner of her eye. Erin took a few steps across the courtyard toward it, and as she approached, she was vaguely aware of a shuffling sound on the terrace directly above her. She looked up.

What happened next was a blur. She was aware of something hurtling down toward her from the balcony, followed by a pounding blow as the object hit her on the top of her head, and then blackness overtook her.

Chapter Thirty

~

"Erin! Are you all right? Erin! Wake up, please wake up!"

She opened her eyes to see Khari kneeling by her side. She sounded panicked, and looked utterly terrified. She was gently patting Erin's cheek, and the first thing Erin did was reach out and grab her wrist. Her head pounded, and even the light touch of Khari's hand on her cheek hurt.

"Thank God!" Khari said. "I was just about to call 999."

"No," Erin said quickly. "I'm fine." To demonstrate, she started to sit up, which brought on a wave of dizziness.

"Mind you don't try to move too quickly."

"I'm all right, really," Erin said, lifting onto one elbow before sitting up all the way.

"Steady on," Khari said, sitting beside her. "What happened?"

"I'm not sure," Erin said, and told her of following the light down the alleyway, then of being struck by something falling from the balcony above her.

"Let me see your head," Khari said, examining it.

"Ouch," Erin said when her fingers touched a spot in the front, near the top of her forehead.

"There seems to be a bump. No blood, though. What do you think hit you?"

"I don't know, but it should be on the ground somewhere."

"There's nothing nearby."

"It has to be here! It can't have gone far."

Khari took a small torch from her pocket and walked up and down the courtyard, shining it on the cobblestones. "I don't see anything."

"Let me look," Erin said, getting to her feet slowly. She was hit by another wave of dizziness, and Khari grabbed her arm to steady her.

"Are you sure you should be on your feet?"

"I'm all right," Erin said, looking up at the balconies overhead. There was no movement, and no one was out on their porches. Several of the windows were dark; a few were dimly lit behind pulled curtains, but no sign of anyone moving around inside or peering out the window. Erin thought briefly about knocking on each door to ask if anyone had seen anything, but knew such an intrusion would not be well received in a city overrun with sightseers. The locals already had a love/hate relationship with the tourists who crowded their streets and pubs, roaming their neighborhoods day and night, aware that their influx of money supported York's businesses and merchants, and buoyed up their property values.

"May I borrow your torch?" she asked.

"Of course," Khari answered, handing it to her.

Erin walked up and down the courtyard, shining the torch in every corner of the small area. Khari was right—there was nothing. The ground was completely clear of objects; in fact, the cobblestones looked especially clean, as if they had recently been swept.

"See anything?" asked Khari.

"This is really strange," Erin said, giving her the torch. "Something hit me. It was hard and heavy enough to knock me out."

"Are you sure you didn't faint and get that bump falling down?"

"Positive. Something fell off one of these balconies and hit me."

"Any idea which one?"

"I think it was that one," Erin said, pointing to a building with dark windows. "But I can't be sure. Everything is a little fuzzy right now."

"Let's get you home," said Khari.

"What about the Ghost Tour?"

"I'm sure they'll manage without us."

"So no one saw me go down the alley?"

"No. We had moved on down the street when I realized you had disappeared, so I came back to the last place I had seen you."

"How did you know to look for me down the alley?"

"I guess I've heard enough about you to suspect you were snooping around on your own."

"Hmm," said Erin. She wasn't entirely sure she believed Khari, but couldn't think of any reason she would lie—unless, of course, she was responsible for the attack. But that seemed a stretch, and Erin couldn't think too clearly just now. "I just don't understand where it could have gone," she said, searching the ground one final time.

"Maybe it rolled underneath one of these old buildings," Khari suggested. "There are a lot of gaps in the foundations."

Erin flashed the torch around one more time. It was true—some of the buildings had gaps and holes where stones were missing or chipped. She rubbed her aching forehead, which was tender to the touch. She needed to get back to the hotel, to be alone in her own room, to sort out what had happened.

"Should we call an Uber?" asked Khari.

"All right," Erin said, casting one last look around the courtyard before following Khari back down the alley and into the crooked, twisted streets of York.

Chapter Thirty-One

❧

"You must tell Detective Hemming!" said Farnsworth, spearing a forkful of rocket from her salad plate. She and Erin were having dinner at The Rise—or rather, Farnsworth was. Erin felt queasy, and didn't have much appetite. After their return to the hotel, Khari had retired to her room for a hot bath, and Erin had accepted Farnsworth's invitation to join her for a late dinner.

The room was sparsely occupied; most people had eaten earlier. A couple of Society members Erin had seen in the audience at panels were finishing their dessert. Both ladies were from the Southern branch, and seemed to be having a lovely time, laughing and chatting over crème caramel and espresso. Christmas music played softly over the loud-speakers—Harold Darke's setting of Christina Rossetti's poem "In the Bleak Midwinter." Hearing it, Erin tuned out what Farnsworth was saying for a moment—she had always thought the choral piece was the most perfect setting of one of the best poems ever written.

"Are you even listening to me?" Farnsworth snapped.

"Sorry," said Erin.

"Seriously," Farnsworth continued, "it doesn't sound like an accident. It sounds like someone is out to get you."

Erin had to agree there was something fishy about the whole thing. She didn't like to admit it, but she was frightened.

"On the other hand," said Farnsworth, "I remember a few years back a woman was killed in New York by an ornamental bit of mortar that fell off a building."

"That's the thing. It was a windy night, and I might just have been unlucky."

"Do you remember an especially strong gust of wind just before it fell?"

"Not really."

"How long were you out?" Farnsworth asked, tearing off a piece of hot homemade bread from the loaf in the basket and smearing it with yellow butter. Inhaling the yeasty aroma of fresh bread, Erin's mouth began to water—maybe she was at bit hungry after all.

"I don't know. I didn't look at my watch before I was hit."

"So it's possible someone removed the object from the courtyard?"

"Definitely."

"And that someone could have been Khari Butari."

Erin frowned. She knew Farnsworth was jealous of her new friend, but she had to admit Farnsworth was right. Khari *could* have removed the object that hit Erin, which would mean she was . . . Erin didn't like to think about that. She liked Khari Butari, and wanted very much to believe in her innocence.

"Where's Grant?" she asked.

"Still nursing his gout. I think he's embarrassed about it. Apparently it's very painful."

"Where does he have it?"

"His big toe—can't wear shoes or put any weight on it. I offered to bring him dinner, but he said he'd just call room service." Farnsworth took a bite of vol-au-vent, a puff pastry stuffed with chicken in creamy béchamel sauce with leeks. "What about Jonathan—where did he go off to?"

"I haven't seen him since our walk this afternoon."

"I wonder what it's like to know your father was . . . well, you know."

"A murderer?"

"Does he ever talk about it?" Farnsworth said, squirting lemon juice over her roasted asparagus.

"No."

"I wonder if it runs in families."

"Even if you inherit a propensity toward violence, genetics isn't destiny."

"Do you feel safe around him?"

"I do, yeah."

"So where is he?"

"He probably just fell asleep," Erin said, yawning.

"You look like you could use some sleep, pet," Farnsworth said, wiping her mouth delicately with a linen napkin.

"That smells amazing," said Erin.

"Are you sure you don't want anything to eat?"

"You know, I think I'll have something after all," Erin said, signaling the server. It was the same waifish blonde girl she had questioned earlier in the day. "Hello, Christine," she said as the girl approached.

"Hello, Miss." Christine's eyes looked redder than before, as if she had been crying. Erin wondered if Hemming had informed the hotel staff about Sam's death.

"Are you all right, Christine?"

"Yes, Miss," she said softly. Her presence was wispy as a whiff of smoke, as if she might vaporize any minute.

"You look tired."

"It's been a long day, is all. Sam didn't show again t'night, so I had t'cover his shift."

So the staff didn't know yet. Erin wondered what Hemming was waiting for—surely they had notified the family by now.

"I'll try not to be too much trouble," Erin said.

"Oh, it's no trouble, Miss. What would you like?"

"A bowl of soup would be lovely, if you don't mind."

"What kind would you like?"

"Cream of asparagus, I think."

"Yes, Miss—right away," she said, turning to Farnsworth. "Can I get you anything, Miss?"

"No, thank you—everything is lovely."

"I'll be right back with your soup, then," she told Erin, and turned to go.

"Oh, Christine?" Erin said.

"Yes, Miss?"

"Thanks for your help this afternoon."

Fear flitted across her face. It was just for an instant, but it was unmistakable.

"You're welcome, Miss. Please let me know if you hear anything about Sam."

"I will, thank you."

When she had gone, Farnsworth leaned in toward Erin. "What's with her? She looked like a pack of devils was after her."

"Didn't she just," Erin agreed.

"And what's with the Oliver Twist routine?"

"What do you mean?"

"She's like someone straight out of Dickens. 'Yes, Miss' and 'No, Miss' and all the rest of it."

"Maybe it gets her bigger tips."

"What were you thanking her for?"

"I asked some questions of the wait staff this afternoon, and she was helpful."

"Oh?" Farnsworth said, taking a sip of Malbec. "What about?"

"Sam."

Farnsworth sighed. "Poor fellow. The staff don't know yet, do they?"

"No, and I promised Detective Hemming I wouldn't tell them."

"How's your head, pet?"

"Fine," Erin said, but the truth was she had a pounding headache, and her vision was a little blurry.

"You really should get it checked out in hospital. What if it's a concussion?"

"Then you'll have to stay up all night with me making sure I don't fall asleep."

Farnsworth laughed. "Don't threaten me, pet—I'd be only too happy to stay up watching Christmas movies."

"Now *you're* threatening *me*," Erin said as Christine arrived with her soup.

"Thank you," she said when the girl set it down in front of her, but Christine lingered by the table as though she wanted to say something. "This looks brilliant," Erin said, but still the girl stood where she was.

"Uh, Miss?"

"Call me Erin."

"I didn't want to say so in front of Bridget, but, well . . ." She swallowed hard. "Sam seemed—well, spooked, I s'pose."

"When was that?"

"Sunday. It was around brunch time. I noticed he just seemed frightened. Like he was lookin' over his shoulder or somethin'. I don' know if anyone else noticed, but . . . well, I thought you might like to know."

"Thank you, Christine—I appreciate it."

"You're welcome, Miss."

"Erin."

"Right—sorry," she said, her pale cheeks flushing red as she scurried away.

"Sunday," said Farnsworth. "That's the day before he—"

"Yeah," said Erin, looking down at her soup, her appetite vanished. The pale-green liquid with bits of asparagus floating in it suddenly looked utterly unappealing, and she fought to contain her nausea as she wrestled with the idea that whoever killed Sam had just tried to kill her.

Chapter Thirty-Two

Erin intended to call her father, but by the time she reached her room, barely had enough energy to pull off her clothes before falling into bed. She awoke ten hours later, her neck stiff and sore. Her forehead was still tender to the touch, but the headache had largely disappeared. And she was utterly, undeniably ravenous. After a quick shower, she pulled on a powder-pink jumper over black jeans, ran a brush through her tangled hair, and headed out to breakfast.

When she got off the lift, she was startled to see a familiar Citroen parked in front of the hotel. She was halfway across the lobby when she heard a voice behind her.

"What were you *thinking*?"

She spun around to see Detective Hemming coming toward her. He looked terrible. His usually tidy blond hair was uncombed, his jacket rumpled, his face was pale and drawn. Clumps of snow clung to his shoes.

"Excuse me?" she said.

"You should have gone straight to hospital! You could have a concussion, for God's sake!"

"I'm fine."

"How do you know? You could have at least had a doctor look you over. A concussion is no laughing matter—you might have *died*."

She was aware the nosy hotel clerk, Tricia, was listening to every word, even as she pretended to file a pile of papers behind her desk.

Erin fought the urge to laugh, an unfortunate reaction she sometimes had to stress. Hemming looked so overwrought, standing there in his wrinkled jacket and damp shoes. Looking at him, she melted a little.

"I'll go soon—I promise."

"People have died from ignoring concussions, you know."

"How did you know what happened?" she asked.

"Your friend told me."

"Farnsworth?"

"Yes."

Erin frowned. *Your friend.* "She has a name, you know."

"I'm sorry—I'm just . . . it's been a long—I have a lot going on right now. Please accept my apology."

"Okay," she said, feeling like a cad for confronting him. It was obvious he was distressed, distracted, and not at all himself. "You didn't come here just to talk to me?"

"No," he said, wiping the sweat from his forehead, even though the lobby was not warm. "I have to inform the staff about—you know."

"I understand," she said, glancing over at Tricia, who immediately looked away, caught in the act of eavesdropping. A flush crept up her neck, reaching her highlighted blonde curls.

"Look, I'm sorry," Hemming said. "I just—I don't want anything to happen to you."

"Did Farnsworth call you?"

"No, I saw her in the restaurant when I was getting coffee." He lowered his voice. "Was it an accident, or do you think someone . . . is there a reason someone would want to hurt you?"

She faced a conundrum. If she told the truth—that she indeed suspected someone was after her—he would ask why, and she would either have to tell him or lie about her attempt to track down a potential killer. On the other hand, maybe she was completely mistaken, and the Ghost Walk incident was an accident. Maybe the object that hit her really did roll underneath a building, as Khari suggested.

"No," she said. "It was an accident."

He gave her a searching look. "Are you sure?"

"Absolutely. Those old buildings, you know—and it was a windy night."

"All right. Look, I'm . . . I shouldn't have come on so strong the other night. I mean, what you did was wrong, obviously, but—"

"It's all right. I deserved it."

"Still," he said. "I . . . well, I've not slept much lately."

She laid a hand on his arm. "I can see that."

To her surprise, he seized her hand in his own and pressed it tightly. "You mustn't think I'm angry with you. It's just—"

"I understand. You're under a lot of pressure."

He looked down at her with such tenderness it was all she could do to return his gaze. "Uh, you probably shouldn't be seen holding hands with a potential suspect," she whispered.

"Quite right," he said, pulling away. "Forgot where I was for a moment. I'd best get on with it," he said, glancing at his watch. "I need to get back to the station."

"Are you investigating this as a suspicious death?"

"We will be interviewing anyone who knew Mr. Buchanan, including hotel staff and guests."

"Have you tested for aconite in Barry Wolf's death?"

"The lab is backed up, as usual. I'm sorry, but I have to inform the staff about their colleague."

"I understand."

"You will get checked at hospital?"

"I will."

"All right," he said, and walked toward the front desk, startling Tricia. Erin watched as he spoke a few words to her. Nodding, she knocked on the manager's office door. Erin turned and walked quickly toward the restaurant. She had no desire to watch the manager's face when she heard the news. She dreaded seeing the staff's grief—Sam was obviously well liked, and his death tugged at her own past, reminding her of the bleak, lost days following the death of her mother. Sometimes she could think about it without caving in to the pull of grief; other times she felt as if it could swallow her. She walked toward the dining room pondering the randomness of life and death. Cancer had no conscience, no reason; it could come for anyone—unpredictable and ruthless, just like a murderer.

Back in her room, she took out her laptop and opened the photos she took of Luca and Stephen on her phone. Loading her web browser on the laptop, she went to images.google.com, and uploaded the picture of Luca and Stephen together from her phone. She got a few hits of celebrity couples they resembled, and one of a runway model and her fashion designer, but nothing useful. Then, when she uploaded the picture of Stephen by himself, she hit pay dirt. In a Hungarian publication, she found an article about an art gallery showing in Budapest. There he was, standing in front of a canvas of violent and disturbing images of police attacking a crowd of unarmed protesters. Blood trickled down the side of the canvas, as if it would drip onto the viewer.

When she translated the page, the headline read "Gallery Shows Controversial Artist's Subversive Work, Braving Government Censure."

Beneath his picture, the caption identified him as Hungarian artist and sculptor Andras Varga.

"Bingo," she murmured. "Gotcha."

It didn't take her long to find out from the front desk which room Luca was staying in, and when she knocked on the door of the third-floor suite, it opened almost immediately to reveal Stephen—aka Andras—in jeans and a fitted black shirt.

"Andras Varga?" she said, and his face registered shock, then resignation.

"So," he said, "you have been snooping around the internet, I suppose?"

"Something like that. May I come in?"

He opened the door to admit her to a suite even larger than Farnsworth's. Seated on the striped lavender silk sofa, a tea service on the coffee table in front of her, was Luca. The two exchanged a look, and once again she was struck by the obvious intimacy between them.

"Would you care for some tea?" asked Luca.

"Thank you, no," she replied. "I just wanted to ask you a few questions."

Luca tilted her head to one side, her smooth black hair grazing one shoulder. "How can we help you?"

Erin gathered her courage. "Look," she said. "It's been clear to me from day one there's something going on between you two. You can't hide the truth forever. I already know your name, so you might as well tell me everything."

Luca frowned and bit her lip. Andras bent down and whispered something in her ear, and she shook her head. "Come on," he said. "She's right, you know."

He met Erin's gaze, his face expressing resignation. "You might as well know," he said, standing next to Luca. She placed a hand on his arm, and he patted it gently. "There can be no harm in it now, can there?" he said to her. She looked down, still biting her lip.

Around him, she was different from the cool, self-possessed woman Erin had first seen in the bar.

"Look," Erin said. "I couldn't understand what you were saying in that room. I don't speak Hungarian."

"No," said Andras. "I don't suppose you do."

"But I have ways of finding things out. I already know your name."

"We have heard of your exploits as a crime solver," he said.

"Really?" Erin said, surprised. "Who—"

"Everyone talks of how you solved the murder in your town."

"And we know you think Barry was murdered," Luca blurted out. "This is true?"

"Yes. I do think it's likely."

"It wasn't us," said Andras.

"What was it you were about to tell me? Maybe it will exonerate you."

Luca's grip on Andras's arm tightened. She whispered something to him in Hungarian, and he nodded solemnly. Then he turned back to Erin.

"We like you," he said slowly, "so we will tell you, but you must not divulge this to others. Do I have your word on that?"

She thought about Hemming, and what would happen if she withheld information from the police, but curiosity was burning a hole through her forehead.

"I promise," she said, her voice tight with anticipation.

"You already know my name is Andras Varga. You have probably guessed I'm Hungarian, not English."

Erin remained silent, waiting for the rest.

"Luca is my sister."

Once he said it, it seemed so obvious—they shared the same slim build, straight dark hair, and full lips. Suddenly, it all made sense—the physical intimacy around each other wasn't sexual at all; it was familial. Erin chided herself for not realizing it earlier.

"Luca married Barry Wolf to save me," he said. His sister put a hand up to stop him, but he took it gently in his. "She might as well know the whole thing, Luca." He turned back to Erin. "I became Barry's assistant after a TED Talk he gave in London. Luca came to visit me about a year later, and Barry . . ." He cleared his throat before continuing, his voice thick. "He discovered I had fled Hungary because I was being pursued by the government. I was in fear for my life."

"Barry Wolf blackmailed me into marrying him!" said Luca. "He said if I didn't, he would send Andras back to Hungary."

"I was on a work visa as his assistant. All he had to do was fire me, and I would have to leave the UK."

"Why was the Hungarian government after you? Did it have something to do with your artwork?"

"My painting was controversial. They viewed it as politically dangerous."

"Andras is a great artist!" Luca declared. "He was doing important work, resisting the authoritarian regime, criticizing them with his paintings and installations."

"I was a thorn in their side," Andras agreed, looking rather pleased with himself. Erin couldn't blame him—she admired political activists.

"Is that why you drink?"

His face darkened, and she was afraid she had made a mistake. His jaw tightened, his body stiffened, and She expected him to explode at her. He took a step toward her. Her instinct was to shrink back, but she held her ground.

"Have you ever been persecuted by your own government?" he asked softly.

She swallowed hard. "No. You must be very brave."

"Not so brave, since I fled my homeland. If I were really strong, I would have stayed—"

"No, Andras!" Luca said, her dark eyes glistening with tears. "You must not return!"

"Now that you have no employer," said Erin, "how will you stay in the UK?"

"I don't know, but I hope to find something."

"If you go back, I go with you!" his sister said, clutching his hand.

"No, Luca. We will find a way. Now that we have told you," he said to Erin, "you must not tell anyone."

"I won't," Erin said. She was still suspicious of them both, but she had to admire their sacrifices. Andras had jeopardized his safety, and Luca had given herself to a man she loathed for her brother's sake. It was like something out of a nineteenth-century novel. "One question," she told Andras. "Why don't you have an accent like hers?"

"I was educated here. Our father was a diplomat. I lived with him here, and attended a public school. I lost my accent, and started sounding British. Luca grew up in Hungary with our mother."

That all made sense, Erin thought, as far as it went. But none of it gave them immunity from suspicion. In fact, she thought, they had just given themselves something key to any murderer: motive.

Chapter Thirty-Three

꙳

After leaving their room, Erin wandered the halls until she came to the bookstore. It was a little after ten, and the room was quiet, a few people perusing the tables of books and Jane Austen–related knickknacks—tea cozies and tea towels, aprons and hot pads, as well as various office supplies, boxes of stationery, greeting cards, key chains, and Regency era jewelry. A young woman Erin recognized from the Southern Branch was minding the cash box, her nose buried in a book. She glanced up when Erin entered, and after giving a brief smile, returned to her reading.

At a table near the back of the room, Winnifred Hogsworthy sat amid baskets of knitted goods. She was clad in a multicolored sweater, its rainbow pattern an advertisement for her work. She was busy knitting something new, the long needles clicking as her fingers moved nimbly on her lap. She smiled as Erin approached, and picked up a deep burgundy scarf from one of the baskets.

"This color suits you, don't you think?"

"It's very nice," Erin said.

"I just thought it would look good on you."

"How much is it?"

"Take it as a gift," she said, holding it out.

"That's very kind, but I want to pay you for your work."

"Please. It would be my pleasure. You have been so kind to me, and I'd like to thank you."

"Cheers," Erin said. "It's beautiful. Thank you so much."

"Appreciation is all the thanks I need. I'm not addicted to money, like *some* people I know." She sighed. "Sorry. Shouldn't speak ill of the dead."

"No need to wrap it," Erin said. "I'll wear it. I'm feeling chilly today, and it's just the thing."

"Lovely," said Winnie as Erin wrapped it around her neck. "It looks perfect on you. That's a nasty bump on your head. What happened?"

"Oh, it was an accident."

"That's quite an accident."

"I hit my head on the . . . shower handle," Erin said, realizing it was a lie she might have to tell more than once. She wished she had given it more thought before being put on the spot, but she was stuck with it now.

"Did you go to hospital?"

"Not yet."

"You should. Head injuries can be insidious, you know."

"I will," Erin said, anxious to leave so she didn't have to explain further. "And thank you for the scarf. It's gorgeous."

"Glad you like it," Winnie said, returning to her knitting.

As she walked away, she wondered if Winnie's curiosity about her head injury was just a little too . . . focused. Or was she overreacting? As she headed down the hallway past the meeting rooms, Erin wondered what Winnifred Hogsworthy was capable of. Or had her wariness of everyone turned into full-fledged paranoia? It was unlikely that Winnie would have ventured out into the cold night just on the off chance she might have an opportunity to kill Erin. She had to admit the most likely person to have attacked her—if that's what it was—was Khari.

As she swung around the corner to the wide hallway leading to the main ballroom, she inhaled the dark, inviting aroma of coffee coming from the small antechamber Charles had shown her. Ducking inside, she saw the stainless steel urn, full of freshly brewed coffee. Taking a cup from the stack, she filled it with the steaming dark liquid. As she added a dollop of cream, she heard Jeremy Wolf's voice in the hallway outside. Erin was about to go say hello, when something stopped her. Instead, she stood where she was, the cup of hot coffee warming the palm of her hand.

"I don't know what I'm going to do," Jeremy said. It sounded like he was speaking with someone on the phone. "It's just him, isn't it? Stupid blighter." He said something else she couldn't understand, and the conversation ended; she assumed he had hung up.

For a moment Erin thought Jeremy might enter the little room where she stood eavesdropping, and her throat tightened, as she thought about what to say to him. To her relief, though, his footsteps retreated down the hall. It wasn't until she released the air in her lungs that Erin realized she had been holding it.

Gulping down her coffee, she waited until she was sure the coast was clear before venturing into the hallway. The floral pattern on the carpet was suddenly blurry, and she blinked to clear her vision. The colors were too bright—the blend of lime and dark blue was nauseating. Saliva spurted into her mouth, and she felt her stomach contract violently. Clutching her mouth, she staggered back into the little room, and through the door leading to the ladies' room. Throwing open the door to the first stall, she vomited profusely into the toilet.

She waited a few minutes before emerging to rinse her mouth out in the sink. Thankfully, she was alone—no one had entered while she was there. Walking shakily toward the lobby, she dug her mobile phone from her jacket pocket and dialed Farnsworth.

She answered on the second ring. "Hello, pet."

"Are you free right now?"

"What's wrong?"

"I need someone to drive me to hospital."

"Where are you?"

"I'm headed toward the lobby now."

"Do you have your car keys on you?"

"Yes."

"I'll be right there."

Erin took a deep breath. The pattern on the carpet still seemed unappealing, so she looked away as she walked slowly down the hall. Her whole body felt unreliable and fragile, and it was as if a fog had enveloped her brain. Peter Hemming was right, she thought, feeling sheepish and angry at herself for waiting so long. If she died, she thought, he would be furious.

Chapter Thirty-Four

"Thanks for doing this," Erin said as Farnsworth turned out of the hotel parking lot onto Station Rise Road.

"It's what friends are for, pet. How do you feel now?"

"Woozy." She did not mention that her head was pounding.

"I'm glad you decided to get checked out," Farnsworth said. "Remember the tragic death of Natasha Richardson after that skiing accident? She refused medical help, and died from that concussion."

Erin didn't answer. She remembered it all too well. Though not about to admit it, she was frightened.

"York Hospital isn't far," Farnsworth said, making the turn onto Station Road.

"We'll be mostly retracing our steps to Sam's flat, I think."

"Poor Sam," Farnsworth said, shifting into third gear and revving the engine.

"Steady on," Erin said as the little car accelerated rapidly. "We're not in that much of a rush."

"You're lucky I drive a stick shift. If I weren't so old—"

"You're not old," said Erin. "And plenty of people drive a standard transmission."

"Times are changing, pet. The kids these days want automatics."

Erin looked out the window as they passed the Yorkshire Museum, with its art gallery and extensive gardens. She had seen pictures of the Roman ruins on the museum grounds, but had never visited them in person. *Not on this trip*, she thought grimly as her headache intensified.

A few flakes of snow flittered by as they pulled into the hospital driveway.

"I'm going to drop you off at the Emergency entrance," said Farnsworth, swinging into the circular drive in front of the glass and brick building.

"You don't have to—"

"Nonsense. You go register and I'll join you straightaway," she said, shifting the car into park. "Go on—in you get."

"All right," Erin said, climbing out of the little sports car. She swayed a little taking the first few steps, blinking to clear her vision. She turned back to see if Farnsworth was watching, but she had already driven off toward the carpark.

Registration didn't take long, and Erin was seated in the waiting room when Farnsworth entered.

"Did they say how long it would be?" she asked, lowering herself onto one of the yellow plastic chairs.

"No, but it's not very crowded," Erin said, looking around the sparsely populated room. The only other people in it were a young man holding an ice pack on his elbow, and a little girl with her mother.

"I think I'll see if I can scare up a coffee," said Farnsworth, getting up. "Fancy one?"

"That would be brilliant," said Erin, thinking it might help her headache. "It's on me," she said, handing Farnsworth a ten-pound note.

"Ta very much, pet," she said, heading for the lift.

A nurse in blue scrubs came in from the hallway with a clipboard. "Mr. Hawkins?" she said, and the young man rose, cradling his arm with the ice pack.

Erin settled in her chair and flipped through emails on her mobile phone. When she looked up, she was startled to see Detective

Hemming coming through the double doors leading to the wards. He looked just as surprised to see her, even though he had insisted she visit the hospital.

"Hello," she said.

"Hello," he said, clearing his throat. "I'm, uh, glad you took my advice."

"Always," she said. "But what are you doing here?"

"I'm visiting . . . my mother." The words came reluctantly.

"Oh," she said. "Is she all right?"

He glanced at the woman with the little girl, who was engrossed in a *Highlights* magazine. The mother looked away, avoiding eye contact with him.

"Mummy, why is Goofus so wicked?" said the girl.

"He doesn't know any better," said her mother. "His parents don't teach him how to behave."

"Why not?" said the girl, squirming in her chair.

"They. Don't. Have . . . *the patience*," her mother said, her jaw tight. Erin wondered how long her own patience would last with a small child. If childcare was easy, she thought, everyone would do it well.

"I can't believe they still have *Highlights* magazine," she said to Hemming. "I read it when I was her age."

"Someone should tell her Goofus might have been born wicked," he murmured, too low for the mother to hear.

"Do you believe that some people are born bad?"

"I'm not a social scientist. But if you're around criminals long enough—"

"It shakes your faith in human nature?"

"It certainly doesn't improve it." He ran a hand through his hair. She could smell his aftershave, woodsy and clean like a forest after a rainstorm.

The nurse in blue scrubs came in again and called the young mother and her child. "We're a little short staffed," she told Erin. "It won't be much longer."

"No worries," Erin answered. She turned to Hemming, wondering a little bit why he was still there. She decided to take a chance. "Your mother isn't doing well, is she?"

She thought he might deny it, but, biting his lip, he shook his head. "No, she's not. That's why I brought her here from Manchester."

"Are you all right?" she said, avoiding saying *I know just how you feel. I've been through it myself.* Precisely because she had been through it herself, she did not want to mention it. This was his struggle, not hers, and she had no desire to revisit her own loss.

"It's so strange," he said, "suddenly realizing that someone you thought would always be there . . . I mean, you knew intellectually she'd die someday, but you put it off as being in the future, until one day you actually face it as reality. You've been walking this nice predictable path all your life, and suddenly someone's built a concrete wall in front of you, and it stops you cold. All you can do is stand there and stare at the wall."

"I'm so sorry."

"Family, you know . . . it's in your bones."

"Yeah," she said. "I know what you mean."

He passed a hand over his forehead, damp with sweat. She noticed he had been speaking of himself in the second person. It was remarkable enough he was willing to share this much. Most British people would rather pull out their fingernails than talk about their feelings.

The bell on the lift door dinged and the doors slid open to reveal Farnsworth holding two coffees and scones with cream.

"It's a decent cafeteria, surprisingly. Oh, hello," she added, seeing Hemming. "Sorry—I would have brought you a coffee."

"I'm fine, thanks. Good to see you."

"Here you are, pet," she said, handing Erin her coffee, as the nurse entered again.

"Erin Coleridge?" she said. "You can come through now."

"Here, have my coffee," Erin said, handing it to Hemming. "You look like you could use it."

"But—all right, thanks," he said, taking it.

Erin followed the nurse through the double doors.

Dr. Choudry, the resident on call, examined Erin and listened carefully to her symptoms, a thoughtful look on his face. He was young, thin, and intense, with deep brown eyes and thick black hair. "I'd recommend a CT scan just to be sure. At the very least, you need to rest up and take it easy."

Erin frowned. "Exactly how easy do I need to—"

"No strenuous activity, avoid eye strain and bright light, and get plenty of sleep. Tell you what," he said. "Let's send you up for a scan, all right? It won't take long."

"All right," she said, and followed the nurse to the radiology department on the fourth floor. She actually found the process very interesting, and it was quick—she was back in about ten minutes. Dr. Choudry informed her she would receive a follow-up call the next day once the radiologist had read the results. He gave her an information sheet titled "Concussion Treatment at Home," basically repeating his instructions.

"Don't be overly worried," he said. "Just keep an eye out for a worsening of symptoms, and I'll call you tomorrow."

"Thanks very much," she said, and returned to the waiting room, where Farnsworth was sitting in a yellow plastic chair drinking coffee and reading *Highlights* magazine. There was no sign of Detective Hemming.

"He had to leave," Farnsworth said as Erin approached. "He really does fancy you, you know."

"Oh, I'm not—"

"Everything all right in the noggin department?"

"It's all sorted," Erin said. It wasn't exactly the truth, but it wasn't a lie either.

"What's that in your hand?"

"Oh, just some instructions—"

"Let me have a look," Farnsworth said, grabbing it before Erin had a chance to object. "Hmm, this doesn't sound like you at all," she remarked, studying it. "Good thing you have Aunty Farnsworth to help you."

"Look, I'll be—"

"Fine? I'll make certain of that. Come along—it's time we get back. I'm famished."

"What about the scone?"

"That was lunch, pet. And now I'm thinking about dinner. Duck with sage and prune stuffing. Roasted rosemary potatoes, courgettes in fennel and garlic."

"That sounds heavenly," Erin said, realizing she was incredibly hungry too.

"I think I've memorized the menu by now," Farnsworth said as they left the building and headed to the carpark. It was colder now—there was no sign of the sun behind the cloud cover, and the wind had whipped up. Farnsworth shivered as she unlocked the car. "I hope we're not in for another storm. So odd to have such a cold winter, with global warming and all."

"Actually, global warming leads to extreme weather in both directions," Erin said as they slid into their seats. The interior of the car was so cold their breath fogged the windows, forming ice crystals on the glass.

Farnsworth blew on her hands to warm them. "Good lord, you are a—what is it you call it again?"

"The term is 'weather geek.'"

"You know," she said, buckling her safety belt, "I was thinking about reading *Highlights* magazine as a girl, and how I always used to turn immediately to 'Goofus and Gallant.'"

"Me too," said Erin. "I think everyone did, didn't they?"

"Yes, but why?"

"It's something to do with the struggle of good and evil—Goofus represents our worst impulses, whereas Gallant displays our better side."

"But he's not entirely likable, is he?" said Farnsworth, pulling out of the carpark. "Gallant, I mean. I always thought he was a bit of a twit."

"Too much virtue signaling?"

Farnsworth laughed. "Something like that."

"I have to admit, reading about Goofus was more fun."

"Exactly. Who on earth wants to be around someone who acts appropriately all the time? That's just irritating."

"Rascals have a certain appeal, at least in fiction."

"Some women have an affinity for them."

"Not you, surely."

"Perish the thought. Though Dick Deadeye was a bit of one," Farnsworth said, referring to her late ex-husband. She had a number of unflattering nicknames for him—Dastardly Dick, Dick the Prick, Quickie Dickie, and so on. Dick Deadeye was the villain in *H.M.S. Pinafore*, one of Gilbert and Sullivan's most popular operettas.

"But that's not what you liked about him, was it?" Erin said as they drove past the fish and chips shops, cafés, and Chinese takeaways frequented by the city's large population of college students.

"It's hard now to remember what I liked about him."

"Rascals can be amazingly charming. That's how they're successful, in life and in fiction. Look at Willoughby in *Sense and Sensibility*, for example."

"But he really does love Marianne."

"He loves money more."

"He's just weak. I think he's rather tragic, actually. By marrying for money, he's doomed to live the rest of his life with a woman he doesn't even like."

"He has only himself to blame," Erin said as they pulled up in front of the hotel.

Farnsworth unbuckled her seat beat and turned to study her. "How do you feel, pet?"

"Better, thanks—but I could sleep for days."

"Do me a favor and have an early dinner with me first, would you?"

"Right. I'm actually quite peckish myself."

"Let me check on what Grant's up to and I'll meet you in the restaurant in half an hour?"

"Perfect," Erin said as the parking valet approached the car, a hooded parka obscuring his face. Walking toward them in the gathering gloom of twilight, hands shoved in his pockets, she thought, he could be anybody—Goofus or Gallant. And before you knew which one he was, it might be too late.

Chapter Thirty-Five

~

"Oh, I shall miss this," Farnsworth said, taking a bite of duck with prune and sage stuffing. It was an hour before the dinner rush, and the two had the room nearly to themselves. Chandeliers sparkled cheerfully overhead, long white candles on the table glowed softly; outside the windows snow fell gently, a few puffy white flakes cascading from the sky, caught briefly in the floodlights stationed along the building's eaves. Erin's breath slowed and deepened; she felt safe, sitting here with her friend, comforted by the hotel's elegant furnishings. The darkened courtyard behind Mad Alice's Lane seemed far away, as the pounding in her head subsided and the sense of the world as a dangerous place receded behind the sturdy walls of the Grand Hotel.

"Grant's gout is still bothering him, then?" she asked Farnsworth.

"He's a bit better, but apparently his toe is still swollen. I told him it's the disease of kings, but that didn't cheer him up much."

"Is he taking allopurinol?"

"He's taking something—not sure what."

"My uncle used to get it, and that's what he took."

"Oh, look who's here," said Farnsworth.

Erin turned to see Khari Butari enter the dining room, dressed in knee-high leather boots over black pants and a canary-yellow jumper that brought out the mahogany highlights in her lustrous skin.

"Shall we ask her to join us?" said Farnsworth, her jealousy toward Khari apparently softened by a glass or two of pinot grigio.

"Sure," said Erin, waving at her.

Khari walked toward them, and Erin was struck once again by her beauty and long-limbed grace.

"Care to join us?" asked Farnsworth.

"I don't want to intrude," said Khari.

"Not at all. We're becoming quite bored with one another, aren't we?" Farnsworth asked Erin.

"Massively bored," she agreed.

"We're like an old married couple," said Farnsworth. "We've run out of things to say to each other. We could use some new blood."

"How are you feeling?" Khari asked, taking the seat nearest the window.

"Better, thanks."

"She went to hos—" Farnsworth began, but Erin locked eyes with her, shaking her head, and Farnsworth covered by having a small coughing fit.

"Sorry—what?" asked Khari.

"Are you all right in that spot?" Farnsworth said. "It's so near the window, and it's cold outside."

"Fine, thanks—I'm actually quite warm-blooded." She smiled. "Strange, I know, since I come from a tropical climate."

"I'm like you," said Farnsworth. "But Erin is like a lizard—she needs to sun herself every day to survive."

"Really?"

Erin laughed. "She's talking rubbish."

"I am not. You're always sitting in the sun when I come over to see you."

"Where is it again you live?" said Khari.

"Kirkbymoorside," said Erin. "It's a market town just off the North Yorkshire moors."

"She runs a used bookstore there," said Farnsworth.

"How lovely," said Khari. "I've always thought that would be the most idyllic job in the world. Maybe I should do a documentary about you."

"I'm not that interesting," said Erin. "I live a pretty quiet life."

"Except when she's out solving murders," Farnsworth remarked as their server arrived. On duty tonight was Bridget, Christine's plump, curly-haired colleague. Her mood was understandably depressed following the news of Sam's death, but she forced a smile as she approached the table. Erin and Farnsworth had already expressed their condolences, but Erin felt guilty about knowing the news earlier but having sworn not to tell anyone.

"What can I get you?" Bridget asked Khari.

"What are you having?" she asked Erin.

"Grilled sea bass and asparagus with hollandaise."

"I'll have that, please," Khari told Bridget, who gave a little nod, turning to Erin and Farnsworth.

"Do you need anything else?"

"We're fine, pet," said Farnsworth. "Everything is lovely."

"I'm glad," Bridget said, but looked as if she was about to burst into tears.

"What's the matter with her?" asked Khari when she had gone.

"Have you not heard?" said Farnsworth.

"Heard what?"

They told her about Sam's death, leaving out the details, merely saying he was found dead in his flat.

"How terrible," said Khari. "He was such a nice young man. Why would someone like that kill himself?"

"What makes you think it was suicide?" asked Erin.

"Well, I mean, he was so young. People like that don't just fall down dead, do they?"

"Sometimes," Farnsworth said ominously. "It's not unheard of, you know."

"Have they determined the cause of death?"

"Not yet," said Erin. "It's under investigation."

"That's so tragic," she said, though it didn't seem to dampen her appetite. When the fish arrived, she tucked into it like she hadn't eaten for days. Erin and Farnsworth exchanged a look as she reached for the bread basket, breaking off a large chunk of freshly baked *pain de campagne.*

Erin wasn't sure, but it seemed to her that her friend's expression said *I told you so.*

Chapter Thirty-Six

After dinner Erin felt drowsiness overtake her, like a heavy cloak being slipped over her shoulders. She rose from her chair and yawned.

"I'm all in—think I'll head off to bed."

"I'll walk with you," said Khari.

Taking out her mobile phone, Farnsworth waved them on. "You two go ahead. I'm going to check with Grant and see if I can bring him anything."

As they walked down the hall toward the lobby, Erin saw Charles Kilroy coming toward them, head down, immersed in a book. Seeing them, his face broke into a smile.

"Why, hello, ladies—what a vision of loveliness in these otherwise mundane corridors."

"Hello, Charles," said Erin.

"Ah, Goddess of Grace as always," he said, looking at Khari. Coming from most men, this would sound creepy or clueless, Erin thought, but Charles presented such an odd combination of awkwardness and innocence that it actually came off as rather charming.

"You may call me She Who Must Be Obeyed," Khari said with a smile.

"Ha! Ha, ha—well done!" Charles said. His laugh was rather like what Erin imagined the guffaw of a bull rhino would sound like—a low, percussive hoot. She recognized the reference to the cult film classic—Charles did look like someone who would appreciate a classic horror movie. "Where are you off to?" he said. "I mean, if you don't mind my asking."

"Bed," said Erin. "I'm knackered."

"That is a rather nasty bump on your head. I trust you had it examined by a medical professional."

"I just need a good night's sleep. Good seeing you."

"And you," he said with a little bow to both women. "Good night."

"He's an odd duck," Khari said when he had gone.

"He is," Erin agreed. "But quite harmless, I should imagine."

"Look, I'm not certain, but I caught a glimpse of someone who looked like him on the Ghost Walk."

"Really? Why didn't you tell me before?"

"It was just before you disappeared down the alley. I completely forgot about it until just now. And I'm not even sure it was him."

"Where was this?"

"Just before we stopped at Mad Alice's Lane. I was going to draw your attention to it, but the tour guide started talking, and I didn't want to be rude. Then with all that happened, it slipped my mind until now."

"What was he doing?" Erin said as they reached the lobby.

"He seemed to be following us, but at a distance."

"Thanks for telling me. Are you coming up?" she asked, standing in front of the lift.

"I think I'll have a coffee in the bar. Spike makes a good macchiato."

"Good night, then," Erin said as the lift doors opened.

"See you tomorrow."

Alone in the lift as it rose slowly to the top floor, Erin thought about what Khari had said. She didn't exactly suspect Khari, but she didn't entirely trust her either. Claiming Charles was on the

Ghost Walk gave her deniability, establishing another possible per-petrator in the attack on Erin—if that's what it was. As the lift stopped on the fifth floor, she had to admit there was a possibility the whole thing was an accident. Farnsworth was right—things fall from balconies, bits of buildings crumble, and sometimes people get hurt. But Erin didn't think it was an accident.

Back in her room, she opened her laptop. Feeling somewhat reluctant and conflicted about what she was about to do, she typed "Khari Butari" into the search engine. The first few hits were announcements of the release of *Girls of Dakar*, a link to her web-site, and below that, reviews of the film. One link caught her eye. It was a review of the movie by Professor Barry Wolf, PhD, Faculty, Trinity College, Oxford.

Taking a deep breath, Erin clicked on it. To say that he didn't like the film was an understatement. He eviscerated it. Point by point, he picked it apart, and finally dismissed it. The last sentence of the review read, "The young women of Senegal not only deserve a better representation of their lives, they deserve a more honest one."

Erin's head felt hot and her vision blurred, though whether from her injury or emotion, she couldn't tell. Closing the laptop, she stood and went to the window, gazing out at the starless night. If she were Khari Butari, she thought, she wouldn't just dislike Pro-fessor Barry Wolf, PhD. She would loathe him with every bone in her body.

*   *   *

After falling into bed and sleeping soundly for some hours, Erin awoke to the sound of an owl hooting softly outside her window. Putting a pillow over her head, she rolled over in bed, but she could still hear the owl. Throwing off the pillow, she sat up and looked at the bedside clock. 3:00 AM. *The witching hour*, her mother always said, when the membrane between the living and dead is thinnest. Erin's father dismissed this as "Celtic superstition," a reference to Gwyneth's Welsh ancestry, but her mother always just smiled and laid a finger next to her nose, indicating her father was the crazy one.

The owl hooted again, and Erin couldn't help feeling it was summoning her. She thought of the owlet in her famous ancestor's poem, calling out in the dead of night while the other inhabitants of his cottage lay sleeping, with only the solitary writer at his desk as witness. Perhaps it was a metaphor for the artist in society, the poet attentive to sounds others missed—awake and attuned to Nature while everyone around him slept. The poet and the detective, she thought, ever vigilant, alert to the possibility of as yet undiscovered truth.

Rising from her bed, she threw open the curtains. There, in the gnarled branches of an ancient yew outside her window, caught in the glow of the building's floodlights, was a solitary tawny owl. Her mother, something of a birder, had taught her to recognize various owl species. Its great dark eyes pierced the night, and seemed to be staring directly at her. Its eyes were less round and more deep-set than other owls, with furrowed brows giving it the appearance of deep contemplation. The animal continued to peer at her, unblinking, and she had the feeling she was gazing into the eyes of an ancient Druid reincarnated in the form of an owl.

"What have you come to tell me?" she murmured, and the bird raised its powerful wings, fluffing its mottled brown and white feathers. For a moment she feared it would take off, but it settled back onto the branch, preening itself before resuming its study of her.

The owlet's cry
Came loud—and hark, again! loud as before.
The inmates of my cottage, all at rest,

Have left me to that solitude, which suits
Abstruser musings

    She listened for any noise from her fellow humans, but the hotel was quiet as the grave. She imagined them all sound asleep in their beds, feeling once again the connection to her ancestor and fellow poet. Rifling through the drawer in the bedside table, she pulled out a pad of monogrammed hotel stationery and a pen, and scribbled a few lines.

The owl's cry in the dark of night
Disturbs my soundest slumber
And calls me from my bed
Suddenly alert to what lies in the darkness

    Standing there in her bare feet and flannel pajamas, she shivered. What lay in the darkness, she wondered, and how could she find it, alone while everyone else slept? She looked back at the tree, but the owl was gone. Creeping back to bed, she pulled the covers up to her chin, but sleep did not come easy, as the events of the past few days tumbled around in her mind. Their meaning remained elusive, evading her grasp; as she stared into the darkness, a solution seemed more remote than ever.

    When finally she did sleep, she dreamed of being pursued down crooked cobblestone streets by unknown assailants, while a tall, bearded man in a top hat cackled loudly, his laughter echoing down endless corridors of an ancient, inscrutable city with a violent past.

Chapter Thirty-Seven

The mercury dropped precipitously overnight. The next morning dawned bright and cold, a chill wind whipping across the River Ouse, frothing its normally sluggish water into jagged little whitecaps. Erin could feel the change in temperature as she padded over to plug in the teakettle; the wind whistled in the eaves, needles of cold air slipping through tiny gaps in the window panes. Waiting for the water to boil, she gazed out at the old yew tree. There was no sign of last night's owl, and as the morning sun streamed into the room, her mood of the night before suddenly felt remote.

The sun was too harsh for her eyes, still sensitive to bright light, so she pulled the filmy white inner curtains close to block the glare. Hearing the water burbling in the kettle, she rose just as the automatic safety switch turned off with a soft click. Still groggy from her exertions of the previous day, she added an extra teabag to the pot. Yawning, she stretched her sore muscles, feeling the cold deep in her bones.

Her mobile phone played the familiar opening strains of the Bach B Minor Fugue. She picked it up and flopped onto the bed.

"Good morning, Pumpkin."

"Hello, Dad," she said, stifling a yawn.

"You sound tired. Did you get enough sleep?"

"I haven't had my first cuppa yet."

"Should I call back later?"

"No, it's all right," she said, looking up at the by now familiar ceiling stain. It looked even more like the outline of a body in the light of day.

"Did you get my package?" he said.

"Not yet. What did you send?"

"A yearbook."

"Of what?"

"You'll see."

She sat up abruptly. The sudden movement made her head swim a little, and she felt a bit queasy. "Why are you being so mysterious?"

"Just let me know when you get it."

"But—"

"Talk later," he said, and hung up.

She picked up the hotel phone next to the bed and called the front desk.

The concierge picked up on the second ring. "Grand Hotel, Harriet speaking." It was the nice middle-aged woman who wore too much pancake makeup.

"This is Erin Coleridge. Do you have a package—"

"Oh, yes, dear—I was going to ring you but I didn't want to call too early."

"When did it arrive?"

"Let me see . . . yesterday afternoon. Tricia signed it in."

Figures, Erin thought. Tricia never struck her as someone who could be trusted.

"Thank you," she said.

"Shall I send it up?"

"I'll come get it." She didn't want to risk it getting lost in transit. Safer to fetch it herself, she thought as she pulled on her jeans. She gazed longingly at the teapot as she left the room. Tea would have to wait.

The package, a large manila envelope, seemed to be a book of some kind, her name on the address line in her father's familiar scrawl. His handwriting was full of fanciful loops and expansive whorls, as if it was trying to escape the confines of the page.

After collecting the package from the front desk, she saw Jeremy Wolf lounging on one of the benches lining the alcoves along the wall. He was on his mobile, talking loudly, the way young people did, so it was impossible not to overhear.

"Yeah," Jeremy said. "Can't believe we got away with it." He laughed. "I know—right? I doubt that mystery will be solved. Well, I've got to go—talk to you later." He laughed again. "Yeah, right—bye."

He rang off and waved at Erin as she headed for the lift. "Hold it for me, would you?" as she pressed the button. He loped across the lobby, and by the time the lift arrived he was standing beside her. She felt her forehead grow clammy. She wiped the sweat off as she entered the lift, Jeremy so close behind her she could feel his breath on the back of her neck.

"I was talking to a college chum," he said, pressing the button for the third floor. "On the phone just now."

"No problem," she answered. There was an uncomfortable pause. "None of my business," she added, as the door opened on the third floor.

"Hang on a minute," he said, letting the door close.

She felt trapped, and tried not to hyperventilate as they proceeded to the top floor.

"Hang on," he said. "You don't think I did in my own dad, do you?"

"Why should I think that?"

"Everyone knows you've been snooping around," he said, looming over her. She swallowed hard, her heart suddenly beating in her throat. "Look, I was talking about a prank we pulled in school, see?"

"What sort of prank?" she asked as the lift door opened on the fifth floor.

"We snuck into the dining room," he said, blocking the door from closing. "We played a prank on the chef, see—he was a mate of ours."

"What kind of prank?" she asked, trying to remain calm.

"We put chili pepper in the tomato sauce. We were just having him on," he added as the lift door began dinging. "Look," he said, holding out his phone, "you can call my mate to check on it if you don't believe me."

"It's all right," she said, backing out of the lift. "I believe you."

"It was just a stupid practical joke," he said as the lift doors closed behind her.

Taking a deep breath, Erin stood for a moment to clear her head before walking down the hall to her room. She was inclined to believe Jeremy—though even if he was telling the truth about the phone call, it didn't mean he was innocent of murder.

Back in her room, she tore open the envelope to find a 1986 year-book from Trinity College, Oxford. Her father had taped a yellow sticky note to the cover. "Look at page 27." Hands trembling, she turned to the page as instructed. There, in the center of a layout devoted to the school literary magazine, the *Monthly Review*, was a photo of a much younger Terrence Rogers, his arm around an equally fresh-faced Barry Wolf. Towering over them, his hand on Barry's shoulder, was Grant Apthorp. All three men smiled broadly at the camera, as if pleased with themselves and their position in the world, poised at the beginning of what promised to be glittering careers. Next to Grant, wearing a slightly less confident smile, was Judith Eton. The caption beneath the photo read "Monthly Review Editorial Staff."

Apparently a lot had happened since those halcyon school days, some of which she knew about. But clearly there was a lot more to it than she realized. "Thanks, Dad," Erin murmured, studying the latest piece in what was becoming an increasingly complicated puzzle.

Chapter Thirty-Eight

⤳

The first thing she did was to call Prudence to find out Judith's Eton's room number. Pru was in charge of making sure the VIPs got the best rooms, and she informed Erin that Judith was on the third floor, her son in an adjoining room. Erin didn't fancy interrogating Grant, and Terrence's rather imposing reserve made him an equally unattractive source. While Judith wasn't exactly the touchy-feely friendly type, at least she was another woman. Leaving her phone in the room to charge, Erin slipped out and took the stairs down to the third floor.

The halls were quiet; most people had probably left their rooms for the day. The morning panels had already begun, and the restaurant was still serving late breakfast. Judith's room was at the far end of the hall, and Erin walked down the long corridor, keenly aware of the creak of old floorboards beneath the crimson carpet with its gold trim. She didn't expect Judith to be in her room, but it was worth a try. This was not the kind of thing you talk about over the phone—she needed to have this conversation face to face.

Room 332 was the last one on the left before the fire exit at the end of the hall. Ignoring the Do Not Disturb sign dangling from the doorknob, Erin lifted her hand to knock on the door, but it seemed to be slightly ajar. When there was no response to her knock, she pushed it gently, and saw that it was indeed unlatched. Opening it slowly, she poked her head into the room.

"Hello? Judith?" she called. "It's Erin Coleridge."

No answer. She could hear the faint clanking of the wall pipes as steam made its way through to the radiators. Taking a deep breath, she stepped into the room.

Erin had a disquieting feeling that something was wrong. The air itself was unnaturally still. There was a stuffy smell, as if no window had been opened in a long time, and nothing fresh had entered the room for quite a while. The queen-sized bed was rumpled, the sheets and blankets in disarray, as if someone had had a bad sleep, tossing and turning all night. Closing the door behind her, she took a few more steps into the room. The smell seemed to intensify, reminding her of . . . what? A hospital.

When she reached the far side of the bed, she realized why. Lying on the floor between the bed and the window, a dark red stain spreading from her head, was Judith Eton. Erin knew without touching her that she was dead, her blood already soaking into the plush carpet. But Erin bent down anyway and put two fingers to her neck. Her skin was already cool to the touch, and there was no pulse. Kneeling next to the body, Erin attempted to locate the source of the wound without touching anything. It wasn't difficult. Dried blood encircled a small hole in the right side of her neck, and judging by the pattern on the carpet, it seemed to be the source of the blood. No other wound was visible, nor was there any sign of a weapon under the bed or anywhere else. The amount of blood in the carpet suggested the weapon had pierced the carotid artery— she would have bled out fairly quickly.

Erin avoided touching anything as she examined the room. She knew it was important to keep everything as pristine as possible for the police, but since she was there anyway, she figured it wouldn't hurt to have a look around. Once the cops arrived, her access to the crime scene would be over. Judging by the blood spatter on the nearby wall and bedspread, Judith had fallen where she was attacked. There seemed to be little or no staging of the crime—the killer likely fled quickly, taking the murder weapon. An examination of the room and bathroom showed no signs of a fight or struggle, and Judith's fingernails were all intact, with no visible defensive wounds. It seemed to have been a blitzkrieg attack, indicating that she knew her killer, and trusted them enough to let them into her hotel room.

Nothing seemed out of place either in the room or the closet, where Judith's clothes hung neatly from wooden hangers. Her purse dangled from the hook on the closet door, her wallet poking out of the top, and an expensive set of jade jewelry lay on the dresser. The heavy necklace, bracelet, and matching earrings were laid out in a way that suggested they were to be worn with the green and black pantsuit Judith was wearing. Her clothes were untouched, and there was no other evidence the assault was sexually motivated.

The truth was obvious and grim. Someone had simply wanted her dead, badly enough to take the tremendous risk of killing her in her own room. And whoever had killed her knew enough about anatomy—or was lucky enough—to hit the carotid artery. Her death would have been swift, Erin thought—at least she didn't suffer much.

Not wanting to touch anything in the crime scene, Erin avoided using the hotel phone next to Judith's bed to call the police. Tiptoeing from the room, Erin closed the door softly behind her and slipped out, taking the stairs to the top floor. Letting herself into her room, she scrolled through her phone's contact list until she came to Det. Peter Hemming. He answered on the third ring.

"Erin?"

So she was in his contact list as well, she thought with satisfaction.

"I think you'd better send someone over here as soon as you can."

"Why?"

"There's been another murder," she said, emphasizing *another*.

"Who?"

"Judith Eton."

"Are you sure it's—"

"I discovered the body. She was killed in her room."

"Are you there now?"

"I'm in the lobby."

"Can you go back up and make sure no one disturbs the crime scene? I'll be there as soon as I can."

"All right."

"Don't tell anyone about it, okay?"

"Sure."

"And don't touch anything."

"I won't," she said, pretending to be irritated. She had no intention of telling him she had already examined the crime scene, though she had avoided touching anything.

"And Erin—?"

"Yes?"

"Please be careful."

"I will," she said, pleased by the concern in his voice. As she was slipping the phone back into her pocket, Jonathan Alder entered the lobby from the hallway. Seeing her, he waved. Normally she would be happy to see him, but now he was an obstacle to her mission.

"Hello," he said, approaching her, smiling. He looked fully rested, as fresh and bouncy as his sleek black curls. He wore black trousers and a powder-blue button-down shirt that set off the deeper blue of his eyes. In contrast to Peter Hemming's rumpled exhaustion, Jonathan looked as if he had just had about nine hours of sound sleep.

"Hello," she said.

"Good morning, Miss Coleridge," he said in a posh accent, with a little bow. "I must say, you are a veritable breath of fresh air."

"Thank you," she said, heading toward the lift.

"I'm practicing my Regency speech, to get in the mood for the ball tomorrow," he said cheerfully, walking alongside her. "Hetty suggested it."

"Good idea," she said, distracted.

He frowned. "You all right?"

"Sorry, I'm just—"

"Did you hurt your head?" he said, peering closer. "It appears you have a bruise."

"Yeah, I just bumped it on the, uh, bedpost."

"Ouch. Did you have it looked at?"

"I did, thanks," she said, ringing for the lift.

"Head injuries are no joke. You know, once in a rugby match, I made the mistake of tackling a bloke with my head. Broke my nose, had to leave the game."

"That must have hurt," she said as the lift arrived.

"There was a lot of blood, but it wasn't as bad as it looked."

"See you later," she said, stepping inside.

"Wait—I'll join you," he said, and her heart sank. Jonathan's room was on the third floor. She would have to ride up to the top floor and circle back. "I'm looking forward to the ball," he said. "Even if I missed the dance lesson."

"Why didn't you show up?" she asked. The machinery whirred softly as they ascended slowly to the third floor.

"I lay down for a few minutes, and that turned into an hour. I guess walking the wall with you wore me out. I heard you went on the Ghost Walk later on."

"Yeah," she said as the door opened on the third floor.

"Can't keep up with you," he said, cocking his head to one side so a loose lock of hair fell over one eye. He looked like he was waiting for an invitation.

She gave only a vague smile in response, but a part of her contracted with disappointment when the door closed, leaving her alone in the lift. When she reached the top floor, she walked to the end of the hall and took the back stairs down to the third floor. Peering through the glass at the top of the fire door, she waited until the hallway was empty before slipping into the corridor. Positioning herself next to the room, she switched her phone from ring to vibrate and leaned against the wall, standing guard until the police showed up.

She didn't have long to wait. The lift soon arrived, carrying Detective Hemming, Sergeant Jarral, and several crime scene techs in white jumpsuits. Jarral was dapper as ever in a russet-colored suit and matching tie; his smooth black hair appeared freshly cut. He greeted her with something less than his usual friendliness, and she felt a little guilty about pumping him for information about Sam's death—but not too guilty. Each turn of the screw proved her initial suspicions correct.

"You all right?" Hemming said when he saw her.

"Fine, thanks."

"I never should have asked you to watch the room—I'm sorry."

"No harm done."

"It was too dangerous."

"I'm *fine*," she repeated.

"No one's been in or out of the room?" Hemming asked as Jarral opened the door with a master key card.

"Not that I saw," she said. "I went here straightaway after we spoke."

"Thanks," he said as Jarral and the crime scene technicians entered the room.

"I'll leave you to it, then," she said, turning to leave as her mobile vibrated in her pocket. She switched it off without looking to see who was calling.

"Hang on a minute," he said. He looked even more haggard, with gray circles under his eyes, his thick blond hair shaggy, in desperate need of a trim. "I just have a few questions."

"All right."

"You found her directly before you called me?"

"Yes," she said, not mentioning the ten minutes or so she spent poking around.

"And you touched nothing?"

"No." That, at least, was true. "Other than to check for a pulse. Her skin was cool to the touch, so—"

"What were you doing in her room?"

"I came to talk to her about something, and found her dead."

"How did you get in?"

"The door was ajar. I went in and saw her on the floor."

"Did you see anyone in the corridor?"

"No."

"All right," he said, rubbing his eyes. "That's all for now, thanks."

"Let me know if I can help in any way."

"You can help by keeping this to yourself."

"How long do you think it will be before word gets around that a couple of coppers with a retinue of crime scene technicians just happen to be poking around the third floor?"

"I'd appreciate it if you would avoid revealing any details about the crime scene, at least for now."

"Including the fact that I discovered the body."

"Especially that."

"I can't even tell Farns—"

"Please don't tell anyone."

"Okay," she said. "I won't."

But even as she said it, Erin realized it was easier said than done.

Chapter Thirty-Nine

~

Erin took the back stairs up to her room, thinking that Farnsworth could read her like a book. The only way to keep secrets from her was to avoid seeing her altogether. But when Erin arrived at her room, her friend was standing outside the door.

"There you are!" she said. "You weren't answering your mobile. What on earth is going on?"

"What do you mean?"

"He told you not to talk about it, didn't he?" Farnsworth said, following Erin into the room.

"Who?"

"Come along, pet," Farnsworth said, closing the door behind her. "Detective Hemming's car is right outside, with a big white police van parked behind it."

"I can't tell you anything."

"Someone's dead, aren't they?"

"I can't—"

"Is it murder? It *is*!" Farnsworth said, studying Erin's facial expression. "Who's the victim?"

"I can't—"

Farnsworth went pale. "Oh God—it's not Grant, is it?"

"No, it isn't him."

Farnsworth sank into one of the armchairs. "Thank God. I mean, it's not good for anyone to die, obviously, but—" She looked at Erin slyly. "You more or less just admitted someone's been killed. You might as well—"

"Look," said Erin. "I'm not going to tell you who it is, but I will say that we'll have to cancel tonight's keynote speech."

Farnsworth's jaw went slack. "It's not—oh. It's Judith Eton, isn't it?"

"Whether or not you're right, we'd have to cancel it anyway."

"It *is* Judith, isn't it? Poor Judith," Farnsworth said mournfully. "I liked her. Who do you suspect? Whoever it is, we have to assume they also killed Barry and Sam."

Erin shook her head. She dearly wanted to join the conversation, but not until Hemming told her the coast was clear.

"Look," she said finally. "I gave my word that I—"

"Say no more," said Farnsworth, lowering herself into the armchair nearest the window. "I understand. You told him you'd stay silent."

"I can show you this, however," Erin said, handing her the yearbook. "Look at page twenty-seven."

Farnsworth did as instructed, staring at the page for a long time before speaking. "Wow," she said finally. "Where did you get this?"

"My father sent it," Erin said, plugging in the electric kettle. "Did Grant ever tell you that they all knew each other at school?"

"No. I knew he and Barry both taught at Oxford, but he never mentioned that the three of them attended the same college, let alone working on the same literary magazine."

"Has he talked about Barry or Terrence at all?"

"Not really."

"What a strange omission," Erin said.

"Maybe they weren't such great chums as the picture suggests."

"Or maybe they were once, but not anymore."

"This is a three cup problem," Farnsworth said as the water came to a boil. "Shall I go fetch some of my private stash?"

"Not unless you want it. The hotel tea is decent."

"Oh, all right," Farnsworth said, sighing. "Are there biscuits?"

"There are indeed," Erin said, producing a packet of McVitie's. "Chocolate digestives."

"Well done. I'm glad you came prepared."

"It's possible there's nothing sinister at all about the picture," Erin said, preparing the tea. "Maybe they just drifted apart over the years."

"I've barely seen Terrence and Grant exchange a single word this whole time," said Farnsworth. "Doesn't that strike you as strange?"

"Certainly neither of them seems fond of Barry."

"I'll see if I can get more out of Grant."

"I'm not sure that's a good idea."

"Nonsense. I want to help. Ta," she added as Erin handed her a cup of tea. "You're right, this isn't bad," she said, taking a sip. "And the chockie bickies make up for anything it lacks."

There was a knock at the door. Erin opened it to see Sergeant Jarral standing there.

"Oh, hello," she said. "Would you like to come in?"

"Just for a moment," he said, stepping into the room.

"Hello, Sergeant," said Farnsworth. "Good to see you again."

"Hello, Ms. Appleby."

"Please call me Farnsworth. How about some tea?"

"Thanks, no," he said stiffly. "I just came to ask a few questions of Ms. Cole—"

"Call me Erin."

"Detective Hemming has a few more questions, so if you don't mind—"

"Look," Erin said. "I owe you an apology. My actions got us both in trouble."

"It's my fault," he said, looking down at his shoes. "I never should have—"

"But I'm the one who plied you for information, and I'm sorry."

"You *are* persuasive," he said, his lips twitching into a smile.

"Am I forgiven?"

"I should have known better, obviously."

"Now that's settled, how about a cup of tea?" said Farnsworth.

"I could really use one—thanks."

"Milk, sugar?"

"Both, thanks."

"Detective Hemming doesn't let up once he's on a case, does he?" Farnsworth said, pouring him a cup.

"Actually, I'm worried about him. He's not himself. He seems . . . I don't know, ragged."

"He looks exhausted," said Erin.

"It's this business with his mother," said the sergeant. "It's wearing him down."

"Please, sit down," said Farnsworth.

"I shouldn't—"

"Just for a minute," said Erin. "We won't tell."

"You are allowed to enjoy your tea, aren't you?" said Farnsworth. "Have a biscuit."

"All right," Jarral acquiesced, perching on the edge of the desk chair.

"You had some questions for me?" said Erin.

"Both of you, if you don't mind."

"Happy to oblige," said Farnsworth.

"Did you notice any unusual behavior on the part of the victim?"

"Such as—?"

"Did she seem nervous or threatened in any way?"

"No—in fact, she seemed quite relaxed, in spite of being tapped last minute to give the keynote speech."

"When was that to be?"

"Tonight, as a matter of fact," said Farnsworth. "Do you think the timing of her murder is significant?"

"I couldn't say," said the sergeant. "It does seem odd someone would kill a person to prevent her giving a speech."

"Unless they thought she might reveal something they wanted kept secret," said Erin.

"How many people knew she'd been drafted to do the speech?"

"Everyone, I suppose," said Farnsworth. "We made the decision two days ago."

"Was there an official announcement?"

"No, but word got around. It certainly wasn't a secret."

"Did she have any enemies that you knew of?"

"Not exactly," said Erin.

"But she did have a past," Farnsworth added.

"How do you mean?"

They explained what they knew about Judith's history with various other Society members, including the fact that she was Barry Wolf's first wife. The sergeant listened carefully, jotting down notes on a pad he balanced on his knee.

"You can use the desk, you know," said Erin.

"Oh, right," he said. "Good idea."

"I don't know if I should say this," she ventured. "It's just a suspicion—more in the realm of gossip, but I have reason to believe Terrence Rogers may be her son's biological father."

"That would be . . . Jeremy Wolf?" Jarral said, consulting his notes.

"Right."

"What makes you think that?"

Erin told him everything she had observed, including her attempts at eavesdropping.

"You're what my mum would call a curtain twitcher," Jarral said.

"She's always poking her nose in where it doesn't belong," Farnsworth agreed.

Erin rolled her eyes. "That's a load of—"

"It's true, pet, and you know it. How about some more tea?" she asked the sergeant.

"I'd best be getting on," he said, rising.

"You know where to find us," said Farnsworth, escorting him to the door.

"Right," he said. "Thanks for the tea and biscuits."

"Did you see his hands?" Farnsworth said when he had gone.

"What about them?"

"They were perfectly manicured. Like a model."

"You fancy him."

Farnsworth smiled. "No. All right, maybe a little."

"What would Grant say?"

"God, I wonder if he's heard yet. I should call him. Shall I help tidy up first?"

"I'll sort it. You go on."

"I'll check in with you later, pet."

After Farnsworth had gone, Erin sat down to study the yearbook, but found it hard to concentrate; Peter Hemming's drawn face kept swimming through her consciousness. Finally she got up to put away the tea things.

"He's a grown man," she muttered as she rinsed out the pot in the bathroom sink. "He can take care of himself."

But with an increasingly bold killer stalking the conference, she wondered if any of them could take care of themselves.

Chapter Forty

After she finished tidying up, Erin sat down in an armchair and gazed out the window, trying to quiet her mind. There were so many disparate elements—three deaths, all of them totally different: poisoning, strangulation, and a stabbing. What was the pattern? What kind of killer uses such varied methods?

She wondered if there was more than one murderer. Statistically unlikely, perhaps, but it might be a better explanation than the idea that this was all the work of one person. She knew it was important not to get too attached to any one theory of a crime. That could lead you to miss important clues just because they don't fit your assumptions.

Taking out her poetry notebook, she drew her own version of a murder board. In the center she put the three victims, along with the manner of death. Fanning out from the center, she listed potential suspects so far. To make it more visual, she drew a little sketch of each person. A real police bulletin board would include pictures of the victims and suspects, but lacking that, she could at least do her own version of it.

The obvious suspects included Society members attending the conference, of course, but then she wondered if she should include hotel staff—or any of her friends from the North Yorkshire Branch. She tried to picture friendly, bouncy Jonathan Alder or vain, man-obsessed Hetty Miller as a murderer, but that seemed highly unlikely.

None of her friends had a history with any of the victims. Neither did the hotel staff that she knew of, but one of the victims was Sam Buchanan, after all. Was it possible he was the intended victim all along, and the other deaths were just ancillary? Maybe Barry Wolf overheard something he shouldn't have. But Judith Eton . . . if she was a witness to the crime, why keep quiet until she herself was murdered?

Pondering these questions, Erin heard the flapping of wings outside her window. Looking up, she saw the owl from the previous night sitting on the same tree branch. At least it looked like the same one—definitely a tawny owl, easily recognizable from its large round head and light brown and white mottled feathers.

But what was it doing out in broad daylight? Tawny owls were nocturnal, hunting at night and roosting during the day. The animal sat very still, looking back at her, as if it wanted to tell her something. She dismissed the thought as supernatural nonsense, but a shiver threaded its way up her spine as she gazed back at her watchful visitor. The owl blinked once, its long lids closing over the large, perfectly round eyes, so dark she couldn't make out the pupils.

She remembered a quote from John Ruskin: "Whatever wise people may say of them, I at least have found the owl's cry always prophetic of mischief to me." There had been so much mischief already, she thought—what more could the owl portend? Was he there to warn her that she was in danger?

Her right leg began to cramp, and she rose to stretch it. As she did, the bird spread its long wings and took flight. She watched it swoop toward the River Ouse, a silent hunter, approaching its prey so quietly that the unsuspecting animal would be unaware of the owl's presence until it was too late. She remembered her mother telling her that the bird's ability came from its small body and large wings, as well as its extremely soft feathers and special sound-dampening wing design. Her mother had imbued Erin with a love of nature and science—her father was more bookish, most content in his study with his feet up on the grate. If it weren't for her mother, he would rarely have left his office overlooking Oxford's High Street. Now that she was gone, it fell to Erin to pry him from his beloved books and manuscripts.

As she watched the owl disappear behind low-hanging clouds over the river, Erin wondered what enabled this predator to sneak up on his victims. What made his flight so silent, the strike so deadly? Judith Eton had no visible defensive wounds, which meant her attacker would have pounced as quickly as an owl on an unlucky vole, its talons closing around the animal's neck before it had a chance to cry out. Judith's neck had been pierced with deadly precision by something long and thin, by the look of the entrance wound—not a talon, of course, but what?

She wished she could discuss it with Farnsworth, but her lips were sealed, at least for now. She glanced at the blue-striped teapot and matching mugs, drying on the coffee service area over the mini fridge. Over it was a little cupboard well equipped with napkins, a set of small plates, bowls, and silverware. *Almost like a miniature kitchen . . .* an image floated into her head, of an item that would certainly be in a well-stocked restaurant kitchen.

Throwing on her cardigan, Erin grabbed her key card and left the room, hurrying down the hall without looking back.

Chapter Forty-One

～

When Erin reached the first floor it was clear word had gotten around about the police presence in the hotel. A small crowd had gathered in the lobby; some clustered in groups, talking softly, while others stood, arms crossed, staring out at the lineup of police vehicles. Behind Hemming's Citroen were a couple of yellow and white police cars, the white crime scene van, and behind that, an ambulance. Erin's stomach tightened when she saw the ambulance. She hoped to avoid Shanise. She knew the medic didn't like her, but Erin was also angry at being ratted out, and wanted to avoid the temptation to confront her. She imagined the city of York had enough EMT workers that someone else was probably on duty, but she scurried through the lobby, just in case.

As she entered the dining room, Erin realized she hadn't eaten a proper meal all day, and the buttery smell of simmering soup made her mouth swim with saliva. The lunch service was over, which Erin saw as an excuse for poking around. The wait staff was nowhere to be seen, and she slipped through the swinging door into the large, well-equipped kitchen. A couple of young men wearing rubber aprons were rinsing dirty plates and loading them into the large stainless steel dishwasher at the far end of the room, with more dirty dishes lined up on the conveyor belt.

On the other side of a center island, gleaming pots and pans hanging from its racks, a young man in a white apron and matching cap over a mass of ginger curls was chopping herbs on a wooden cutting board. He looked up as Erin entered.

"Can I help you, Miss?"

"I missed the lunch service," she said, her eyes roaming the room. "Would it be possible to get a bowl of soup?"

He put down his knife as a brisk, middle-aged blonde woman in a chef's hat entered from the pantry.

"What is it, Billy?" she said in response to his look, not seeing Erin.

"She asked if she could have some soup," he said, indicating Erin.

The woman bent down and gazed at her through the gap between the counter and the hanging pans.

"I don't see why not. Fancy some cream of broccoli?"

"Brilliant, thank you."

"I'll fetch it," said Billy, going to the pot simmering on a large gas stove next to an industrial double sink. On the other side of the stove, Erin saw what she was looking for—a stoneware crock containing several dozen long metal skewers.

"Mind if I ask a question?" Erin asked the chef.

"How do we feed so many people from this kitchen?" she said, coming around to Erin's side of the island. Her name tag identified her as Constance Moore.

"Well, that's massively impressive, obviously. But I was wondering if you were missing any skewers," she said, pointing to the stoneware crock on the counter.

"Why?"

Erin realized she had no ready lie prepared. "I may have seen one in one of the meeting rooms. Don't know how it go there, but—"

Constance Moore laughed. "You wouldn't believe what disappears from this kitchen, and the strange places where things turn up."

"So are you missing one?"

"I don't keep track of how many we have at any given time—do you know, Billy?"

"Sorry, no, Chef," he said, bringing Erin her soup. "Would you like it to go, Miss?"

"Yes, please, if you don't mind."

He poured the soup into a lined cardboard container and put that in a paper bag. "Crackers?"

"Lovely, thanks. What about ice picks?" she asked. "How many of those do you have?"

"Two."

"Either of them missing—"

"Both accounted for," said the chef. "You're with the conference, aren't you?"

"Yes, I'm one of the organizers."

"Why all the questions?"

"Well," Erin said, stalling for time. "The fact is—"

"What's goin' on with all the coppers runnin' around?" said Billy, handing her the bag of soup and crackers.

"I can't really say," said Erin. Technically, it was the truth, as she had promised Hemming to remain silent.

"Is that what all these questions are about?" asked Chef Moore.

"The police have asked me not to divulge anything at this time."

"Strange, innit?" said Billy. "I mean—"

"You have a lot of prep work," the chef told him. "You'd best get back to it."

"Yes, Chef," Billy said, scurrying back to his post.

"I'll get out of your hair. Thank you so much for the soup," said Erin. "You and your team are doing brilliant work. Your trout almondine is a spiritual experience."

"Kind of you to say so," Constance Moore said, pulling an enormous slab of pork ribs from the refrigerator.

"Mind if I ask just one more thing?"

"Fire away," she said, hacking at the ribs with a meat cleaver. Her blows were skillful and perfectly aimed, and Erin couldn't help thinking what a lethal killer the chef would make, as she sliced off ribs with surgical precision.

"I was wondering if you—or any of your staff—saw anyone in the kitchen in the last twelve hours or so. I mean, someone who didn't belong."

"I can't say that I did," she replied, setting aside the butchered meat before starting on another slab. "Who did you have in mind?"

"Maybe one of the guests, or—"

"Hang on a minute," said Billy, putting down his knife. "I saw someone in 'ere last night. A woman, it was."

"Can you describe her?"

"That's easy enough. She was pure dead gorgeous—red lips, hair black as night. Looked like a model or somethin'. A bit on the skinny side, but—"

"Did you speak with her?"

"I asked her what she wanted, an' she said she'd lost an earring, wondered if I mighta found it. Struck me as odd, but I was in no hurry for her to leave. She seemed antsy, though, an' didn't say much else."

"What time was this?"

"Round about midnight."

"Look," Chef Moore said to Erin, "not to be rude, but we have work to do."

"I promise this is the last question."

"And what is all this about?" the chef said, frowning.

"Is it to do with all the coppers swarmin' around?" asked Billy.

"Not really," said Erin. "It's . . . Society business. So is there anything else you noticed about her?"

"Yeah—she had an accent a' some sort. Not sure what—sounded Polish or somethin'."

"Thank you," said Erin. "You've been very helpful."

"So what's she done?" Billy asked.

"That's enough, Billy—back to work," said Chef Moore.

"I very much appreciate your time," said Erin, and clutching her now soggy bag of soup, fled the kitchen.

There was little doubt the person Billy described as being in the kitchen around midnight was Luca Wolf. The question was, what was she doing there?

Chapter Forty-Two

Luca Wolf twisted a strand of smooth dark hair between her fingers. "I was hungry," she said in a sulky voice. They were seated in the parlor of her hotel suite, the fanciest the Grand had to offer, which, as their Guest of Honor, the Society had reserved for Barry Wolf. Luca was relaxing in an overstuffed armchair, clad in a thick white bathrobe, the hotel's name monogrammed in gold on the lapel. Her slim legs rested on a matching footstool, her freshly polished toenails the color of bright-red holly berries. Erin didn't blame her for sticking around after her husband's death—the luxurious surroundings included a massive bouquet of flowers in a cut-glass vase, velvet curtains, and an eighteenth-century French armoire.

Though Judith's body had finally been removed, the room was still cordoned off with yellow crime scene tape, and no one at the hotel could talk of anything else. Hetty and Prudence had notified Society members of her death via email, though at the request of Detective Hemming, no mention was made of how she had died. The keynote presentation for the evening had obviously been canceled, and conference members were informed there would be further updates as more was known. Erin's phone had started ringing minutes after they sent the email, until she finally turned it off. She took the stairs from her room to avoid running into conference attendees who, understandably, would be full of questions.

"Is it crime to be hungry?" Luca said, a pout on her pretty face.

"If you were hungry, why not take something from the mini-bar?" said Erin.

"Too expensive," she said, flipping the corner of her terrycloth robe over her tanned ankles. Erin wondered how she had a tan in the middle of an English winter. "I don't know what Barry left me in his will—maybe nothing. I have to be careful."

"There's a vending machine."

She made a face. "All junk."

"If you were so hungry, why not ask Billy for something to eat while you were in the kitchen?"

"He make me uncomfortable."

"So you left hungry."

Luca shrugged. "I got crisps from vending machine."

"Then what?"

"I went to bed."

"So you didn't steal a skewer from the kitchen and stab Judith Eton?" Erin said it just to watch her reaction. She had to hand it to Luca. If she was guilty, she managed to look appropriately shocked.

"Of course not!" she sputtered. "What are you talking about—did someone stab Judith?"

"Didn't your brother tell you?"

"No. I haven't seen him since breakfast."

"You didn't read our email?"

"I just wake up from nap. What has happened?"

Erin told her of Judith's demise, without mentioning details, but it was too late—she had spilled the beans, and Luca knew it.

"So she was stabbed? With a skewer?"

"No one knows how she died," Erin said, feeling foolish.

"You just ask me if I stab her."

"I was just fishing. I don't know how she died."

"But she was murdered?"

"I honestly can't say," Erin said, but knew Luca saw through her.

"She was—otherwise you wouldn't ask me that question."

"Look," Erin said, her palms beginning to sweat. "Just forget what I said, all right?"

"How can I forget when you accuse me of murder?"

"I didn't—I just had to be sure." Erin was keenly aware she was losing, and that the power had shifted to Luca. "Look," she said, feeling sweat prickle on her neck, even though the room was cool. "I would really appreciate it if you didn't repeat this conversation to anyone."

Luca studied her, and Erin sensed something coolly predatory in that gaze. Maybe Luca's protests were the reaction of a very clever and collected killer.

"Why are you afraid of what I might say?" said Luca.

Erin decided to bare her throat. "Because I promised the police I wouldn't say anything."

"How is it you—oh, you discovered body, didn't you?" said Luca with a triumphant little smile.

"Yes. I did."

"And they don't want the public to know details—like police shows on the television."

"Right. So do you think you can—"

"Don't worry," Luca said. "I grew up in Hungary—I am good at keeping secrets. And I did not like that Judith Eton. I am sorry she was killed, but she was not nice person to me or my brother."

"Really? How so?"

"She made us feel we were hired help. Treated us like servants. Barry noticed but never said anything." She pulled an emery board from her pocket and swiped at her fingernails. "He was a—what is it you British say? A wanker. Do they think this person also killed Barry?"

"They're not convinced he was murdered."

Luca put down her emery board. "But you are?"

"I think there's a good chance. Did he see a lot of his ex-wife?"

"No. But she brought their son over sometimes."

"Can you think of anyone who might want to harm Judith?"

"Not especially. I didn't know that many people. I think Barry wanted it that way." She stretched and yawned. "And now, if you don't mind, I have appointment at spa."

"Thanks for your time," Erin said, rising.

"I hope they catch this person. Barry was not good person, but no one deserves to die like that."

As she left the expensive suite, Erin had to agree. No matter who or what Barry Wolf had been in life, he did not deserve the fate that she increasingly believed had befallen him.

The minute she entered the hallway, Erin nearly ran into Sergeant Jarral.

"Sorry," he said, stepping out of her way. He seemed to be in a great hurry, and she decided to follow him. She didn't have far to go. At the end of the corridor, near the fire exit, a room door opened and Detective Hemming emerged with Winnifred Hogsworthy in handcuffs.

"Anything you say may be given in evidence," he was saying as he led Winnie down the hall.

He was in such a hurry to arrest her that he was still reading Winnie her rights, Erin thought as they came toward her.

"What's going on?" Erin asked. "Why are you arresting Winnie?" she demanded when Hemming didn't answer.

"We'll be giving a statement later this afternoon," he said, avoiding eye contact as they passed.

"Winnie—?" Erin called out. "What's going on?"

She twisted around to face Erin, her face a mask of sheer panic. "I didn't do it!"

"Why do they think you're guilty?" Erin asked, following after them.

"They found one of my knitting needles in the room—they think it's the murder weapon!"

"Please let us do our job," Hemming told Erin as Sergeant Jarral rang for the lift.

"Where did they find it?" Erin asked, ignoring him.

"Under the bed," Winnie said. "They claim it was covered in blood. I didn't do it!"

"We'll be releasing a statement at five o'clock," Hemming said as he and Jarral escorted Winnie onto the lift.

Erin watched as the doors closed behind them. She felt bad for Hemming—she knew from his gray pallor and beads of sweat on his forehead that he wasn't well. But she also knew someone had planted evidence against Winnifred Hogsworthy. Erin had looked carefully under Judith's bed, and saw no knitting needle, bloody or otherwise. The problem was, if she told the police, it was an admission she had snooped around before calling them—either that, or she was implicating herself as the murderer.

Chapter Forty-Three

～

"Is it true they arrested Winnie Hogsworthy?" Hetty Miller said breathlessly, rushing into the dining room. The members of the North Yorkshire Branch of the Society were meeting over dinner that evening to discuss how to proceed after Judith's sudden death.

"It's true, pet," Farnsworth said, spearing a pat of butter with her fork. "Pass the bread, please." Judith's death did not seem to have affected her appetite.

"Why?" asked Jonathan, handing her the basket of fresh, yeasty rolls. "What do they have on her?"

Erin was silent. This was no time to involve other Society members in what was, at best, a highly charged situation. Anyone she told could immediately be put in danger.

"Do you know?" Farnsworth asked her.

"I'm as confused as you are," she replied, which was the truth.

"I heard they're to release a statement soon," said Hetty, glancing at her phone. "I keep checking their Twitter feed but haven't seen anything." Hetty was quite the devotee of social media—she was responsible for the branch's online presence, and Erin had to admit she did a brilliant job. Her posts were witty and informative, which made Prudence quite jealous. Erin thought Pru was also secretly proud of her friend, though she would never admit it.

"What are we going to do going forward?" said Jonathan. He tended to sprinkle his conversation with phrases like "empower," "pivot," and "going forward," which Erin attributed to the administrators in the public schools where he taught.

"What I'm hearing is that people don't want to cancel the ball tomorrow," Pru said, taking a large bite of linguine primavera. "There seems to be a general opinion that Judith would want us to carry on."

"How strange," said Jonathan. "Why would anyone—"

"Her son actually asked us to hold the ball," said Hetty, picking at a plate of crudités next to the bread basket. She and Erin had ordered the trout, which hadn't yet arrived. "He claimed his mother would want us to."

"Doesn't that strike you as odd?" asked Farnsworth, reaching for the pinot grigio. She had ordered a bottle each of red and white for the table. Unlike the parsimonious Prudence, and Hetty, who was always dieting, Farnsworth was all about abundance, one of the many things Erin loved about her.

"Grief strikes people in strange ways," said Prudence as the server arrived with the fish entrées.

"How's your head, dearie?" Hetty asked Erin.

"Better, thanks," she said, gazing longingly at the Shiraz. She still had a bit of a headache, and thought it best to abstain until she was entirely recovered.

Prudence plucked a piece of broccoli from her plate. "Those who do not complain are never pitied." Erin recognized it as an Austen quote, though she couldn't place it.

Hetty put down her stick of celery. "Why on earth would anyone want to be pitied?"

"I'm just saying," Prudence replied, wrinkling her nose as she sniffed at a carrot. With her dull brown hair and scruffy beige cardigan, she reminded Erin of a small burrowing animal.

"I did have an interesting sighting, though," said Erin, inhaling the scent of almonds, lemon, and butter emanating from her plate. The trout was as exquisite as ever, she thought as she took bite of the tender white flesh.

"Did it involve your sexy detective, shirtless maybe?" asked Hetty.

Everyone laughed except Jonathan, who pretended not to hear. Seizing the bottle of Shiraz, he poured himself a rather reckless amount.

"It was an owl, actually," Erin said. "Perched in the yew tree outside my window."

"That's very portentous," came a deep voice behind her.

Erin turned to see Grant Apthorp hobbling toward them, leaning heavily on a cane. His bandaged right foot was clad in a hotel slipper.

"The dead have arisen!" Farnsworth exclaimed, her cheeks flushed from more than just the wine.

"Please join us," said Jonathan, rising to fetch an extra chair.

"Your poor foot," said Hetty, clucking her tongue. "Does it hurt much, dearie?"

"Not nearly as much as two days ago," he said, lowering gingerly into the chair Jonathan provided, next to Farnsworth.

"We've missed you," she said, passing him a menu.

"You did not want to be around me during the worst of this, I can promise you that," he said, taking it.

"Oh, surely you're exaggerating," said Prudence, a blush creeping up the yellowish skin of her face. Even she seemed enlivened by Grant's presence.

"Pru is right," Hetty said. "You are always delightful."

"If you enjoy the company of a very irritable and hungry bear just coming out of hibernation," Grant said.

"Didn't you want someone to comfort you in your misery?" asked Prudence.

"Men are different, pet," said Farnsworth, reaching for the pinot grigio. "They prefer to suffer in silence."

"Is that true?" Hetty asked Jonathan.

"I can't speak for other men," he said. "But I generally don't enjoy being around other people when I'm not feeling well."

"You see?" Farnsworth said smugly. "Just as I said."

"Two people hardly comprise a scientifically supportable conclusion," Prudence remarked.

"Call it a representative sample," said Erin. "My father is the same way. Best to leave him alone when he's under the weather."

"Your father's a clergyman, isn't he?" Grant asked.

"Yes, in Oxford."

"He's a veritable fount of information," said Farnsworth. "Knows everyone in Oxford."

"Oh? What kind of information?" said Grant.

"For her *investigation*," Hetty whispered. "You know, into the *murders*."

"It sounds to me like the police have everything well in hand," he said as the waiter approached their table.

"You must be so devastated about Judith," said Prudence. "I mean, you and she go back so far."

"Yes," Grant replied sadly. "It hardly seems real. I'll have the salmon," he said to the server, who stood waiting patiently, his weight on one hip.

"Yes, Sir," he said. He was new, maybe Sam's replacement, Erin thought glumly. "Is everyone else all right?"

"Yes, thank you," said Jonathan.

"Everything is lovely," Farnsworth added.

"If you ask me, the coppers jumped to a conclusion awfully quickly," said Hetty. "I mean, aren't they meant to interview people?"

"They interviewed me," said Prudence.

"And me as well," said Farnsworth.

"What about you, Erin?" asked Hetty. "Did they speak with you?"

"Yes," she replied, hoping no one would press for details. She exchanged a glance with Farnsworth; only she knew Erin had discovered the body, and Erin intended to keep it that way.

"What about you?" Hetty asked Jonathan. "Did they interview you?"

"I don't know that you could call it an interview, but yes, they did reach out to me," he said, taking a bite of rocket salad. Erin shuddered at the sight of the dark green leaves. Normally she loved its bitter taste, but hadn't ordered rocket salad since then Barry Wolf's death.

All eyes turned toward Terrence Rogers as he entered the dining room. He was nattily dressed as usual, in a burgundy dinner jacket and matching bow tie, but he looked haunted. His whole body slumped forward, his shoulders narrowed inward, and his remarkably youthful face looked a decade older. His red-rimmed eyes darted around the room, as if unable to focus, and fine lines in his face, nearly invisible before, had deepened. He was the very picture of walking grief.

Studying him as he was escorted to a table, Erin couldn't help wondering if it was all an act to divert suspicion away from himself. Was he the one who had pointed the police toward Winnie—had he planted the knitting needle during the time Erin was away from the room? Anyone could have gotten into the room during that time; she had left the door ajar, just as she found it.

Shortly after Terrence was seated, Jeremy Wolf entered the room. He too looked as if he been crying, but by no means as devastated as Terrence. He nodded at Erin's table as he passed; she caught his eye and nodded back.

"Do you think we should speak to him?" Hetty said as he walked away.

"Best leave him be for now, don't you think?" said Grant.

"Poor boy," said Hetty. "Lost his mother and his father in the same week."

If Barry Wolf was really his father, Erin thought.

The sound of raised voices made them all turn and look at the back of the room, where Jeremy was standing over Terrence, talking so loudly everyone in the restaurant could hear.

"It's all your fault!" Jeremy shouted at him. "You convinced her to come to this bloody conference!"

"I did nothing of the sort," Terrence replied. "She came of her own free will."

"That's bloody nonsense and you know it!"

Terrence looked around nervously. "You're making a scene. Everyone can hear you."

"Let them, then! I'm sick and tired of secrets!"

"Jeremy, please—" Terrence said, rising and taking the boy's elbow.

"Don't you touch me!" Jeremy said, pulling away.

By that time, the beefy security guard had reached them, covering the length of the restaurant so quickly it looked as if he was on wheels. Swooping down on Jeremy, he clapped a heavy hand on the young man's shoulder.

"Come along, now, laddie," he said softly, but there was no mistaking the implied threat in his voice.

"I'm not going anywhere!" Jeremy said, pulling away.

The guard grabbed both of his wrists, pinning them behind his back in one swift movement, so quickly Jeremy had no time to react.

"Ow!" he said. "Loosen up, will you?"

"You can either come now quietly, or I can remove you by force. Your choice, mate."

"Let me go," Jeremy said between clenched teeth.

"You going to behave?"

"All *right*. Just don't *touch* me!"

The guard released his hold slowly, and Jeremy complied. Head down, he shuffled out of the room, with his escort right behind him.

"*That* was interesting," Hetty remarked when they had gone.

"Poor Terrence," said Farnsworth.

"I wonder what that was all about?" Prudence mused.

"Emotions are running high," said Jonathan. "You can hardly blame the lad for being upset."

"But why take it out on poor Terrence?" asked Hetty.

Erin had an idea of why, but remained silent. Glancing over at Terrence Rogers, she saw him rise from his table and signal for the check.

Erin yawned. "I'm knackered. I think I'll turn in," she said, signaling for the bill.

She finished paying it just in time to follow Terrence Rogers as he left the restaurant.

"Professor Rogers," said she, catching up with him in the hall.

"Oh, please call me Terrence," he said. All the vinegar had drained from his personality; he seemed meek, defeated. "How's your head? I heard you got a bit banged up."

"Better, thanks," she said, wondering how much he knew. But only she, Farnsworth, and Khari knew what actually happened—apart from whoever had tried to kill her.

And Detective Hemming, of course. She wondered what he was up to now—and whether he believed her now that a multiple murderer was roaming the York Grand Hotel.

Chapter Forty-Four

❧

"You know," said Terrence. "I don't much fancy being alone just now. How about a nightcap?"

"Why not?" she said, and they turned their steps toward the 1906 Bar.

The bar was quiet; a few conference members had gathered in front of the fire, and everyone looked up when Erin and Terrence entered. They chose a table by the window, far enough away so the group at the fireplace couldn't hear them.

"You didn't seem to have much appetite tonight," Erin said as Terrence brought their drinks to the table. Spike was on duty, and it was hard to resist one of his signature cocktails, but she avoided temptation and ordered a macchiato. Terrence was apparently a gin man—the aroma of juniper berries was unmistakable, and four fat olives swam at the bottom of his glass. Martini on the rocks with extra olives, she thought, a drink her father might have ordered— very dry. And definitely stirred, not shaken. She remembered his verdict on Ian Fleming's notion of how to prepare a cocktail: "Fine, if what you want is a watery, weak martini."

Terrence leaned back in his chair and rubbed his temples. "I'm just utterly gutted by what happened . . . good Lord, poor Judith."

"Were you and Judith close?"

"Not really, but we shared . . . a past. I heard they arrested Miss Hogsworthy."

"I heard the same thing."

"Good lord." He shook his head. "Still waters run deep. Never would have thought her capable of that."

"You knew her at school, I believe?"

"Yes."

"And she was suspected of vandalizing your office."

"No one ever proved she did it. I never believed it was her."

"So you and Grant and Barry and Judith were all at school together?"

He took a long drink from his glass before answering. "Why are you so interested?"

"You just don't seem very close anymore."

"I'm not best mates with everyone I was at uni with."

"But you worked on the literary magazine together."

"How do you know all this?"

"I saw the picture in your yearbook."

"Why on earth were you looking at our school yearbook?"

"Barry Wolf was our guest of honor. You and Grant Apthorp are conference VIPs. I was doing my homework." To her relief, he didn't question this.

"That was all donkey's years ago," he said, staring off in the distance.

"The three of you look pretty chummy in the photo."

"I suppose we were."

"What happened? I hope you don't think I'm being too intrusive," she added quickly.

"You are. But I've got nothing much on my plate tonight," he said with a wry smile. "It's a fairly long story—I hope you don't have somewhere you have to be."

"Only bed. But that can wait."

"It's late," he said, sipping his drink. "I'll give you the shortened version. Fancy another coffee?"

"Thanks, but I'd be up all night."

"I don't imagine I'll sleep much myself. But the basic story is that Barry is—was—a real piece of work, something that only became clear to me much later, sadly."

"What do you mean?"

"Oh, I knew he was a bit dodgy, you know—not above cheating on the odd exam, that sort of thing. I didn't approve, but I thought loyalty was one of his virtues. It wasn't until later I discovered it was all a front. He was all style and no substance."

"What do you mean?"

"I wondered for years why I didn't get a teaching post at Oxford. After all, I graduated summa cum laude with a double first," he said, swirling the remaining ice cubes in his glass.

"But you didn't?"

"I didn't even make it as far as the interview. Which seemed odd, since Barry had been there two years and could put in a good word for me."

"So what happened?"

"I'll never know exactly, but I learned later that Barry Wolf wouldn't lift a finger for anyone unless there was something in it for him."

"Including you getting a teaching post at Oxford?"

"Apparently."

"That must have made you angry."

He popped the remaining ice into his mouth, chewing it. "That would be a fair statement."

"Angry enough to kill him?"

"If I had, do you think I'd tell you all this?"

"You said you learned later that Barry—"

"Last call, ladies and gentlemen," Spike called from the bar.

"Sure you don't fancy another?" Terrence said.

"No, I—oh," Erin said, as the right side of her forehead began to throb.

"What's wrong? Is it your head?"

"Yeah," she said, rubbing her temples.

"You must get to bed," he said. "I shouldn't have kept you up."

"I'll be all right."

"I know a little something about head injuries," Terrence said, rising. "Come along. I'll see you to your room."

Erin knew he was right. Her curiosity had gotten the better of her. She had ignored her fatigue, and now she was paying. She was still full of questions, but followed him meekly out of the bar, and didn't object when he gently took her elbow, escorting her down the corridor to the lift. As he walked her through the quiet halls to her room, it occurred to Erin that if he was the killer, she would be utterly at his mercy.

Chapter Forty-Five

But, for whatever reason, Terrence Rogers behaved like a perfect gentleman, making sure she got into her room before turning to head back down the hall. She watched him until he was halfway down the long corridor, half afraid he would turn and charge toward her, a murderous expression on his face. But when he did not even look back in her direction, she closed the door softly behind her, slid the safety bolt over the lock, and exhaled deeply.

After taking two paracetamol, she slipped on her pajamas and slid between the sheets with a sigh of deep contentment. Nothing—but nothing—she thought, had ever felt better than the clean cotton sheets and soft, yielding mattress of her bed in her attic room at the York Grand Hotel. The last thing she remembered was thinking she should turn off the bathroom light, but before she could act on the impulse, sleep claimed her.

She awoke to bright sunshine streaming through her windows. Cursing herself for forgetting to close the drapes the night before, she crawled out of bed and stumbled over to the windows, closing the curtains just as her mobile phone beeped, indicating there was a text message. She peered bleary-eyed at the bedside clock. The red numerals on its screen proclaimed it to be just short of seven AM.

"Sod off," she muttered. Grabbing her phone, she was about to turn it off and bury it in the drawer next to her bed, but curiosity got the better of her. She glanced at the screen, and was surprised to see the text was from "P. Hemming." She clicked on it with trembling fingers.

Tox screen back—aconitine poisoning. Score one for you. Please keep it to yourself!!

"Told you," she mumbled. "Triple murderer." Said out loud, the words sounded harsh, unreal. *Triple murderer.* Technically, that meant they were dealing with a serial killer. The manner of Sam's death wasn't official yet, though—or if it was, no one had told her. Wide awake now, she gripped the phone in both hands and texted a reply.

What about Sam Buchanan's Manner of Death?

She sat on the edge of the bed, the phone next to her, gnawing on her fingernails as she awaited his reply. Her phone dinged and she snatched it up eagerly.

That's not official yet

Was the hyoid bone intact?

She knew fracture of the tiny, U-shaped bone in the throat was highly unlikely in a suicide hanging, but common in strangulation. When there was no reply, she texted him again.

Please? Promise I won't tell anyone. Girl Guide's honor.

Again she awaited his reply. "Come on, come on," she murmured, pacing back and forth in front of the windows, her palms sweating so much she had to put the phone down. Finally her phone beeped. Her breath shallow, she stared at his reply.

Hyoid fractured

"Yes!" she said, her momentary feeling of triumph followed by sadness, then fear. What were the chances little Winnifred Hogsworthy was capable of strangling the wiry young Sam Buchanan? Cases of women strangling men were not unknown, but they were rare, and would likely involve the man being incapacitated in some way—injury, drugs, alcohol, or some form of disability. She had an impulse to text Hemming back, but he had to be thinking the same thing she was: If they had the wrong person in custody, the killer was still at large.

Chapter Forty-Six

After dressing hastily, Erin went down to the dining room, where she saw Khari Butari sitting at a table by the window. Seeing Erin, she waved.

"Good morning," she said when Erin approached. "You look tired. How's your head?"

"All things considered, could be worse."

"Care to join me?"

"Sure, thanks," Erin said, sitting with her back to the window so she could watch the room.

"Coffee?" Khari said, picking up the gleaming metal pot from the table.

"Yes, please," Erin said, watching as Khari filled her cup with the steaming liquid, pausing to inhale the rich dark smell before drinking. The first sip of coffee always tasted so good that she liked to prolong the moment, savoring the anticipation nearly as much as the coffee itself.

"I'm totally gobsmacked about Judith," Khari said, shaking her head as she filled her own cup. "I really liked her."

"I know," said Erin. "Losing someone is hard enough, but murder . . . it's a whole new dimension of horror."

"And Winnie—good lord! Do you think she did it?"

"The police seem to think so."

"But Winnie? She just doesn't seem the type."

"One thing I've learned is that anyone is capable of anything."

"It seems so odd that we're going ahead with the ball tonight. I heard her son wanted us to hold it to honor her memory."

"And the police have asked us not to leave, so what else are we going to do?" Erin said as Charles Kilroy entered the room. He wasn't dressed in his usual safari gear—he had ditched the leather vest and hat. His khaki shirt and cargo pants still gave the impression of someone about to head into the Outback, even though Charles looked as if he would be more comfortable in a library cubicle than in front of a campfire.

Seeing the two women, he approached them hesitantly. "Good morning, ladies. I don't mean to intrude—"

"Not at all," said Khari. "Why don't you join us?"

"I don't want to impose—"

Khari smiled, showing brilliant white teeth. "You are a fan of our work, are you not?"

"Well, yes, but—"

"Then by all means, please sit."

"That's very kind of you."

"Not at all—maybe we just like our egos massaged."

"Or maybe we just enjoy your company," Erin added quickly. In spite of his intellectual bravado, she thought, Charles was rather shy and insecure.

"Terrible news, isn't it?" he said, sitting across from the two women. "Shocking, just shocking."

"Yes," Erin agreed.

"I mean, one doesn't ever expect someone you know will be murdered."

"Least of all by someone else you know," Khari said, handing him the bread basket.

"I can't imagine," he said, taking an almond scone. "Do we know why they arrested Winnie?"

"I heard something about evidence found in the room," said Khari.

"What kind of evidence?"

"I don't know."

"Maybe something belonging to Winnie," he said, buttering the scone. "Or fingerprints."

"Maybe DNA."

"Couldn't be that," said Erin. "It takes too long to analyze. When did you say you and Barry first met?" she asked Charles.

"Let's see . . . a literary convention about two years ago, I think. In Edinburgh. Or was it Glasgow? I've been to conventions in both of them. No, it was Glasgow—I ran into him at the Willow Tea Room."

"That was the first time?" asked Erin.

"Yes—why?"

"Just wondering."

"I live in London," Charles said. "He lives in Oxford. Why would our paths have crossed?"

"Let's order," Khari said as their server approached the table. "I'm starving." After refilling their coffee, she took their orders. Erin and Charles ordered the eggs Benedict, while Khari opted for eggs Sardou.

"That's an unusual brooch," Erin said, pointing to the lapel pin Charles wore on his khaki jacket. It consisted of a large amber stone lined in silver, crafted in the shape of a seahorse.

"Tiger's eye, isn't it?" said Khari, studying it.

"Yes."

"To help you ward off the evil eye?"

"It belonged to my sister," he answered softly. "I wear it in her memory."

"Oh," Erin said. "I'm so sorry. What was her name?"

"Sarah. It was many years ago."

"It is right that you honor her," said Khari. "It is wrong for someone to just disappear from the earth without memory."

"It keeps her near to me," he said, his voice thick. Clearing his throat, he reached for the coffee pot. "Right, then," he said in the best tradition of British forced cheeriness. "Who's for more coffee?"

Later, back in her room, Erin flipped open her laptop and typed "Sarah Kilroy" into the search bar. She scrolled past an Instagram account belonging to a pretty, dark-skinned teenager, and skipped past several other links, including the profile of a psychology professor on LinkedIn. Finally, at the bottom of the page, she saw the article: "Suicide of Oxford Student Raises Alarm on Campus." Her breathing became shallow as she scrolled down, looking for Barry's name. It did not appear, but when she was identified as a "first year comparative literature student at Trinity," Erin leaned back in her chair. What were the chances she *didn't* come across Barry Wolf at some point? She devoured the article, which coyly omitted certain information, like how she died, who found her, and so on.

She reached for her mobile and pressed the first number on her Favorites list. He answered on the second ring.

"Hi, Dad."

"Hello, Pumpkin. I wondered when you'd call."

"Don't tell me you were sitting by the phone waiting for it to ring."

"Tragically, I have no life."

"If you were any busier, you'd need an extra set of hands."

"What a good idea. Remind me to call the plastic surgeon tomorrow. Now, how can I help?"

"Do you remember a Trinity student named Sarah Kilroy?"

"Yes—tragic story. What about her?"

"What can you tell me?"

"I never knew her, but by all accounts she was quite gifted but troubled. She killed herself at the end of her first year."

"Was there an inquest?"

"Yes. The verdict was suicide."

"How did she die?"

"I think she hanged herself. It was about ten years ago, as I recall."

"Nine, actually. Do you know if she studied with Barry Wolf?"

"I can ask around."

"Thanks, Dad—you're a dear."

"So you're still at that hotel?"

"Yes. Oh, almost forgot to tell you—there's been another murder."

"What?" His voice rose an octave.

"Sorry, Dad, gotta go—I'll call you later."

"You stay out of trouble—" he began, but she rang off, turning off her phone just in case he tried to call back. She didn't need her father nattering at her about staying safe. She had work to do.

Chapter Forty-Seven

~

When Erin knocked on Farnsworth's door, she heard voices on the other side. One was Farnsworth's—the other was a man's voice, and she had a pretty good idea who it belonged to.

"Hello?" Farnsworth called from inside the room.

"It's me. I can come back later."

She heard the sound of the safety bolt sliding off, and the door swung open.

"Hello, pet." Farnsworth was clad in a pale-yellow silk kimono with blue and pink peacock feathers—a Christmas gift from Erin.

"I don't want to interrupt anything," Erin said, trying to peer around her shoulder.

"Nonsense," Farnsworth said, holding the door open. "Nothing to interrupt. Come in."

Erin entered the sitting room to see Grant Apthorp stretched out in an armchair, his bandaged foot resting on the matching leather hassock.

"Hello," he said, struggling to rise.

"Please don't get up. How's your foot?"

"Better, thanks."

"He thinks he's going to be ready for the ball tonight," Farnsworth said with a sigh, but her expression was more admiring than disapproving.

"How's your head?" Grant asked Erin.

"Better, thanks."

Farnsworth took a pile of clothes off another of the chairs and tossed them on the back of the couch. Even in a hotel room, she was not the tidiest person—her belongings had a tendency to spread out like weeds in a garden, until there were few clear surfaces left.

"Now that you're both so much *better*," she said, escorting Erin to the chair, "why don't you rest so you don't get worse?"

"Is she always like this?" Grant asked Erin. "A compulsive mother hen?"

"*She* can speak for herself," said Farnsworth. "And no, she is not always like this. Sometimes she is needy and vulnerable. But when some people aren't good at looking after themselves, she will step in and do the job."

Grant raised his hands in surrender. "Message received. And I will avoid talking about you in the third person in the future."

"You and Judith go a way back, don't you?" said Erin.

"She was my research assistant during my graduate training. I still can't believe she's gone. I think I'm in shock about it. It feels so . . . surreal."

"I'm sorry for your loss."

"Jeremy's the one I feel bad for," he said. "He must be utterly gutted. I can't believe he wants us to have the dance."

"He thinks it will honor her memory, pet," Farnsworth said, switching on the electric kettle.

"Are you really going to the ball?" Erin asked.

"Absolutely, even if I end up just sitting on the sidelines."

"How do we know your gout attack wasn't just an excuse to avoid dancing?" said Farnsworth.

"Do you want to see my toe? It's still swollen."

"That won't be necessary," Farnsworth said, wrinkling her nose in disgust. "I believe you."

"I don't know if you'll believe me when I say I'm not a bad dancer, at least under normal circumstances."

"Which this certainly is not."

"Do the police have any new leads?" he asked Erin.

"If they do, they haven't told me."

"But they did arrest Winnie," said Farnsworth.

"They can only hold her for twenty-four hours without charging her with a crime."

"You mean they haven't charged her yet?" asked Grant.

"I don't know. They can apply to hold her longer for a serious crime like murder, but they have to get approval to hold her for longer than twenty-four hours."

"They must not think the crime is solved if they're keeping us all here," he remarked as Farnsworth busied herself making tea. She looked happy, Erin thought, in spite of all that had happened, and it was fairly obvious why. Her friend hadn't so much as dated anyone since Erin had known her, insisting she would never trust a man again, that she had no need for them. But now here she was bustling over a tea tray, arranging cups and saucers in a display of domesticity. With a man to fuss over, Erin saw a side of her friend she never realized existed, and it was touching to see how natural it seemed. Farnsworth wore her happiness like a well-made suit of clothes.

"Even if they're sure Winnie is guilty," Erin told Grant, "they still need to collect all the evidence they can."

"Which is where we come in," Farnsworth said, bringing over a brimming teapot and a plate of Scottish shortbread.

"You come prepared, don't you?" Grant said as she placed it all on the coffee table. "Were you a Girl Guide?"

"Me? No, pet—that was more Erin's thing. She's the outdoorsy one."

"Were you still at Oxford during the Sarah Kilroy incident?" Erin asked Grant.

"Was that the girl who—"

"Killed herself."

He shook his head. "No, I was gone by then, but I heard about it. It was a big story, even in Cardiff."

"Sarah Kilroy?" said Farnsworth, stirring the pot. "Any relation—"

"His younger sister," said Erin.

"Oh my God. Poor thing."

"Do you know if she was Barry's student?" Erin asked Grant.

"You think Barry had something to do with her death?"

"I'm just trying to follow a lead. It seems like too much of a coincidence."

"Erin doesn't believe in coincidences," Farnsworth said, handing him a cup of tea.

He stared out the window at the wintry landscape. Erin followed his gaze. The feeble sun was holding its pale head up just a little longer before sinking over the horizon of the ancient city, as it had during times of Roman legions, Viking invasions, and Norman conquests.

"You know something you're not telling me," she said. "Why would you want to protect him?"

Putting down his cup, Grant heaved a deep sigh. "Barry Wolf was a ruiner of women, in the nineteenth-century sense of that phrase. He seduced and destroyed them, a feat made possible only through his utter lack of conscience. He preyed on younger ones, and once he had them in his power, he could do whatever he liked. His instinct was unerring—he had a talent for sensing who was vulnerable, like a tiger choosing which gazelle to take down in a whole herd of them."

"Is that why Judith left him?" asked Farnsworth.

"One of many reasons, yes."

"So you think he might be responsible for Sarah Kilroy's suicide," said Erin.

"I wouldn't be surprised if he was involved in some way."

"If he was so terrible, why wasn't he booted out of the college?" said Farnsworth. "Or arrested?"

"This was all before the MeToo movement. It wasn't so easy to get rid of a tenured professor, especially when he's chairman of the department."

"It sounds like you hated him," said Erin.

Grant smiled. "It's impossible to hate a cypher. He wasn't really human—he was a ghost. Oh sure, he walked around breathing and eating and doing all the things people do, but he was a hollowed-out shell of a person."

"Except he didn't seem to know that," said Farnsworth.

"Ghosts seldom know they're ghosts. They think they're as solid as the rest of us, but they cast no shadow, no reflection in the mirror."

"Like vampires," said Erin.

"Barry Wolf *was* a vampire—he sucked the life out of people, and when he had drained them dry, moved on to find another victim."

"So do you have any actual information about Sarah's death, maybe something that wasn't in the paper?"

"Talk to her brother. He initiated an investigation of his own. Couldn't accept the police ruling that it was a suicide, and spent thousands trying to prove them wrong."

"But he never succeeded?"

Grant shook his head. "He couldn't convince them to change the ruling."

"How do you know all this?"

"I remained close to Judith after I left."

"But nothing romantic?"

"I was extremely fond of her, but there was never anything between us. Poor Judith," he said sadly. "She didn't deserve to die like this."

"No," Erin said. "Nobody does."

It seemed like such an obvious statement, and yet someone lurking in the corridors of this venerable building did not agree.

Chapter Forty-Eight

~

After tea, Grant returned to his room to take his gout medicine and have a nap. Erin stayed, ostensibly to help tidy up, but in reality she wanted to talk to Farnsworth alone.

"You two seem to be hitting it off," she said as she gathered up dirty cups and saucers.

"Oh, pet, you're so transparent." Farnsworth said, wiping off the coffee table. "Why don't you just come out and say it?"

"Say what?"

"Was I there for him, to comfort him in his loss?" Farnsworth said with a sly wink.

"Comfort him—what are you talking about?"

"It's all right, pet—you can ask. Did we, or didn't we?"

"No—oh God, no!" Erin said. "I wasn't—oh, no. No, no, no."

"Really?" Farnsworth looked disappointed. "You don't want to know?"

"No. I really, *really* don't. Please don't even think of telling me."

"But I thought—"

"What?"

"I thought we were friends."

"We are."

"Best friends."

"Right."

"Then why don't you want to know?" Farnsworth said, crestfallen.

"It's . . . intimate."

"So?"

"Between you and him."

Farnsworth threw herself on the couch, arms crossed. "What's the point of having a girlfriend if you can't talk girl things with her?"

"I just don't need to know every detail—"

"Never mind," Farnsworth said, turning away. "Clearly you're not interested."

"It's not—I'm sorry, I just don't . . ."

"What?"

"It'll make you angry."

"No it won't."

"Promise?"

Farnsworth held her hand up in a three-fingered salute. "Girl Guide's honor."

"You weren't a—"

"Just *tell* me, will you!"

"All right," Erin said reluctantly. "I . . . I'm just not sure this is a good time to get involved with someone."

"Oh, I see," Farnsworth said tightly.

"I mean, with all that's happened this week—"

"What's that got to do with anything?" Farnsworth said, grabbing a tea towel from next to the sink.

"We still don't know who the killer is."

"Surely you don't think Grant—"

"What do you know about him, really?"

Farnsworth put down the tea towel and glared at Erin. "You're jealous, aren't you?"

"No, I just—"

"You don't want me to have any fun."

"I *do*, I just don't want you to get hurt."

"I can look after myself, thank you very much," Farnsworth said, snapping the tea towel as she dried the clean dishes.

"Look, Farnsworth—"

"Since you were so anxious to give me advice, let me return the favor."

"I really don't—"

"You have a problem with intimacy."

"What are you—"

"You avoid emotional involvement with other people. Maybe it's because you lost your mother; I don't know. But whatever the reason, you keep a distance between yourself and people you're supposedly close to."

Erin picked up the tea caddy and began polishing it, just to have something to do. "There's a difference between intimacy and being intrusive, you know."

"Fine," said Farnsworth. "Forget I said anything. Thank you for your help, but I can take it from here. I have to take a shower and have a lie-down. Why you don't go hang out with Khari?"

"You know," Erin said, "Life is not like a Hallmark Christmas movie."

"How would you know?" Farnsworth snapped.

"You're right," Erin said. "I wouldn't."

Putting down the tea caddy, she left the room without looking back.

Chapter Forty-Nine

"Hello again," said her father.

"Hello," Erin said, staring at the ceiling. The water mark was beginning to feel like an old friend, she thought as she traced its faint yellow outline with her eyes.

"Something's wrong."

She sighed. This was virgin territory. They had avoided talking about the aftermath of her mother's death, and here she was bringing it up at a time like this. Suddenly she regretted making the call.

"What is it, Pumpkin?"

Dive in all at once, her mother always advised her when confronted with a cold swimming pool. *It will be a shock, but it will be over more quickly.* "Do you think I have intimacy issues?"

"What?"

"Is it hard for me to get close to people?"

"You've had a fight with Farnsworth, haven't you?"

"How do you—"

"I've seen it coming for some time."

"But how—"

"Just reading between the lines. I'm sorry it had to happen now, with all that's going on."

She swallowed, feeling something stubborn and hard in her throat. "Do you—"

"What, Pumpkin?"

"Do you think it has something to do with . . . Mom's death?"

There was such a long pause that for a moment she thought he had hung up. But she could hear him breathing on the other end—in and out, in a ragged rhythm that resembled sobbing.

"Is that what Farnsworth said?" he said finally.

"I think she might be right."

"Your mother's death was hard on both of us."

Your mother. He always called her that—never "Gwyneth," or "my wife," but always "your mother." It seemed like a way to sever himself from the equation.

"Why don't we ever talk about it?" she said, feeling light-headed and strangely bold.

"We talk about her," he said defensively. He sounded oddly childish, and Erin felt the scales of power tipping in her direction. She took a deep breath and pressed her advantage.

"We don't talk about her *death*. How it affected us, what it meant to live through it. What it's like without her."

"What is there to say?" he asked weakly.

"Oh, Dad," she said softly. "There aren't enough minutes from now till the end of time for all that I have to say."

Another pause. Then, his voice barely a whisper, he said, "I'm sorry, Erin. I just . . . I don't think I can."

"You mean you don't want to."

"No, I mean I can't. I really can't."

"But I *need* to. Otherwise I feel like . . . I might explode."

"If that's what you need, then you'd best find someone you can talk to."

"Like a therapist, you mean?"

"If that's what you need."

"Okay, Dad," she said, feeling a sorrow deep in her chest that was nearly as bad as what she had experienced at her mother's death. "I'll talk to you later."

"Look, Pumpkin—"

"It's okay. I'll catch you later," she said, and rang off.

Tossing the phone onto the chair, she threw herself on the bed. Lying on her back, she stared back up at the ceiling. Even the familiar water mark gave her no comfort. She felt empty, alone. Farnsworth was right. She had somehow managed to alienate the two people who meant the most to her.

> The inmates of my cottage, all at rest,
> Have left me to that solitude, which suits
> Abstruser musings

But unlike her ancestor, Erin had no young child in a cradle by her side. She glanced at the empty branches of the yew tree outside the window; even the owl had deserted her. Sinking into a bath of self-pity, she allowed her body to heave in rhythmic sobs, until, exhausted, head on one tear-stained arm, she fell asleep.

Chapter Fifty

She awoke to a loud rapping on the door.

Opening sleep-crusted eyes, she saw that it was dark outside; according to the red numbers on the bedside clock it was 7:04, though for a moment she wasn't sure if it was AM or PM.

"Erin! Are you in there?"

The rapping continued more insistently. Pulling herself into a sitting position, she called out, "Coming!"

She opened the door to find Hetty Miller, elegant in a long, apricot-colored Regency dress, the traditional high bodice tied with a pale matching ribbon. She held a pair of white dress gloves in one hand and a black lace fan in the other.

"Don't you look smart," said Erin, wiping the sleepers from her eyes.

"Well? Aren't you coming to the dance?" Hetty said impatiently.

"Has it started?"

"It starts in half an hour, and nearly everyone is already there!"

"All right," Erin said. "I'll get dressed."

"Do you have something to wear?"

"Farnsworth got me something at a charity shop."

Hetty snorted. "Charity shop! One can splurge every so often for important occasions, you know."

"Actually, it's very nice. Really," she added in response to Hetty's disapproving look.

"Well, come along quick as you can. Everyone's asking about you—including Jonathan," she said with a sly smile. "Wait till you see him. Positively dashing. Regency dress suits him."

"I'll be down straightaway."

Still sleepy, she walked barefoot to the closet and took out the royal-blue, short-sleeved gown Farnsworth had bought her, admiring the satin finish as she slipped it over her shoulders. Pulling her thick ginger hair up into a chignon, she wound it with a pale-blue ribbon that matched the bodice ribbon on her dress—also courtesy of Farnsworth. After applying a touch of mascara and rouge, she slid her feet into a pair of pink satin slippers and grabbed the matching purse, into which she stuffed a pair of long white gloves, her key card, lipstick, and a mirror. She was nearly out the door when she remembered her mobile phone—not very period appropriate, but she had come to rely on it, perhaps too much. In the back of her mind was the thought that Peter Hemming might try to contact her.

It was close to seven thirty when she slipped out of the room and hurried down the hall toward the lift. She could hear the faint sound of music coming from the grand ballroom as soon as she stepped into the lobby, passing several uniformed officers. It sounded like a Regency era waltz, she thought as she walked down the carpeted corridor leading to the main ballroom. More policemen were roaming the hall, which should have been reassuring, but only made her feel jittery.

Pushing open the heavy door, Erin was amazed to see how the room had been transformed. Chandeliers sparkled overhead, white lace bunting hung from the tall French windows, and the inlaid marble fireplace was draped in dark-blue velvet. Tables covered in pristine white linen cloths lined two sides of the room; an ensemble of half a dozen musicians sat on a low stage on the far wall. Flowers were everywhere—on the tables, overflowing from tall floor vases tied with pale-blue chiffon, the air thick with their fragrance. Waiters in formal wear circulated with trays of refreshments. Nearly everyone in the room was elaborately clad in period clothing. Maybe it was the festive atmosphere, but Erin thought almost everyone looked better in Regency apparel. The ladies sparkled nearly as brightly as the chandeliers, and the men looked dashing in buttoned trousers, waistcoats, and tails. She looked around for Farnsworth, but didn't see her.

Khari Butari approached, radiant in a long-sleeved silver gown with black trim. She smiled when she saw Erin admiring the surroundings. "Like it?"

"It's breathtaking," Erin answered. "You've done an amazing job. It must've cost—"

"We had a budget. Raised quite a bit of with jumble sales and charity events."

"Well, it's brilliant," Erin said as the musicians struck up a lively mazurka. No one was dancing yet, but the ball had only just begun. People seemed more interested in the fancy hors d'oeuvres piled on the silver trays carried by the waiters slipping in and out of the crowd of people.

"How about some punch?" Khari said, leading her to a corner table with two huge glass bowls filled with pink liquid. One was labeled "Virgin," the other "Spiked."

Khari took two punch glasses from the stack on the table. "Virgin or spiked?"

"Definitely spiked. What's the base, pink lemonade?"

"And a few other ingredients," Khari. "We found a recipe for orgeat."

"Isn't that a syrup involving orange flower?"

"And almond extract. We added it to the lemonade, as they would have done, along with soda water, and—" she said, dipping the ladle into the "Spiked" bowl, "in this one, plenty of brandy, as well as eighty-proof rum."

"Cheers," Erin said as Khari handed her the glass.

Khari lifted her glass. *"A votre santé."*

The punch was deeply satisfying, sweet and somewhat floral; the sour lemonade provided a refreshing contrast. Erin realized she was incredibly thirsty after her long nap, and poured herself a second glass.

"Oh look, there's Jonathan," Khari said, pointing to a group of ladies flocking around him like gaily colored sheep, fluttering and tittering in their pastel dresses and ribbons. Jonathan was prettier than any of them, in a burgundy-striped waistcoat, charcoal-gray pants, and black frock coat. The red waistcoat brought out the rose in his cheeks, and the black coat set off his glossy curls and porcelain skin. He really was like a Gainsborough painting come to life. Seeing Erin and Khari, he smiled and waved. Erin waved back, though perhaps not as enthusiastically.

"He fancies you," said Khari.

"I don't know about that," Erin said, greedily gulping down her second glass of punch.

"Go easy on that," Khari said. "It has more of a punch than you think."

"No pun intended," said Erin.

Khari shuddered. "Good lord, no."

The pun made her think of Peter Hemming. She wondered what he was up to, when, to her surprise, she saw him across the room. Taller than most of the people in the room, in a simple white button-down shirt and dark trousers, he stood out amid all the fancily dressed partygoers. A suit jacket was slung over his shoulder; the room was warm, and as she watched, he wiped his brow with a white handkerchief. He did appear somewhat more rested, though. His wheat-colored hair was neatly combed, and his keen pale eyes scanned the crowd. She wanted to run up to him and fold him in her arms, but instead, she plucked a canapé from a silver tray held by a passing waiter.

"What is it?" Khari asked.

"Caviar. With sour cream and lemon."

"Lovely," she said, taking one.

Erin also took one, savoring the salty plumpness of the caviar, perfectly balanced by the lemon and sour cream. Before the waiter had turned to leave, she helped herself to another.

"Good, isn't it?" said Khari.

"I'd eat this every day if I could afford it," Erin admitted, popping the second one in her mouth.

"Ready to join the dance?" said Prudence, coming up to them. Even she looked better in Regency attire; though she had managed to pick an unbecoming beige-colored frock, her hair was done up nicely, her cheeks were rouged, and she even wore a touch of lipstick.

"You look nice," said Erin.

"So do you both, but that's not much of a challenge for the likes of you," Prudence answered cheerily. "So are you going to join the fun? It seems Hetty has appointed herself dance mistress, and she's asked me to drum up some support."

"How very public spirited of you," said Khari.

"After all, to be fond of dancing is a certain step towards falling in love," Prudence said with a knowing smile.

"Well done," said Erin. "Hetty may be dance mistress, but you retain your title as mistress of Austen quotes."

"Come along as soon as you can," Prudence said, bustling off to entreat another group of people to join the fun as the musicians launched into a charming country dance. Between Hetty and Pru's efforts, a line of dancers was forming. Erin couldn't hear what Hetty was saying, but she could see her coaching and encouraging the more hesitant participants.

"Good for Hetty," Khari said. "Shall we lend some moral support?"

"Why not?" said Erin, and the two of them went to join the line of women standing opposite their partners.

"Oh, look who your partner is," Khari whispered as Jonathan slipped into the line across from her. "Lucky you."

Erin couldn't help feeling a surge of satisfaction as envious feminine gazes turned toward her, bodices heaving and eyelashes fluttering in Jonathan's direction. He was so much like Jane Austen's easygoing Mr. Bingley that it was impossible not to like him, but even as she admired his beauty, her eyes searched the room for a glimpse of the moodier, Darcy-like Peter Hemming. Not seeing him, she turned her attention back to the matter at hand just as the line of men and women bowed and curtseyed to each other to signal the beginning of the dance.

After a rather rocky start, things settled down. While they didn't exactly look as though they'd done this their entire lives, after the first couple of patterns, people began to loosen up, remembering the steps Judith had taught them.

As if reading her mind, Jonathan whispered "Judith would be proud," as he and Erin took hands to skip between the row of other dancers to take their place at the other end of the line.

"Yes," she agreed as Khari and her partner did the same, following them down the line to end up standing next to them. People seemed to be having fun now, their faces shiny and glistening as they glided around the room with increasing abandon.

As they turned to start another pattern, Erin saw Farnsworth enter the room with Grant Apthorp at her side. Splendid in a rich green gown, her hair upswept in an elaborate layered bun, layered through with pale-green ribbons, Farnsworth had never looked lovelier. She also looked happy, holding Grant's right arm, his free hand gripping the handle of an elegant carved wood cane Erin had recognized from the dealer's room. Grant was resplendent in a red cutaway frock coat, snowy white shirt, simple black neck stock, and matching breeches. His bad foot still swathed in gauze inside an open-toed slipper, he sported a gleaming black riding boot with red trim on his good side.

To her surprise, as the dance ended, Grant and Farnsworth headed toward the group of dancers. Grant was walking better than earlier, but still appeared to need the support of his cane.

"Shall we do another?" Jonathan asked, and Erin nodded. She was enjoying herself, and wasn't going to be put off by Farnsworth, no matter how much of a row they had. She wasn't about to let it spoil her fun.

The ensemble struck up a charming tune that Erin recognized as "The Duchess of Devonshire's Reel."

"Let's do the cotillion!" Hetty called to the assembled company, and there was some milling about as people struggled to remember Judith's instructions, but they settled into the right configuration just in time to begin the first steps. To Erin's relief, Grant and Farnsworth started on the far side of the room, but she knew that the dance would eventually ensure that their paths crossed more than once. To her left, Hetty had partnered with a fresh-faced man young enough to be her grandson. She was glowing, her expression triumphant as she held the young man's hand. Erin had to hand it her—Hetty was indefatigable.

The assembled company handled the fairly complex patterns pretty well, emboldened by their success in the first dance. Sure enough, in the third pattern, Erin and Jonathan linked arms with Farnsworth and Grant, who was handling himself well, using the cane deftly as he moved about the dance floor.

"So," Farnsworth said as she breezed past Erin, "I hope you don't disapprove of my dancing."

"Don't be absurd," Erin said, as the four of them joined hands in a circle before breaking off to join a larger circle of dancers.

"Or my partner," Farnsworth whispered as the group of dancers circled to the right.

"You're being childish."

"Am I?" Farnsworth replied as the circle of dancers reversed direction.

"You're just trying to punish me," Erin said as they entered the dance's final pattern.

There was no more opportunity to exchange barbs with her friend before the dance ended. Relieved, Erin excused herself before Farnsworth could say anything more as the music ceased. The musicians stood up, apparently ready for a break. Seeing Peter Hemming lurking near the punch table, she excused herself to Jonathan and made her way over to him.

"Keeping an eye on us?" she asked, filling a glass from the large bowl marked Spiked.

"Mind how much you have of that," he said. "I hear it packs quite a—"

"Punch? Been there, done that."

He sighed. "That's the trouble with puns. You've heard one, you've heard them all."

"And most you wish you'd never heard in the first place."

"The unkindest cut of all," he said, miming being stabbed with an invisible knife.

"I'm sorry," she said. "You're only allowed to quote Austen here."

"In that case, I defer to you."

"There is safety in reserve, but no attraction. One cannot love a reserved person."

"Do you find me reserved?"

"I was accused of it myself recently."

"Well, then, can two reserved people love each other?"

Oh yes, she thought, sipping her punch, but she said, "I'm afraid Jane Austen is silent on that subject."

"I thought she had something to say about everything."

They both watched as Charles Kilroy wandered into the room. Clad in Regency period dress, he was transformed. In striped breeches, deep-green waistcoat, and black frock coat, he actually looked quite elegant. A watch chain dangled from one pocket; he held a pair of kid gloves in one hand and a riding crop in the other. Seeing Erin, he gave a brief, dignified nod. The costume seemed to have transformed his personality as well.

"What do you know about him?" Hemming asked.

"Didn't you interview him?"

"Of course, but clearly he knows you."

"We only just met, but I can tell you he's a bit of a character. Smart, but odd."

"The riding crop is a bit of a giveaway there."

"Unless he has a horse waiting outside."

"I'm guessing that's not the case."

"I doubt he's ever been on a horse. Why are you here, if you already arrested your prime suspect?"

"We haven't arrested her yet—we're holding her on suspicion."

She looked out over the crowd, her head agreeably fuzzy from the punch, and everything suddenly seemed less dire. A warm haze settled over her as she relaxed into the music, letting it carry her into a place where everyone was a character out of Jane Austen, life was full of Regency ballrooms and rum punch, and murder didn't stalk the halls of the York Grand Hotel.

Chapter Fifty-One

❧

Shaking herself out of her happy reverie, Erin turned to Peter Hemming. "Someone planted that knitting needle at the crime scene," she said, surprised to hear the words coming from her.

He turned to look at her. "How on earth would you know that?"

"I looked under the bed when I found Judith's body."

"You might have missed it."

"Miss seeing the murder weapon? Does that sound like me?"

He frowned, the lines in his forehead deepening. "Why didn't you tell me before?"

"I didn't want to admit I was snooping around."

"Were you?"

"I didn't touch anything, mind you, but I certainly looked under the bed."

"So when could they have planted it there, if you discovered the body and called me right after?"

She told him about going upstairs to fetch her phone. "I'm sorry—I should have closed the door after me, but I left it the way I found it. I don't know why."

To her surprise, he didn't seem angry. "Never mind—the killer might have had access to the room anyway."

"You mean they might have got a copy of the key card?"

"Or bribed the cleaning staff. Or picked the lock. Hotel rooms aren't that hard to break into. A good stiff bobby pin or a rubber band and a credit card is all it takes if you know what you're doing."

"But don't you think the discovery of the needle makes it *less* likely Winnie is the killer? What kind of murderer incriminates herself like that?"

"People leave all sorts of ridiculous things at crime scenes, especially when murder is involved. Unless they're professionals, most people aren't prepared for what it's like to kill someone. It's incredibly hard, physically and emotionally. And up close like that—it's pretty shattering, even if you really hated the person. People think they can handle it, but more often than not, it hits them harder than they thought, and they make stupid mistakes."

"Seen a lot of murders in York, have you?"

"I worked a London beat for a while before coming here."

"Why did you leave?"

"To be closer to my mother. And I missed Yorkshire."

"I like it here too," she said, feeling the heat of his body next to her. She moved a little closer, and he didn't back away as the back of her hand touched his. She breathed a deep sigh of contentment as they watched the scene together. It felt so natural standing next to him, familiar somehow, as if she had been expecting this moment all her life. She took the opportunity to study his face. It wasn't perfect, but in the flaws lay his perfection. His cheekbones were undeniably prominent, and his nose flawless. But his mouth was perhaps a little too full, his eyes too far apart. It was, she decided, the most wonderful face she had ever seen.

She looked up to see Hetty vigorously beckoning her to the dance floor. The musicians had returned from their break, and were gearing up for another set. Hetty and Prudence were prowling the crowd, collecting participants for the next dance as the band struck up a lively Irish tune Erin recognized as "The Haymaker's Jig."

Hemming touched her arm lightly. "Your friend is summoning you. Looks like the jig is up."

Erin groaned. "That's my cue to leave. Thanks for making it so easy for me."

"Any time," he called after her as she bounded onto the dance floor, as if the combination of music, alcohol, and the lively crowd could relieve her of the heaviness she had felt ever since Barry Wolf's death. She looked back at Hemming, who was scanning the crowd, apparently having forgotten about her.

He hadn't really, though. She knew it as well as she knew every inch of her beloved bookshop back home in Kirkbymoorside. She could feel an invisible force connecting them, as if she had always known him. *What a cliché*, she thought as she crossed to join the dancers, and yet she could not escape the feeling.

By this time, everyone had been dancing long enough (combined with sufficient amounts of alcohol) that they were loose and relaxed. Hetty beckoned Erin to a spot next to Jonathan, whose cheeks were becomingly flushed, his eyes bright. Opposite them were Grant and Farnsworth—Hetty had no doubt placed the two couples together, not knowing Erin and Farnsworth were at odds at the moment.

Grant bowed graciously to Erin, who curtseyed in return. Farnsworth and Jonathan did the same, and they began the lively steps Judith had taught them. Grant did well, minus the kicks and hops, but he was able to move around the room tolerably well with his cane—rather better than earlier in the evening, Erin thought. Farnsworth didn't make any more snide comments, but Erin still sensed an aloofness in her friend's attitude toward her. Still, she enjoyed the dance, and was sorry when it was over. Hetty swooped in and commandeered Jonathan's attention, drawing him toward a group of women from the Southern Branch

"I've got to spend a penny—be right back," Farnsworth told Grant, and threaded her way through the crowd toward the exit.

He turned to Erin. "How about a libation?"

"Why not?"

Grant escorted her to the punch bowl, where he poured them both generous servings.

"I see the police are staking us out," he said, handing her a glass. She was impressed at his dexterity, as he was wearing white dress gloves as he poured the punch.

"Just keeping an eye on things," she said, drinking deeply. It was even more delicious than before, and she refrained with difficulty from having a second glass. She looked around for Detective Hemming, but didn't see him. Sergeant Jarral stood at the far side of the room, chatting amiably with a young blonde woman who seemed to have attached herself to him.

"I hear you're conducting your own investigation," Grant said. "How's that going?"

"Oh, it's—" she began, breaking off when she saw Terrence Rogers approaching them. She hadn't noticed him during the last few dances, and wondered where he had been all this time.

"Hello, Miss Coleridge," he said.

"Hello."

"Hello, Terrence," Grant said amiably.

Rogers peered at him coldly. "Why don't you just save everyone time and tell them what you've done?"

Grant laughed, though it was somewhat strained. "Whatever do you mean, old boy?"

"Oh, come off it. It's no secret you couldn't stand Barry Wolf."

"Neither could you. After all, he got you sacked from Oxford."

Terrence reddened. "I wasn't 'sacked.'"

"'Let go,' then. A rose by any other name—"

"Smells rank to heaven," Rogers snapped back.

"I appreciate your thinking me capable of such a clever crime," Grant said. "But we may as well face it—no one liked Barry Wolf."

"But who had an actual motive to kill him?"

"From what I hear, pretty much everyone. He didn't win any popularity contests."

"But why Judith?" Terrence said, his eyes narrowing as he studied Apthorp. "Who was anxious to remove her from the picture?"

"Your guess is as good as mine," Grant replied as Jeremy Wolf entered the room. He looked utterly gutted, his already pale face drawn and lined with grief. Dressed in normal street clothes, jeans and a black shirt, he wandered aimlessly through the crowd, which parted for him as if aware of his suffering.

"Excuse me," Terrence said to Erin. "I have to go," he added, walking swiftly toward Jeremy.

"Poor lad," Grant said when Terrence had gone. "Do you believe the rumor?"

She watched as Terrence approached Jeremy, putting his arm around the boy's shoulders. To her surprise, Jeremy did not shrug him off, and even seemed to welcome the gesture. "Which rumor are you referring to?"

"That Terrence Rogers is Jeremy's real father."

"I haven't heard that one," she lied.

"Yes, you have," he replied smoothly. "You've been snooping around here all week."

This caught her off guard. Her head cloudy from the effects of the punch, she stammered a feeble reply. "I . . . wasn't aware it was—"

"Never mind," he said with a little chuckle. "You don't have to explain. Like a good detective, you're withholding key information from the suspects."

"Are you a suspect?"

"Isn't everyone in this room? Or have you eliminated some people?"

The way he said "eliminated" made her shiver. "What happened between you and Terrence Rogers?"

"How do you mean?"

"You worked together on the literary magazine all those years ago. You thanked him in your first book, but not the second."

"Ah," he said. "You are a good sleuth, aren't you?"

"What happened to your friendship?"

"Let me show you something," he said, taking her by the elbow, as the band struck up another mazurka.

She followed him from the ballroom and into the little ante-chamber around the corner, where Charles had shown her the coffee urn. It was quiet and secluded; she could barely hear the music coming from the ballroom. An abandoned tray of plates and silverware sat in one corner.

"What did you want to show me?" she said as he turned toward her.

She realized too late she had made a terrible mistake. All the wry humor had evaporated from his face. His eyes were opaque, as if a membrane had been pulled over the pupils, transforming them into the black, lifeless eyes of a shark. She turned to flee, but a strong hand gripped her arm and spun her around, pulling her toward him. She opened her mouth to scream, but his hands were already around her throat, squeezing hard, cutting off her air. As he forced her to the ground, she flailed wildly at the tray of kitchen-ware, bringing it crashing down; she hoped someone would hear the sound and come to find out what had caused it.

"Foolish girl," he muttered as he pressed the breath from her body. "Did you really think you could bring me down? I could have finished you off on that bloody Ghost Walk, if it weren't for your little friend showing up."

"Why . . . Sam?" she gasped, thinking she could perhaps stall him long enough for rescue to arrive—all the while realizing it was probably a vain hope.

"Stupid busybody," he muttered. "Nearly caught me in the act, then blabbered to everyone about the bloody salad after bumping into me."

"So . . . you—"

"I had to be sure, didn't I? Now just stop struggling, and this will go much easier," he said, pressing down.

She reached up to scratch his cheek—thinking she could at least embed his DNA under her nails—but forgot she was wearing gloves. Her last thought before blackness closed around her was that his own white gloves would leave no fingerprints when they found her body.

Chapter Fifty-Two

❧

Erin was brought back to consciousness by the sound of a woman screaming. Her first thought was that it might be the sound of her own voice, but when the attempt to breathe brought a violent fit of coughing, she realized she had no breath in her body to speak, let alone scream. Sucking in more air, she opened her eyes to see Farnsworth Appleby standing over her, bellowing like a bull elephant. Farnsworth emitted no words, just the throaty, primal sound of pure rage.

Struggling to sit up, Erin looked around for Grant Apthorp, just in time to see him stagger and collapse against the far wall, clutching at his throat. A sturdy dinner fork protruded from his neck. His eyes found hers, the pupils widening in disbelief. He opened his mouth in an attempt to speak, but he emitted only a deathly gurgling sound. His hands clawed at the empty air as he slid down the side of the wall, landing in a crumpled heap. And then he was silent, a silence even more terrible than the sound of Farnsworth's screaming, which had stopped. Panting heavily, her friend dropped to her knees beside Erin. Wrapping Erin in her arms, Farnsworth stroked her hair and murmured nonsense syllables, like a mother comforting a sick child.

They remained like that for several moments. Still struggling to breathe without coughing, Erin realized the spray of liquid falling on her face was Farnsworth's tears.

Chapter Fifty-Three

~

"You sure you're all right, pet?" Farnsworth said as the two of them sat huddled in the empty ballroom an hour later. They were both wrapped in blankets, which Hetty had insisted on bringing them—because, as she said, "Trauma makes the blood go cold."

"I'm fine," Erin said, drawing the blanket closer around her shoulders. Hetty had a point, she thought—she couldn't seem to stop shivering. She looked around the deserted ballroom, she and Farnsworth its only occupants. It had a sad, abandoned air, made more melancholy by the remnants of recent merrymaking. Sheets of bunting had come loose, hanging forlornly from the windows or strewn across the carpet. Flowers wilted in their vases; discarded cocktail napkins lay trampled on the floor, along with lost gloves, hatpins, and bits of dress lace.

They had already given their statements to the police, and were awaiting a final interview before being officially released. Erin's hand strayed to her throat, still sore and tender to the touch. The events of the past hour had such a patina of unreality that only the feel of her fingers upon her injured neck convinced her that it had happened at all. She coughed softly, not wanting to alarm Farnsworth, but her friend had the ears of a bat.

"Sure you're all right, pet?"

"I'm fine. But what about you? You must be in shock." In truth, Farnsworth's behavior since rescuing her had been so stoic that Erin was worried, fearing a meltdown was imminent. "If it makes you feel any better, I was as fooled as you were. I just never thought—I mean, for you it must be . . . I can't imagine."

Farnsworth shrugged. "Easy come, easy go."

Erin stared at her, too shocked to reply. She watched as Farnsworth's breathing deepened and sobs shook her body. Her face crumpled as tears cascaded down her cheeks. Erin reached to put her arms around her, but Farnsworth shook her off. "I should have known," she wailed. "It's my fault!"

"Rubbish," said Erin. "He had us all taken in."

"Not me," said a voice at the other end of the room. They turned to see Terrence Rogers, still clad in breeches and waistcoat. The cuffs of his white shirt were somewhat soiled, and his boots were scuffed, but otherwise he did not appear much the worse for wear. "I always thought he was a silly prat," he added, sauntering toward them.

"Terrence," Farnsworth gasped through her sobs. "W—what are you doing here?"

"Just thought I'd see how you were getting on."

"We're just waiting for the police to let us go," Erin said.

Terrence smiled. "That tall blond fellow fancies you, you know."

"She knows," Farnsworth said, drying her tears with a pile of cocktail napkins.

"Why did he do it?" Erin said. "You knew both of them."

"There were always rumors Barry sabotaged Grant's efforts to get tenure at Oxford. No one could ever prove it. If I had to guess, I'd say someone at the conference finally told him."

"Judith?"

"Possibly. Maybe Barry himself—he always was a vindictive little prick."

"Remember that conversation we saw on the first night between them at the bar?" said Farnsworth.

Erin nodded. "Whatever Barry said, Grant did not like it. We were too far away to hear what they were saying," she told Terrence.

Farnsworth sighed sadly. "He obviously killed Sam because he thought Sam was onto him, with the salad and everything. But what about poor Judith?"

"She might have been onto him as well," Erin said. "And he obviously faked the gout attack."

Farnsworth sighed. "I felt so sorry for him, when he actually was out stalking you. He nearly killed you—twice!" She looked as if she was about to cry again.

"Can I get you anything?" Terrence asked.

Farnsworth smiled hopefully. "A cup of tea would be nice."

"I'll see if I can scare one up."

"Have they released Winnie yet?" said Erin.

"Yes, we have."

Erin turned to see Peter Hemming enter the room.

"She was released an hour ago," he said, walking toward them. "I believe she's in her room, if you want to see her."

"What about us?" said Farnsworth. "Are you finished with us?"

"Just one or two more questions, if you're up to it," he said, glancing at Terrence.

"I'll just go see about that tea," Terrence said, leaving the ballroom.

"What did you want to know?" Farnsworth asked Hemming.

He pulled up a chair across from them and sat. "How did you know Mr. Apthorp was, uh, attacking Ms. Coleridge?"

"I was on my way back from the loo, and I heard a crashing noise."

"That would be the tray falling?"

"Right. I went to see what was going on . . ." She paused and swallowed hard. "Well, you know the rest."

"Thank you, Ms. Appleby. And thank you . . . for your assistance."

"Saving Erin's life, you mean?"

He cleared his throat. "Yes."

"Any time," Farnsworth said, winking at Erin. "Should I wait for you, pet?"

"No, you go on ahead," said Erin. "I'll be up in a while."

"You were right in the end, pet," said Farnsworth, standing up somewhat stiffly.

"About what?"

"Life isn't like a Hallmark movie."

"Actually," Erin said, with a glance at Hemming, "I'm not so sure about that."

Farnsworth smiled. "Good night, Detective."

"Good night, Ms. Appleby."

Left alone with Hemming, Erin looked down at her hands, surprised to see they were still trembling. The room was very quiet, and she could hear the faint ticking of the wall clock over the makeshift stage. The music seemed to still linger in the air, and yet it felt to her as if ages had passed since the ball. Time was like an accordion, compressed one moment, stretched out the next.

"Your hands," he said.

"Yes," she answered, gazing at his face, trying to memorize it in case she didn't see him for some time.

"Are you cold?"

"No," she lied. Then, gazing into his deep-blue eyes, the color of the North Sea on a cloudy day, something inside her melted and she no longer felt the need to hide anything from him—her vulnerability, weakness, even her deepest fears and desires. "Yes," she said. "I'm cold."

Leaning forward, he wrapped her in his arms. "There," he said after a moment. "Is that better?"

"Oh, yes," she said. "Much better."

Outside, she thought she heard an owl hooting softly, and she gave a little laugh.

"What is it?" he asked.

"Just an owl," she said. "Now then, where were we?"

"I believe I was about to take you into custody. That is, if it's all right with you."

"Will there be handcuffs?"

"That depends on whether you come quietly or not."

"I can't promise anything."

"So you might be bad?"

"Oh, yes," she said. "Very, very bad."

He laughed, and the dark cloud hanging over her cracked and shattered like glass, the pieces cascading to the floor in a dazzling kaleidoscope of possibilities.

Acknowledgments

Thanks to my awesome agent, Paige Wheeler, as always. Deepest gratitude to Jenny Chen, Emily Rapoport and Melissa Rechter for their sage editorial advice, patience, and unwavering support.

Thanks to Anthony Moore, for introducing me to the wonders of the Yorkshire Moors, always sharing my passion and sense of adventure—and to the staff of the Lion Inn, Blakey Ridge, for an unforgettable night, splendid meal, and wonderful gift of A Coast to Coast Walk, by Alfred Wainwright. Deepest thanks to Alan Macquarie, scholar, musician, and historian, for being such a gracious host in his glorious Glasgow flat, and to Anne Clackson, for being such a boon (and bonny) companion. Special thanks to my dear friend Rachel Fallon for her generosity and loyal spirit. And a big shout out to the baristas at Gatehouse Coffee in historic York, the most glorious coffee house I have had the pleasure of visiting.

Thanks to Hawthornden Castle for awarding me a Fellowship—my time there was unforgettable—and to Byrdcliffe Colony in Woodstock, where I enjoyed many happy years of residency, as well as Animal Care Sanctuary in East Smithfield, PA, Craig Lukatch and the fabulous Lacawac Sanctuary, where so much of this was written. I can't wait to return!

Special thanks to my dear friend and colleague Marvin Kaye for his continued support, and for all the many wonderful dinners at Keens. Thanks to my assistant, Frank Goad, for his intelligence and expertise. Thanks too to my good friend Ahmad Ali, whose support and good energy has always lifted my spirits, and to the Stone Ridge Library, my upstate writing home away from home.

Finally, special thanks to my parents—raconteurs, performers and musicians, who taught me the importance of art and the power of a good story.